INTO THE

Nightfell Wood

Also by Kristin Bailey

The Silver Gate

INTO THE

Nightfell Wood

KRISTIN BAILEY

KATHERINE TEGEN BOOKS
An Imprint of HarperCollins Publishers

Katherine Tegen Books is an imprint of HarperCollins Publishers.

Into the Nightfell Wood
Copyright © 2018 by Kristin Welker
www.harpercollinschildrens.com

ISBN 978-0-06-239860-4

Typography by Aurora Parlagreco
18 19 20 21 22 PC/LSCH 10 9 8 7 6 5 4 3 2 1

First Edition

This book is dedicated to Dr. Scarberry, because you saved her life, and to Dr. Boreman, because you saved mine.

CHAPTER ONE

Wynn

WYNN DIDN'T LIKE BEING A fairy princess. She sat on the end of her fluffy bed and kicked the wall with the toe of her silk slipper, making a low thumping sound on the soft wood. Living inside of a giant tree wasn't very nice either. If she were a squirrel, or a bird, maybe she would like it. But she wasn't a squirrel or a bird. She was a girl, and she wanted to go outside.

Before she came through the Silver Gate, Wynn used to go outside every day. She could go outside when she lived with her mother in a hut in the woods. She used to gather sticks for the fire and feed the chickens in the garden. There was lots to do, and her mother was always there. Sometimes her older brother, Elric, would come back from tending the sheep for the village, and they would play in the woods and try to find the gate to the realm of the Fairy Queen.

But then her mother got sick. And the storm came. And Mother didn't get better. She didn't wake up.

Wynn hugged her arms across her chest as she remembered. The shimmering skirts of her dress rustled as she drew her feet up under her and sat on the edge of the bed. Her father had come to the hut. He was angry. He wanted to get rid of her. He didn't like that it took her so long to think, and her words didn't sound right, and her thumbs weren't shaped like other people's thumbs. He thought she was cursed, a changeling child, a monster.

But then Elric came and together they ran away. Wynn followed the clues the Fairy Queen left for her, and she led them to the real Silver Gate, the only place where someone from the Otherworld could cross over to the land Between from the human world. It had been a scary adventure. They almost died. But they found the gate and Wynn was very happy when the Fairy Queen made them prince and princess of the land Between. The queen gave them beautiful and wonderful things and Wynn felt safe again.

Maybe too safe. She looked around her room. A magical tree formed the entire palace. The branches of the great tree were so large they held entire corridors with stairs and bridges. Wynn lived in a little nook, carved into one of the branches. It was a pretty room.

The fairies told her it didn't hurt the tree to live in it. It wasn't like the trees where she came from. This tree was magic, and magic could do strange things.

Sparkling stones had been fixed in the ceiling and walls. They glittered like stars in the night. A large glowing orb traveled across her room every day, following a sun that she could not see. When it stopped glowing and rested on the floor, she had to go to bed.

The magic in the Between was very beautiful. Colorful lights danced everywhere, and there was no dark shadows or mean villagers. But the magic things in her room only seemed magical for a while. Now they were just the same thing day after day, after day. Wynn got up and walked in a small circle around her room. It was very boring. Now no one needed anything from her.

The fairies had given her pretty dresses, funny

puppets to play with, and a toy bird that came alive in her hands and flew around the room. But she couldn't go outside. Not ever. It wasn't safe. She walked over to the narrow slits in the wooden wall and tried to push her hand through, but her palm stuck. She wiggled her fingers outside, but she couldn't feel a breeze. She couldn't see anything interesting through the slits either. All she could see were some big leaves and the pinks, blues, and cool green colors that shifted through the magical dome that covered the fairy lands. She wanted a real window.

"No, Wynn, you could fall. No, Wynn, you can't swim. No, Wynn, it's too hot." Wynn repeated the phrases that came too easily to her mind. She had heard them enough. They made her so angry.

She picked at the soft bark on the edge of the slit pulling it away in strips, then dropping it through the narrow gap. When she lived in the Otherworld, she used to spend her entire day looking for sticks so she and her mother would have enough wood to tend the fire at night. Every day it was the same: go to the woods, pick up sticks, find her way back home. Her pet hen, Mildred, would follow her and eat bugs. Wynn liked finding sticks. It was an important job and she could do it without help. Her mother needed those sticks. Her mother needed the fire. Her mother needed her.

Now she didn't even have a window she could see things out of. The fairies were too afraid she would fall out of it. She knew how to stay inside a window. Wynn kicked the wall hard, and it hurt her foot, so she smacked the wall with her hand.

Elric had a bigger window, and his room was next to hers. She should go see what he was doing.

Wynn carefully opened the door to her room and peeked out. The hollow branch of the tree formed a long, curving hallway. The fairies didn't like her to leave her room without someone to watch her, but there were no fairies in the hall right now. She bunched up her skirts and held them away from her feet, then ran next door and slipped into Elric's room.

"Elric?" She closed the door behind her. His room wasn't as fancy as hers. She stepped over to his bed, but his blankets were messy and he wasn't in it. Where was he? "Elric?" she called again. Usually he came to get her and they would eat together and stay together in the palace. He shouldn't be gone now, and it made her feel upset. She didn't like to be away from him for long anymore. She wandered over to his window, a teardrop-shaped opening in the branch wall.

Wynn stuck her head out and looked straight down, her shoulder-length hair falling around her face. Fairies scurried around like bugs in the courtyards below. She watched them for a second but the silver circlet on her head shifted forward. She slapped a hand on her head to hold it steady and looked up. Hills blanketed with a rainbow of flowers rolled around the great valley. It would be fun to play in them. She could walk with Mildred. She hadn't seen Mildred in several days. Mildred didn't like to be in the high branches of the palace.

And Wynn's room was very high. She could see the tops of the stone towers that surrounded the tree like the old druid circles in the Otherworld. Curling blue designs glowed on the surface of the enormous stones in pretty knotted patterns. Fairies liked circles. The courtyards below were circles, and the dome formed an enormous circle of light.

On the other side of the protective dome, a dark forest waited, and the tall shadows of storm clouds lingered beyond that. The storms couldn't reach them here, and the dangerous creatures of the forest never crossed the line of magic that kept them in their woods.

She needed to find Elric. Wynn crept out of the door and went farther into the palace. She turned and climbed higher in the branch, holding her skirts in a big bunch so she didn't trip on them. They were too puffy and long but her soft slippers made her feet quiet and that was good.

The queen's rooms were nearby. She would know where Elric was.

Wynn reached an alcove at the end of the branch with two doors made from carved wooden screens. One side showed the queen looking down on the palace tree and the fairy lands with the moon behind her. The other side showed a fairy man with the sun behind him and the woods at his feet near a great city with tall stone towers. Light glittered through the screens. Wynn cracked open the door and stepped into a perfectly round chamber with high arching windows and a second set of doors on the other side. Sun streamed in from everywhere, throwing green and gold splashes of color on the pale wood walls. That light danced off the shining treasures filling the room.

What was this place?

An animal skin hung on the wall, but it was different from any animal Wynn had ever seen. It had dark stripes on pale gray fur. The fur was old and worn as it sagged. It made Wynn feel very sad to look at it.

Whatever animal it was might have been very beautiful when it was alive. A long staff with a clear blue gem at the top hung next to it on the wall. Next to that stood a pedestal with a crystal crown on a silk pillow.

"Oh, it's beautiful," Wynn whispered as she stepped closer to get a good look. The crown wasn't silver, exactly. It looked like starlight. It seemed to glow with an inner light, and Wynn thought she heard the sound of tiny bells as a breeze blew over it.

Wynn reached out to touch it and carefully lifted it so she could see it better. She took off her own plain circlet, and reached to place the crown on her head.

Suddenly the golden room filled with an icy blast of air. Wynn gasped and nearly dropped the crown as a flurry of snowflakes swirled over her in a cold and angry wave.

"Wynnfrith!" The voice of the Fairy Queen filled the room like thunder. "Do not touch that."

"Do not touch that!" Wynn repeated. Her body tensed and shook as her thoughts turned into a jumble. The crown slipped in her hands.

The queen rushed forward on a gust of wind, and caught the crown before it fell. Wynn covered her ears and hunched over. The queen placed the crown back on the pedestal, and immediately dropped to her knees in front of Wynn.

She was so beautiful the shadows bowed to her, and light tended her as a handmaid. Her large eyes shifted color, reflecting the magic of the protective dome around them. She reached out to Wynn, her glittering white sleeves floating beside her. "Oh, no, darling. There's no harm done. It didn't break." The queen wrapped her arms around Wynn and pulled her into a tight hug. "I'm sorry I scared you."

"I'm sorry," Wynn repeated again, because her own thoughts still wouldn't work the way they should. One of Wynn's tears fell on the deep brown skin of the queen's arm, and the queen gently brushed her tear away and placed a kiss on the top of Wynn's head.

"I know you're sorry. Don't worry. Nothing was harmed." The queen picked up Wynn's plain silver circlet and placed it on Wynn's head, then smoothed Wynn's hair back behind her ear. The queen began to softly sing to Wynn. The words were new, but she knew the tune by heart.

"My love, my love, my changeling child,
You braved the wind and snow

To find me here within the gate,
And make my magic grow.
Please stay with me, my changeling child,
And for all time I'll keep you."

The Fairy Queen stroked Wynn's hair. Wynn wrapped her arms tightly around the queen's neck, holding on. She was the only mother Wynn had now. Slowly her mind cleared enough that she could form her own words again.

"What is this place?" Wynn asked, looking around the room.

The queen smiled, but it didn't look like a happy sort of smile. "It is where I keep things that are special to me. That crown is the crown I made for my daughter."

"The lost baby?" Wynn remembered the story of the baby the queen lost, but didn't remember all the parts. There were things she didn't understand. She only knew the baby was stolen by the Grendel.

"Yes, she never had a chance to wear it. I keep it here now, to remember her." The queen stood and looked around. Her pure white hair floated around her head as the glittering crystals on her dress seemed to flow like drifts of snow down her body. The golden light shining into the room made the queen glimmer with magic. She gently picked up an amulet with a flower symbol on it lying next to the crown. Wynn thought she had seen one of those before, but she couldn't remember. "Who is this for?" Wynn asked, pointing to the necklace.

"My last changeling son wore a matching one, so I could call him home when he wandered. He fancied himself a brave adventurer." She gave Wynn a sad smile and placed it back down on the pedestal.

"What is this?" Wynn asked, stroking her hand down the striped fur. It felt coarse and dry.

The queen placed her hands behind her back. Wynn couldn't tell if she was happy or sad anymore. She was very still. "It was a gift from someone I thought was a friend. The creature was the last of its kind, a tigereon, a dangerous darkling creature that didn't obey fairy magic."

"That is sad," Wynn said, but the queen did not respond. Wynn moved over to look at the staff. "What is this?"

"That belonged to my . . ." She stopped herself and looked out the window into the dark shadows beyond the shield. "That belonged to a great prince, long, long ago. It was a gift. Elves gave it to him. It is made from the same crystal as the heart of the kingdom." The queen didn't say anything more about the prince, but stared at the staff for a long time before she turned to look at Wynn. "Why did you leave your room?"

"I want to go outside," Wynn said. "Want to play in the flowers. Will you play with me?"

This time the queen smiled as she brushed her hand over Wynn's head. "I wish I could, darling, and I will once things are secure. All the other fairies and I are working to make sure the shield is strong now that my magic is returning. I must protect everyone. When it is safe for you, I will take you outside."

"I want to do magic," Wynn said. "Then I will help."

The queen folded her into a hug. "You can do magic. When you sing, it's magic. When you dance, it's magic. There is magic in the joy and love you share. That magic helped bring you here." She bent down and smiled. "You are my magic. That is why it is so important to keep you safe."

Wynn looked around the room. All of the treasures were from people that made the queen feel sad. She glanced down and kicked off her shoe, picked it up, and set it next to the crown. "There, now you have something that is happy."

The queen laughed. "And I will treasure it always. Come, let's go back to your room now."

"No." Wynn pulled her arm away. "Elric's gone. Where is Elric?"

The queen looked troubled. She twisted her hand and a small ball of light appeared. She flicked it out the window and turned with her hands behind her back. A moment later a raven flew into the room with a loud caw.

The large bird hopped forward, and as he did, his body stretched out and in a blink he became a fairy man with long indigo robes and a cape of shining black feathers. His slick black hair lay smoothly over his head. He lowered his body in an elegant bow. "My queen, you called?"

"Where is Prince Elric?" she asked.

Wynn tucked herself back toward the door. Raven didn't look at her. Wynn didn't think he liked her very much. He never talked to her, but told other people to make her do things. She didn't like it. He cleared his throat, placing one of his pale hands over the other. "Master Elk is teaching the prince fighting techniques this morning."

Wynn held very still and didn't say anything. When

other people talked, sometimes they said lots of things that they didn't know she could understand. She learned new things that way. Why was Elric fighting?

A stiff breeze blew around the queen as she frowned. "I thought his lessons wouldn't begin until we found a way to make the shield completely opaque. There are still spies in the woods. The elves have those peering glasses trained on us at all times." She waved an arm toward the windows, her sleeve billowing beside her.

"The elves won't risk an attack now that the shield is stronger," Raven insisted.

"Have all the cracks and fissures been found and repaired?" the queen asked.

"Of course, it's perfectly safe."

The queen glared at him. "A reaper has prowled along the shield for the past three nights, looking for a weakness in it. I fear the Grendel knows I have another child." The chamber grew cold. A flurry of snow blew across the floor. She looked back at Wynn. Wynn batted at her skirts as if she weren't paying attention.

Raven stepped closer to the queen and lowered his voice. "We both know the Grendel will use his reapers to try to take the children. However, we have one advantage."

The queen turned to him.

Raven continued. "If he sees only one child, he will assume there is only one child. And your deeper bond is with this girl." Raven pointed to Wynn. She didn't like that, either, but he was saying important things, and she was trying to remember them. The Grendel was trying to hurt them. He was bad. And they were teaching Elric to fight. Did Elric have to fight the Grendel?

"I will not sacrifice the boy," the queen said. "I will keep them both safe."

"As you should," Raven said, holding his hands out. "As you should. But if the Grendel only knows of one child, it should be the child capable of defending himself. It does not hurt to let those spying on us get a glimpse of him, rather than her." Raven walked toward Wynn. He peered down at her and held out a hand. "We should keep the other tucked away at all times, like the treasure that she is. Come, little one. I will take you back to your room."

"Here, child." The queen turned to her and produced a pair of crystal bells from the air. They rang with several notes at once as the queen handed them to her. "Go and make me a pretty song in your room. I will come and listen to it at dinnertime. Promise me you will obey the rules. I don't want anything to happen to you."

Wynn glanced out the window. A gust of wind shook the trees of the shadowy woods in the distance. "I promise," Wynn said.

Raven tried to take her hand, but Wynn pulled it away. She followed him out of the queen's rooms and back to hers, still thinking about what she heard. She had to find her brother.

Wynn jingled the pretty bells for a while, long enough for Raven to fly off and boss someone else around. A pretty song wouldn't help Elric. He was in danger. When everything was quiet again, she slowly opened her door. She tiptoed through the corridor, glancing every now and then through the narrow windows cut into the living wood. A gap opened up to her right and she turned. An arching bridge curved over the top of the leafy branches toward the heart of the tree. She hadn't been this way before, but it led to the trunk, and the trunk had stairs, and it didn't seem as busy as the main branch.

She wasn't supposed to cross the bridges without help. This one was very high, and it didn't have rails. Wynn peered through the branches of the great tree. Each leaf was huge, at least the size of the roof of the hut where she had grown up. She took a step out.

Immediately she looked down. Her head spun. The ground was so far below, it didn't look like ground at all. She stepped back into the hall and heard footsteps and voices coming toward her. The fairies would make her go back in her room.

There was only one thing to do. Wynn grabbed her skirts again and ran over the bridge. She watched her feet and tried not to think of how high up she was. The bridge sloped down, and she nearly lost her balance and fell forward, but she caught herself and stumbled, falling through the open doorway into the trunk of the tree. She skidded down a few steps before she picked herself up.

Her heart was racing, but she made it!

Now she needed to find her brother.

CHAPTER TWO

Elric

"GOOD! FASTER, PRINCE ELRIC, DEFEND your weak side," Master Elk Windlight commanded in his deep and booming voice. It carried across the arena.

Elric gripped his staff harder and used it to parry the attack of the fairy boy he was sparring with. The muscles in his arms felt like they were made of gloppy mud, and his thighs burned with pain. His legs shook as he gritted his teeth and tried to find the strength to fend off the new attack. This was his first fighting lesson, and he didn't want to let Master Elk down. They had been working since dawn without a break, and he was both hungry and exhausted.

The sand of the arena shifted beneath Elric's feet and his sweaty palms slipped on the polished staff. The fairy boy tried to dodge Elric's next blow by floating three feet in the air, but Elric swung his own staff, and landed a strike on the fairy boy's weapon. The crack of wood on wood echoed in the arena.

"Zephyr, the prince is a mortal. You must fight like one too!" Master Elk shouted at the fairy boy with a commanding bellow that suited his rank as the captain of the queen's guard. The air around Zeph's shaggy mop of blue-black hair glimmered.

With a flash of light, the boy was gone. A gust of wind buffeted Elric's head as he fell face-first into the sand.

Zephyr reappeared on Elric's other side and laughed. "Remember the first rule of fighting: always keep your balance."

Elric grabbed a handful of sand and threw it at Zephyr. The lousy cheat. The fairy boy flicked his wrist and the wind blew the sand harmlessly to the side.

"That was against the rules, and you know it." Elric dusted himself off and picked up his staff even though his fingers felt too weak to hold it anymore.

"Maybe." Zeph chuckled. "But it was worth it."

Elric bent to catch his breath. He was the prince. The queen had determined he was ready to fight. This wasn't a game. He rose up, swinging his staff in a quick arc to catch Zeph behind the knees. The fairy landed on his rump in the sand. He looked shocked at first, then his eyes flashed from warm brown to bright green. Zephyr crossed his arms over his belly and fell back in the sand, laughing. "Good one, Prince! I can't believe I fell for that." He floated up and dusted off his rump. "Literally."

Elric gritted his teeth. How was he supposed to be a leader—a prince—to the fairies when at every turn their magic put him at a disadvantage? He had to find a way. He was determined to reward the queen's faith in him. Zephyr, on the other hand, hadn't taken anything seriously all day.

It had only been a month since Elric arrived in this realm. In that time he had made no friends. Most of the magic folk either treated him with deference or kept their distance. The morning had started off well, and he thought perhaps Zephyr was different from the others. Zeph was friendlier than most, and didn't seem to mind the fact that Elric was a human boy from the

Otherworld. But it was late, and Zephyr's carefree attitude and pranks were wearing thin on Elric's patience.

It seemed Elric wasn't the only one who was annoyed. Master Elk crossed his arms and glared at them both. "I'm glad to see this is all fun and games to you boys. Zephyr, I thought I told you to remain solid."

"Yes, Master Windlight." Zeph shook the sand out of his hair. The raven feathers tied near his ear fluttered with the motion. "But if Elric is to learn how to defend himself in this realm, shouldn't he anticipate fairy magic?"

Elk's thin braids slid over his shoulders as he leaned forward and brought his sun-browned face within an inch of the younger fairy's. One of Elk's dark eyebrows rose. There was something in the captain's expression that made the hair on the back of Elric's neck stand up. "It's not fairy magic we are preparing him for."

Elk placed his hands behind his back. His long white robes swished around his legs as he strode in front of them. "That shield . . ." he said, pointing to the shimmering colors of the dome of light that protected the kingdom. "It's fragile. And it is under constant attack from both the Grendel and his cursed reapers, and the elves. If the queen suffers another heartbreak, it could shatter. If it does, the darkling creatures of the Nightfell Wood will invade this land." Elk began to pace, his feet lifting a small cloud of glittering dust with each step.

"The Grendel has corrupted all of the wood. He has fed for centuries on the souls of the creatures that live there. Now they are all like him. The elves are treacherous and cunning. They are betrayers and thieves. They will stop at nothing to break the shield, and allow the monsters of the wood to invade."

The sunlight glimmered on the silver thorn branches that crowned Elk's head. The captain stared down his broad nose as if his words were the law.

Elric looked over at the shield and the woods beyond. He didn't know enough about this world to judge what was good and what was dangerous. As he watched the shadows, dread stole through his blood.

Elk moved in front of him, each step falling with careful and quiet grace. The man's enormous shadow fell over Elric, bringing with it a slight chill. "Remember this, my prince—the Grendel seeks to break the heart of the queen, and her power with it. He will stop at nothing to find a weakness. He will send the foulest minions of his army to find you. The worst of them all, are the reapers."

Elric felt a heavy weight press down on him, and he leaned on his staff. He and Wynn almost died trying to find the Silver Gate, thinking they would be safe once they found it. Now they were in as much danger as they ever were.

Zephyr, who had been hovering nearby, sank back to the ground and cast an anxious glance at the distant shield. "Is it true the reapers have been attacking the shield?"

Master Elk turned to look at the shield. It seemed no more substantial than a bubble of air beneath water. "Yes. The fractures in the shield have been repaired. The Grendel knows there is only one way for that to happen. He knows the queen has taken in a new child. His spies are everywhere. The reapers are here, and they are hunting for the new changeling."

He moved closer to Elric and loomed over him. "They will catch you and drag you back to the Grendel so he can leech away your spirit. You will become nothing but an empty shell, trapped for all eternity in the torment of the Dark One's evil shadow. You must learn to protect yourself, Prince Elric. That is what I'm preparing you for." His expression softened. "I made a mistake the last time. I thought I could protect the last changeling prince myself by watching over him personally. I didn't warn him. He didn't know the danger." Master Elk looked away. "I won't make the same mistake with you."

Elric remained silent as his teacher strode away from him. The sunlight returned and warmed Elric's shoulders, but not his heart. From the moment he had found himself in the Between, he wasn't sure how he should fit into this place. The queen had made him a prince, but in reality, he was still just a shepherd boy. He knew nothing about wars, or fighting, or being a leader.

Master Elk circled around to Zephyr. "You need to learn discipline if you ever wish to grow up. You haven't even earned your second name yet after, what? Four hundred years? So I expect to see more effort out of you and less rule-breaking."

Elric stood straighter. "Captain, sir?"

Elk turned his attention toward Elric, who suddenly felt nervous under the scrutiny of the fairy. "How can we possibly fight the Grendel? He is a shadow." Elric remembered the troubles they had encountered on their journey to the Silver Gate, the howling winds, the disease, and death that seemed to follow them. He didn't think the Grendel was real at the time, but Wynn believed the Grendel had somehow followed them, and she had been right about the Silver Gate. He needed to know the true nature of what they both were facing.

Elk bowed his noble head. "The Grendel is not a shadow. Not in this world. He was a fairy once." Elk crushed a clotted chunk of sand beneath his foot. "Our power is driven by laughter, music, and light. But dark creatures from the Shadowfields began to infiltrate the Nightfell Wood. As a powerful fairy, he swore he would defeat them and protect the elves who lived there. During his battles, he discovered the strength of fear, sorrow, and pain."

Elric knew the power of those forces. The lord who had ruled their village used fear to control everyone beneath him.

Master Elk turned away from them, but his voice was no less resonant. "The Grendel became very powerful. When he defeated an army from the Shadowfields, he believed only he was strong enough to be king. But he was not given the crown." Elk turned back, and his eyes glowed white and glittered. "The Grendel tried to prove the queen wasn't strong enough to rule. He attacked her. In that moment, his heart and his magic became as black as the Shadowfields themselves."

Elk looked out at the Nightfell Wood. "Dark fairy

magic is like a disease. Once it gets hold, it slowly poisons the rest of your power. But it is strong, and we have never had to face a dark fairy as powerful as the Grendel before. The light of our magic gets pulled into his shadow and lost. We have no power that can equal dark magic, but if we tried to use our own dark magic against him, we would become like him, poisoned and corrupted. We cannot destroy him. All we can do is protect ourselves against him."

"But surely the magic of the queen—" Elric began.

Elk's eyes flashed red. "The magic of the queen shields us, and in turn, we protect her. Since you are now tied to the queen's heart as her chosen son, you must learn to protect your mortal life at all cost. That is your duty."

Elric twisted the toe of his boot in the sand. He didn't like being called the queen's son. He had only come here to save Wynn, and he had barely ever spoken to the queen. He was here to give Wynn a better life than the one she had in the Otherworld. He thought he had achieved that. But now he was looking toward a lifetime of always waiting for an attack.

"Elric!" Wynn called from somewhere behind him.

He jumped and spun around at the sound of his

sister's desperate voice. He dropped his staff and ran toward her at the edge of the arena. She was running with outstretched arms, already determined to hug him.

"Wynn, what are you doing here?" he asked as she crashed into him and wrapped him in one of her tight hugs. He gave her a quick squeeze, then put her at arm's length. Out of habit he scanned her, looking for anything out of place. "And what happened to your shoe?" he asked.

"Elric! I found you!" She clapped.

Master Elk swung his long cloak from his shoulders and wrapped it around Wynn, covering her head with the hood. "Princess, why are you outside? Does the queen know you are here?" His voice was hushed, but there was an edge of sharp command in it that made Elric's blood run cold.

Wynn looked at him with wide blue eyes. "My brother," she said, her words soft.

The Captain took Elric by the arm and led him a few steps closer to the palace but kept his body between Wynn and the wood. "Get her back to her room immediately. Keep her hidden," he demanded. "Do it now. We will continue training in the morning, and hurry."

Zephyr crept closer. Elk grabbed Zephyr by the ear

and tugged him back. "You still need to work on your healing magic."

Elric tucked Wynn under his arm as they marched back toward the palace. "What is wrong?" he asked. He still couldn't believe she made it to him on her own without getting caught.

"Danger," she said, pushing back Elk's heavy cloak, but he tucked it back up. "They want the Grendel to see you."

Elric's mind tried to puzzle out what she was attempting to tell him. She must have heard something very upsetting to try to find him so far from the palace. "What did you hear?" he asked.

"They want the Grendel to see you. Hide me," she said, still upset. "No fighting."

They passed under the enormous stone archways of the rock towers, and the high branches of the palace tree. They still had to go through the gardens to reach the doors to the throne room in the trunk of the great tree.

"Wynn, I don't understand," he said. She flapped her hands in response and walked around in a short circle. Wynn only did that when her emotions became too overwhelming. She wouldn't be able to tell him what had upset her in this state. It would also be more diffi-cult to lead her to her room. "Look at the gardens. Aren't they pretty?" he asked, to try to distract her.

Flowers bloomed in swirling arcs and circles of color. He glanced around for someone but the gardens were surprisingly empty. That was odd. For the past few days the palace had been mostly deserted too. But he had to focus on his task and find a way to lure Wynn back to her room. "Have you seen Mildred?" he asked.

Wynn shook her head and looked even more upset. "Mildred is not in my room," she answered, her words so unclear he almost didn't understand them.

No, she wouldn't have seen Mildred lately; the hen didn't like climbing the stairs. Mildred was getting fat staying in the kitchens. The first few weeks in the Between, he took Wynn down to the kitchens to visit her, but he hadn't done it in several days. He knew Wynn probably missed her bird. If they stopped by the kitchens, he could pick up Mildred and carry the hen to Wynn's bedroom so she could play with her chicken.

"I can be a prince too." Wynn flopped down on the ground. "I don't want to be the princess."

Elric tried to pull her up, but it was no use. "Wynn, what is wrong?"

"Stay in my room," she said as she wiped her nose on the sleeve of her delicate dress. "I don't like it."

Elric still wasn't sure what she was trying to tell him. "It is better here in the Between. We have plenty to eat, and warm, safe places to sleep." Elric picked up a rock from the path. "Do you remember when we had to sleep on the hard ground in the snow and we were so cold and hungry?"

Wynn looked away.

Elric wasn't sure what to say. He knew she was bored. He couldn't help that. He could set her on useless tasks just to keep her occupied, but he had a feeling she would know what he was up to. Wynn had an uncanny ability to see right through him. Besides, what could he possibly ask her to do that wouldn't get them both in trouble? Clean her room? "Everyone here wants to keep you safe and happy," he said. "We all love you."

She looked up at him, but she didn't say anything.

A sudden gust of wind nearly knocked Elric over. Zephyr appeared in front of him, his eyes burning bright red and yellow. "A darkling creature is attacking the shield to the west of the arena. I think it's a reaper!"

Elric's heart leaped in his chest. He jumped up, and Wynn followed.

"Come on, we have to hurry," Zephyr said as he grabbed Elric's arm and pulled him down the path. "Master Elk needs you there."

"Wynn, stay here," he ordered. He didn't want her crossing any bridges without help, and the garden was both sheltered and safe.

"No, they want to see you," she protested. "They want the Grendel to see you."

He took a step away from her, even as he held his palm out to stop her from following. "You'll be safe right here in the garden. I'll be back in just a moment. Promise me you'll stay here and wait for me. I'll come for you as soon as I can."

Zephyr disappeared again. Elric gave his sister a desperate look.

"I promise," she said. She flopped down in a pile of her silky skirts and crossed her arms. Elric gave her an approving nod and broke into a run. Master Elk had called for him. He glanced back to his sister.

She picked a flower and lazily plucked at the petals. She would stay until he could return for her, and then he would make sure she reached the safety of her room. "I promise I'll come back for you," he whispered to himself as he turned and ran.

CHAPTER THREE

Wynn

WYNN PULLED ALL THE PETALS off a flower. They floated in the air for a moment, before settling in her lap and on her bare foot. The sunlight caught the edges of the petals and made them glow with an iridescent light. She liked watching them twirl and sparkle as they fell into the sand. When they hit the ground, a faint ring of glittering light spread out through the sand, like a ripple in a pool. She pushed the sand with her toe to watch the light spread across the path in front of her. The sunlight felt pleasantly warm on her shoulders. The soft breeze pushed her hair away from her cheek. The sound of chimes surrounded her, filling the garden with music.

It was all very pretty, and it was very nice to be outside. But this was as lonely as sitting in her room all day, and she was worried about her brother. Still, she promised Elric she'd wait for him.

"You just have to wait," she mumbled to herself, repeating a phrase her mother had repeated to her over and over when she was younger.

She hated waiting.

But she made a promise, and Elric would be back soon.

Wynn swiped her hand over the gritty sand of the path and made a pattern watching the glitter in the sand swirl and loop as it spread outward. The trails of light faded, and she reached out to make another one. Just then, she heard a hissing sound behind her, and turned to look over her shoulder. Thick rosebushes created a blanket of flowers that draped to the ground and hid the shadows beneath them.

Squinting, Wynn pushed herself up and stepped closer to the bush as she brushed her dirty hands off on her snowy white skirts. Something rustled. She reached down to the edge of the bush and grasped a low tangle of the rose branches. One of the thorns pierced her thumb, and she drew her hand back. More carefully this time, she reached out and lifted the untamed roses.

A fat black hen rushed out, flapping her brown-streaked feathers.

"Mildred!" Wynn's heart leaped. She had missed her hen so much. Mildred was her best friend. Wynn trotted over to catch up to the hen, but Mildred hopped just out of reach toward the edge of the garden.

Now Wynn felt very happy. Mildred could stay with her and play until Elric came back. Mildred was good at keeping her company, and pecking bugs, and eating, but also keeping her company. Wynn bent down. "Mildred, come here."

The bird stumbled, letting one wing flop listlessly on the ground. She wasn't making her usual clucking noises. Something was very wrong with her. Mildred liked to talk.

"What's wrong?" Wynn hurried closer to the hen, but Mildred ran away, her wing dragging in the sand of the garden path. "You are hurt?"

A sick feeling rose in Wynn's tummy. Mildred was a good chicken. She had to help her. "Mildred, come here!" Wynn demanded, her voice cracking as she chased after her hen. Mildred darted away into fields of tall grasses beyond the edges of the garden. Wynn tried to trill *"Mill-ee-ee-ee"* the way Elric did so Mildred would come, but she couldn't make the sounds right.

Wynn paused at the edge of the garden. She looked behind her. Elric would be angry that she didn't wait, but he'd understand that she had to help Mildred. He loved the hen too. When she caught Mildred, she would bring her along to go to find him. Elric would know what to do to help her.

With one shoe and one bare foot, Wynn crossed through the tall stone towers and sprinted into the fields that surrounded the palace. She ran as fast as she could, but no matter what she did, Mildred raced ahead of her.

"Come back!" Wynn screamed. Mildred was fleeing as if she were very scared. Her head flopped to the side, and her wing looked broken.

Wynn's chest burned. She was tired, but she wouldn't stop running. She had to catch Mildred. She had to help her. She didn't want Mildred to look the way her mother had when she found her after the storm and Wynn knew she was gone forever.

Mildred was the only thing she had from home.

Wynn grabbed her silky skirts. The material slipped

in her fingers as she lifted the skirts away from her feet. Every sharp little stone and scratchy blade of grass cut into the underside of her bare foot, but that didn't matter. She had to reach her Mildred.

Just ahead, the swirling colors of the queen's magic shield rose up. It stood over her like a great wall. Beyond the twisting light of the shield, she could see the heavy branches of the edge of the Nightfell Wood.

Scary things lived in there. Scary things that would eat Mildred.

"Mildred, stop!" Wynn screamed. "No running!"

The hen looked back at her. She fell to her side and wriggled in the dirt. Wynn was almost caught up to her.

But then Mildred popped up and darted through the shield into the shadows on the other side.

"No!" Wynn shouted. Tears streaked down her face. They felt hot on her cheeks as she panted for breath. She wanted her hen back. It was dangerous out in the Nightfell Wood. Bad things lived there. She couldn't cross through the shield to follow her.

The queen had told her to never come here. She needed help.

Wynn turned around, looking frantically for anyone who could help her. She was completely alone. No one could save Mildred but her.

She swiped the back of her hand under her nose. Mildred had saved her once. Wynn could not leave her.

Wynn hesitantly reached out to touch the shield, but felt nothing. Her hand passed right through it as the swirling colors spilled over her palm like flowing water. She took another step closer. The light and color slid up her outstretched arm, but she still couldn't feel it. Going through would be easy.

Wynn took a deep breath and held it, shutting her eyes tight as she marched forward. She counted eight steps, then opened her eyes and took a deep breath. The shield stood behind her, but instead of being filled with beautiful colors, it looked like a storm-gray sky filled with dark clouds. Wynn couldn't see the colors of the fairy realm on the other side of the smoky shield anymore. Everything in the fairy realm looked gray. The air felt cooler here in the shadows of the dark trees. Wynn shivered.

The branches above her reached close to the shield like skeleton fingers. Leaves rustled in the wind. Sounds seemed sharper and hushed at the same time. Wynn didn't want to go any deeper into the woods.

Just ahead in a small clearing, Mildred lay still on

her side. Her head flopped in the dirt and her bright red comb reminded Wynn of a pool of blood.

"Mildred!" She ran to the hen. For the first time Mildred didn't run away.

She looked dead.

Wynn fell to her knees and scooped up the hen. "You are safe, you are safe," she murmured. She couldn't concentrate enough to find different words, so she repeated the same ones over and over. "You are safe."

The urge to cry choked her. "We need to go home now, Mildred."

Wynn carried the hen very carefully in her arms and turned toward the shield. She had to take Mildred and find Elric. He would know how to help. She hoped it wasn't too late.

A strange hissing sound came from Mildred's chest, and she opened her eyes. They flashed bright red and her head stretched forward, her fat body seeming to melt and pull into a long, thin line.

Wynn screamed as Mildred's soft feathers disappeared and scales appeared in their place. Wynn's body froze up and she couldn't move. Mildred's head curved around and formed into a serpent with spines running down its twisted back. The serpent clutched a dark feather in its horrible mouth. It snapped, trying to bite her. The light gleamed on sharp fangs as the feather fluttered to the ground.

Wynn forced her body to move, and threw the snake as hard as she could at the trees and ran toward the shield. It slithered after her through the grass with a sound like the rattling of bones. Wynn glanced over her shoulder. The snake was gaining on her. Suddenly she crashed into something, hard.

She tumbled to the ground, then picked herself up, thinking she had run into a tree. No. The only thing in front of her was the shield. She reached her hand out the way she did before, but instead of passing through the smoky gray shield, her fingers and knuckles crumpled against a hard force, shooting pain up her arm. The stormy clouds felt like they were made of stone.

The rattle and hiss grew louder.

Wynn jumped to her feet and picked up a rock and threw it at the snake. She missed, but the snake had to dodge.

"Help!" she screamed, pounding on the shield with her palm.

The snake lunged again and Wynn had to spring away. It hit the shield where she was standing, then slid toward her along the edge. Wynn backed away from the shield. The serpent slithered in front of her with the shield behind it. She had only one way she could go, toward the dark trees. The heavy leaves of the branches loomed over her head like thunderclouds.

The snake bared its fangs. Its eyes glowed brighter red, and Wynn thought she could hear the echo of a dark and cruel laugh on the wind.

She ran.

Dashing into the shadows of the branches, she ran as fast as she could without looking back. She stumbled and scrambled over knotted tree roots. Whip-like branches tore at her dress and slapped against her arms.

"Help!" she called again, but the sound barely came out of her throat.

The toe of her shoe caught on something and she fell forward in a heap. Her cheek hit the ground and she felt the blow through her jaw and neck. Slimy leaves clung to her face as she rolled over. She curled her arms in toward her chest.

Backing up against a tree, she tried to push herself up, but slipped on the leaves under her feet.

The snake slithered over the curling tree roots. Its eyes narrowed and it seemed to grin. It rattled the spines along its back again as its long, forked tongue darted out.

"Go away!" Wynn shouted at it. She picked herself up, and grabbed a nearby branch. She swung the branch at the serpent, and it hesitated.

She was all alone. No one could help her now.

A loud squawk filled the clearing and a furious ball of dark feathers charged forward.

It was the real Mildred! At least, she thought it was her. Maybe this was a monster too. Wynn's heart thudded as the chicken's white legs slashed out at the serpent. Her comb flushed dark red, and her fiery eyes blazed as her sharp beak pecked at the serpent's head. Wynn's hen was fighting to save her.

The serpent hissed and turned to strike Mildred, but Mildred was too quick. She stamped on the beast, tearing at it with sharp claws. Then, with a furious squawk, she pecked it right in the eye.

It let out a terrible hiss of pain. Wynn jumped forward with her stick and bashed the snake hard on the head. She hit it again and again while Mildred clawed and scratched its twisting body.

Slowly the twisting stopped.

"Come, Mildred, quickly!" Wynn shook and ran

away as fast as she could. Mildred followed at her heels, clucking and chattering at her the whole way. Wynn didn't know if the creature was dead. She didn't want to take a chance.

Out of breath, she stopped at the bank of a dried creek and placed a hand on her chest.

"Mildred?" she asked cautiously. The hen fluffed up the feathers of her chest as if she were deeply offended by Wynn's tone, then snuggled down on top of Wynn's bare foot. She let out an exhausted coo, and her eyes drooped.

Wynn knelt down and cautiously clapped a sharp two claps. Mildred repeated the sound with two crisp clucks. Elric taught her that trick.

"It's you," Wynn said, and scooped up her hen. She buried her face in Mildred's feathers as the hen affectionately pecked at the tips of her hair. This was her hen. She knew it. "Mildred, you saved me."

Awwwwwwk, Mildred cooed. *Tut, tut, tut.*

Wynn tucked Mildred under her arm, glad to have her safe where she belonged.

"We have to go home." Wynn looked up. The canopy of dark leaves towered above her so thick, she couldn't see the sky. She couldn't see the shield.

Wynn took a hesitant step one way. Paused, then took a step in another. All the trees looked the same. The chilly air settled over her.

"Mildred, go home," Wynn said as she gently placed Mildred on the ground. Mildred always knew which way to go.

But Mildred just cuddled close to her leg again and didn't move, glancing warily at the trees.

Wynn scooped her up again and peered into the dark shadows that surrounded them through the thick trees.

They were lost in the Nightfell Wood.

CHAPTER FOUR

Elric

ELRIC RAN AS FAST AS he could across the western fields toward the magic shield, both excited and terrified at the prospect of seeing a real battle. Zephyr flew beside him, stirring a strong breeze at their backs. Elric glanced back at the great tree and gardens. His steps slowed as he had a sudden bad feeling that something was very wrong.

"Why did you stop?" Zephyr floated up ahead.

"This could be dangerous, and I should be looking out for my sister. Master Elk told me to get her to her room right away," Elric said, turning back toward the garden where he'd left Wynn. Nothing was more important to him than her.

Zephyr swooped in front of him on a strong gust of wind. He deliberately floated a few feet in the air right in front of Elric, blocking his view of the palace. The fairy crossed his arms. "Master Elk told me to get you," Zephyr said with a serious expression. Zephyr never wore a serious expression. Something was wrong here. Wynn had left the palace to warn him about something— something about letting the Grendel see him. He had a funny feeling in his gut, and he couldn't ignore it.

"What is really going on?" Elric demanded. "You fly around as a breeze all day and hear everything. Wynn was upset about something. What is it?"

Zephyr rubbed the back of his neck, shifting the raven feathers by his ear. "I overheard Raven Frostrain speaking with Master Elk this morning."

"And?" Elric's heart pounded.

"Lord Raven believes that there is a spy within the dome. He said the Grendel knows the queen has taken in another Otherworld child, and he told Master Elk to dangle you out near the shield so the Grendel thinks it is you." Zephyr looked ashamed. "They won't actually let you fight. They just want the Grendel to believe you are the queen's new child."

"And not Wynn," Elric said. The twisted feeling in his stomach hardened and turned into a rock in his middle. He turned back toward the shield.

"You aren't really in danger," Zephyr said. "The fighting lessons aren't serious. The queen wouldn't let you come to harm."

"Death is not a game." Elric had come too close to it before.

Zephyr tucked his head in a shamed bow. "Look, I like you, Prince Elric. I'm just doing what I was told."

"And allowing me to be a sacrifice," he said.

Zephyr didn't have an answer.

Elric felt as if his heart had slowed to a cold and heavy thrum he could feel in his face and shaking hands. It made sense. As terrible as it was to find out he was a sacrificial lamb, it made sense. His thoughts drifted back to a warm night long ago in the Otherworld when he had been tending his sheep.

He knew a wolf was close. He could feel the beast stalking his flock, and when he saw movement in the woods, he went toward it with his sling in hand. He knew the wolf could attack him at any time, but he had a weapon then, and he knew a wild creature would be scared of him.

Now he had nothing. He had no power in this world, no magic, a mortal life, and enemies who would not be afraid of him. Elric let out a slow breath, pushing the air from his lungs until the lack of it hurt.

By filling this role, he could hide his sister and protect her. No wonder Master Elk had hurried to make sure she was out of sight as quickly as possible. And now was his chance to fool the Grendel and his minions. He could keep her safe. He lifted his chest, drawing in a fortifying breath. "Take me to Master Elk."

Shouts arose from the far side of the hill. Elric froze. A blood-chilling howl echoed in the distance. Zephyr's expression darkened as he rose a few feet in the air. Elric stepped forward, ready for the role he had to play.

There was a rustling in front of them. The dark ears of a red fox peeked over the rippling grasses. She reached a patch of low clover, then collapsed, falling to her side as if she had been struck with a club. Glimmering silver mist streamed from her shoulder.

"Fox?" Zephyr looked as stricken as he watched the other fairy collapse in the clover.

"Hurry!" Elric yelled to Zephyr as he rushed forward.

"Fox, are you all right?" He knelt beside the wounded fox lying in a heap of red fur in the clover. His hands shook as he reached toward her.

In a flash, the fox transformed into a young fairy warrior. Silver light bled from the gash in her shoulder.

"It's not safe for the prince. Don't come closer. Go back!" she shouted, holding her bleeding arm.

"You're wounded." Elric couldn't hide the disbelief in his voice. Fox Snowsong was one of the elite guard. Her shoulder had been torn open. Elric looked for something to tie off the wound. He knew how to stop blood. But he didn't know how to heal a fairy. Magic flowed through their veins instead of blood.

"Zephyr, get over here!" Elric shouted at his friend. "She's hurt. You have to use your magic to heal her."

Zephyr still looked stunned. "But I am not good at healing. Even with Master Elk's lessons, I'm hopeless."

"There is no other choice, so do it!" Elric shouted. He reached up and pulled Zephyr down next to him. "You were working on it right before I left the arena."

Fox's long red braid swung behind her as she cried out and fell back down into the clover. Zephyr came to her side, he stared at his hands, slowly they began to glow. Sweat beaded on the fairy's brow as he reached through the air. He caught the silvery light pouring from her shoulder, and pushed it back toward the wound.

"Good work. Keep trying." Elric moved back to give him room.

Fox hissed in a breath, but did not struggle as Zephyr attempted to heal her. "There's a reaper trying to break through the shield," she said. Fox swiped a hand over her brow, pushing aside her fringe of bangs. Silver light glittered along her brow as well. "It's throwing itself against the shield over and over. I've never seen one so aggressive. It won't stop fighting. It's already formed a crack, and it may break through. Elk and I went through the shield to try to fend it off. It was too strong. Elk is still fighting it."

"Is he hurt as well?" Elric stood and took a step toward the crest of the hill.

"I don't know, but you have to stay back," Fox called to him. "If you fall through the shield, you could be trapped on the other side. Only someone with pure fairy magic can pass through and still come back."

A howling scream filled the air, followed by what sounded like the high trumpeting call of a large deer.

"I have to do something." Elric ran forward. He didn't know what he could do, but he had to help. He couldn't just stand there.

Elric rounded the top of the hill and looked down on the scene below. The colors of the shield shifted in bright blues and greens in front of him as he watched the place where it met the bottom of the hill. It reminded him of bits of colored glass. A crack sliced up the shield, jagged and threatening, like a frozen bolt of lightning.

On the other side of the shield, a creature the size of a bear lifted its head. It was a terrifying mix of beast and man, standing on its hind legs at easily nine feet tall and covered in greasy black fur. It opened its long, bear-like snout, stretching the leathery gray skin of its face as it displayed jagged yellow teeth. Its red eyes glowed like hot coals, while the shaggy fur around its neck stood up in a thick ruff.

It turned toward Master Elk, who was charging at it in the form of a white stag.

Glittering light streamed from several wounds on the powerful stag's snowy hide. Master Elk's silver horns gleamed like blades as the fairy charged with his head bent low so he could skewer the beast against one of the wide trunks of the ancient trees of the Nightfell Wood. He didn't have the safety of the shield to protect him from the beast. He was fighting on the far side of it.

Elric watched in horror as everything seemed to happen with an unnatural slowness. The sound of the Elk's hooves hitting the rocky ground clattered in his ears. The monster's arm swung in a ruthless arc. Claws the size of skinning knives, slicing across Master Elk's neck. The blow sent the stag flying toward the dark shadows of the trees.

"Master Elk!" Elric rushed forward, remembered Fox's words, and stopped himself. There was nothing he could do from this side of the shield.

The reaper stalked forward, its bony shoulders undulating beneath its shaggy hide.

Elk transformed into a fairy warrior and pulled himself to his feet. He braced himself, holding his sword at an angle in front of him. Magical fire reflected in his shining blade. But Elric noticed how low he held the tip. His stance didn't show the strength it usually did as silver light flowed from his neck. He sliced his sword in front of him and a wall of flame appeared between him and the reaper.

The monster reached the wall of fire and roared.

The reaper swung at him, but Master Elk dodged and slashed at the creature, cutting the reaper across its hairy forearm. The creature howled, then snapped at him. It fell onto its bony hands and stalked in a tight circle, walking on all four limbs like a beast, pushing Master Elk closer to the edge of the dark wood.

Elk was trapped. With his back to the wood, he was vulnerable to attack from another beast lurking in the shadows. It was the beginning of an ambush.

The reaper sprang. Master Elk slashed at it with his sword, but it reared up and used the mass of its thick body to knock Elk over. The reaper grabbed Master Elk in its bony fingers, then bared its long fangs.

Elk disappeared, then reappeared as a stag, crashing into the beast with his sharp silver horns. The beast swung its enormous arm into the body of the stag, throwing Master Elk into the trunk of a tree.

The stag collapsed, and didn't rise again. The reaper stalked toward him, letting out a snarling bark.

Elric had to do something. Master Elk was in trouble. He glanced behind him, but there was no army charging through the plains to come to their rescue. Only Fox and Zephyr remained hunched in the grasses. He turned back to the shield. He wasn't a warrior, not yet. But he had never been a coward. If the reaper wanted a good look at him, that was fine by Elric.

"Hey!" he shouted, charging at the shield. "Hey, you

there!" He ran down the slope, waving his arms. "You want to take someone back to the Grendel, why don't you take me?"

If Lord Raven had wanted him to be the decoy that protected his sister, he might as well do it now. The slope steepened toward the shield, and his feet skidded in the loose rocks. The beast turned to him and Elric stared into its cold, dead eyes.

"You heard me, come and get me!" Elric shouted. He scrambled toward the enormous monster that could easily tear him in two. Black blood flowed from its wounds into its matted hair. It charged away from Master Elk and toward the shield. Elric fell on his hip and slid toward the shield. He scrambled to hold on to something to keep himself from sliding through.

His heel caught a stone, and he stopped his slide just inches from the edge of the shield. He was so close that the light of the shield cast his feet and legs in washes of bright color.

The reaper's eyes glowed with a killing light as it slowly took a step toward him.

Elric pushed himself to his feet, his nose nearly touching the shimmering barrier. "That's right!" he shouted, though his arms were shaking. He waved them at the beast. "It's me your master wants. I'm the Other-world child!" Elric sidestepped along the shield, drawing the creature away from his wounded teacher until he came to the large crack.

Elric could feel the beast's low growl rattle through his bones.

The reaper shook out its scraggly black ruff like a wet dog. Its wounds oozed as it snarled and stalked closer toward the shield. Elk staggered to his feet and gave Elric a nod. His distraction was working.

"Come and get me!" Elric shouted again.

The creature threw its head down and crashed into the shield like a battering ram. The crack lengthened. A sound like ice fracturing echoed through the air.

Elric's heart pounded as he took a step back. The reaper threw itself against the shield again, and branches appeared on the crack, limbs on a dead tree.

Elk slipped through the shield to the safety of the open field. "Elric, run!" Elk screamed at him. "It wants you. Run!"

But Elric couldn't move. His legs felt as if they were made of stone, too heavy to lift. The creature's eyes burned brighter, and Elric heard a distant laugh on the wind, dark, cruel, and full of malice. He had felt the chill of that wind before back in the Otherworld.

The Grendel.

The reaper stilled at the edge of the shield, listening to its master's voice on the wind. It tapped a single claw against the crack as if testing the damage it had caused. This wasn't a mindless beast, and that frightened Elric more than anything he had seen thus far. It was plotting.

Fire flashed in the creature's eyes, then it smiled at him.

Its bat-like ears swung forward and it lifted its snout high in the air, breathing deeply. Then the creature howled, a long haunting note that slid deep into the shadows of the wood. Those burning eyes met Elric's again, before it fell on its paw-like hands and loped off down the slope of the bluff. It disappeared deep in the shadows of the woods.

Elric let out the breath he was holding. The creature was gone. They were safe, and yet, he had never felt more vulnerable. The crack in the shield remained.

He turned and ran to Elk's side, lifting his teacher's arm so he could help carry him to safety.

"That was very brave," Elk said, his deep voice resonant, but lacking the strength it usually carried. "Risky, but brave."

"It's still out there, somewhere." As they crested the

hill, he saw Zephyr lift Fox to her feet, then Zepher flew over to them. He carefully tended the wound in Elk's neck, with Elk offering quiet guidance.

Fairies always spoke as if they were immortal. Now Elric wasn't so sure. After all, the queen's daughter had died as a baby.

Zephyr looked over at him. "Are you harmed? I really don't know how to heal mortal wounds."

"I'm fine," Elric mumbled. "Scratched up a little, but I'll live." He brushed grit out of the scrapes on his palms. Something wasn't right. The reaper didn't act as if it had been driven off. Something had distracted it, called it away. A sinking feeling settled in the pit of Elric's stomach, but he did his best to ignore it. This was his first battle. He had won. He had protected the fairy realm. Why didn't it feel right?

Elk's dark eyes met his. His teacher nodded at him in approval.

Elric had done his job. He'd given the reapers a target. Now he had to see to his sister. He turned toward the palace.

Zephyr flew up beside him. "Where are you going?" he asked.

"I need to find Wynn. I left her alone." He jogged

down the hill toward the great tree. "I need to get her back to her room." Really he just needed one of her hugs. The kind where she didn't let go until she almost knocked him over.

Besides, he had promised her that he would return as quickly as he could.

"I'll come too," Zephyr said, flying ahead of Elric and turning backward as the breezes that constantly surrounded him cooled Elric's heated skin. Fox supported Elk, keeping her wounded arm close to her side, even though the silvery light had stopped flowing from her shoulder. The guards spoke together as they started toward the palace. Zephyr stayed close to his side, and Elric wondered if the young and uninjured fairy was on orders to protect him.

It didn't take long before they reached the gardens and found the shimmering sand paths leading through the roses. Elric wound through the garden trails until he reached the place where he'd left Wynn waiting.

She wasn't there.

A scattering of petals blew across the swirling patterns she must have traced in the sand. "Wynn?" he called.

He hated when she wandered off, but she wouldn't

have gone far. "Wynn! I'm back! Wait until you hear what happened."

His voice drifted off over the silent gardens. An uneasy feeling crept over him. "Wynn, where are you?"

"Maybe they brought her inside," Zeph suggested. He rose in the air several feet and looked around. "I don't see her anywhere out here."

"Look." Elric bent down and picked up a dark feather. He touched the sand. It still faintly glimmered from the pronged footprint of Wynn's hen. "Mildred must have found her."

The uneasy feeling lingering in his stomach reached up and grabbed his throat. Wynn would follow that hen anywhere.

Zeph bent down beside him to look at the marks in the sand. He waved a hand over them, and they glowed slightly brighter. One footprint with the impression of toes, and another muffled outline of a foot wearing a shoe. Wynn only had one shoe on. The prints led in a direct path out of the gardens toward the field beyond.

Elric's heart sank. She couldn't have. Wynn wasn't foolish. She wouldn't have left the garden.

He ran to the edge of the garden path, following Wynn's footsteps, only to see another path of trampled grasses leading across the meadow. Zephyr gave him a worried look and followed him as Elric tracked his sister's trail through the grass until it disappeared through the shield.

"Wynn!" Elric screamed. "Wynn! Come back!"

Zephyr blew through the shield, flitting over the small clearing on the other side. He paused and picked up something from the ground, then floated back through the shield.

He was holding up a silk ribbon from Wynn's dress.

Wynn was gone.

CHAPTER FIVE

Wynn

WYNN FELT THE GROUND TREMBLE. Maybe it was her. She felt shaky as she looked up at the branches of the tall trees. They were so thick, like a thatched roof, but ugly and twisted. She was turned around. She didn't know which way to walk to go home. There was no path to guide her. She hadn't been in the dark for a long time. In the Between, everything glowed around the fairies. Even nighttime was full of light under the dome. The woods were full of shadows that made Wynn feel afraid. She had never been afraid in woods in the Otherworld before, even when she was alone. These woods were different. They were cold and damp, like a rainy day in the fall just before the rain turned to snow. The chilled, wet air clung to her face and felt heavy, like sadness.

"What do we do?" Wynn picked up Mildred and cuddled her. She wished Elric were here. She didn't wait for him in the garden. She should have listened. The snake tricked her.

Mildred's feathers felt soft against the side of her face as her tears wet them. The woods were danger. She had to find a way back. Elric would be waiting for her.

When she lived at home with her mother, she used to wander in the woods. She always placed sticks to show her way home. There were no sticks behind her. She ran from the snake too fast.

A loud and scary howl sounded in the distance.

She couldn't stay here.

If you are lost, sit down in one place. I will find you.

She heard the voice of her mother in her head. "If you are lost, sit down," she repeated aloud.

Wynn crossed her legs and sank to the forest floor. The skirt of her pretty white dress billowed around her like a cloud. "Sit down." She held Mildred tighter.

Elric would know she was lost. He would come to find her.

"We will wait here, Mildred." Wynn stroked the

bird's neck. Mildred cooed at her in a soothing way. The howl sounded in the woods again. A shiver raced through Wynn. She looked up. The heavy branches of the trees creaked in the cold wind. Something clattered. A bird's wings flapped frantically.

The light around her dimmed as dark clouds covered the weak light that managed to creep through the branches.

She wished she had fairy magic. She would turn into a bird and fly away from this place. Up high, she could see the way home. But the shield would block her if she tried to go through. Wynn drew herself up into a tight little ball, curling around Mildred. She was scared.

"My queen, my queen . . ." She tried to sing the familiar song to make herself feel braver, but the words stopped coming to her. She wanted to get up, to run, to climb a tree to get away from the dark woods, but there was no way to escape. No. Mother had said that if she was lost, she should sit and wait. Mother always told her the best thing to do. They practiced over and over so Wynn would never forget. She wanted to run so badly. She was so scared.

"Sit and wait," Wynn whispered. "Elric will find you."

A dry branch snapped nearby. Something rustled in the bushes.

Wynn's heart pounded, and she couldn't swallow. What if something else found her before Elric did?

"We need to hide," she whispered to Mildred. Looking around the small clearing, she tucked herself behind the twisted trunk of one of the enormous trees. She remembered hiding before. She got down low and reached for her old gray cloak.

Wynn grabbed a handful of her snowy-white dress. She didn't have her gray cloak. She only had princess things. The dress was pretty, but it seemed to glow in the dark shadows. Wynn took a closer look. It did glow! This was not good for hiding.

Mildred kicked the dried leaves piled near the trunk of the tree. The leaves were dark. Wynn scooped them up and spread them over her skirt, then pressed her body into a nook where the trunk had curved in a gnarled way. "Stay quiet, Mildred. We're hiding."

Her hen listened, and tucked her beak into the feathers of her chest. Mildred mistook hiding for napping, but that was all right. It felt good to hold Mildred close. Wynn trembled as she held her pet. She shook so hard, the leaves covering her skirt shivered in the darkness. Something was coming.

Wynn pressed her eyes tight shut, and hugged Mildred.

She heard the rustling. It came closer . . . closer.

"And what is this?" a squeaky little voice called out. Wynn peeked around the trunk of the tree.

There, in the clearing, stood a strange little creature the size of a large cat. He picked up a torn piece of her skirt and turned it over and over in his hands. He had the face of a man, with a long nose, pointy teeth, and large amber eyes that took up most of his face. Fox ears poked up through a mop of black hair, and they twisted this way and that. But the strangest part of the little man was his legs, which were like a rabbit, and covered in dark red fur. Maybe that wasn't the strangest part. He also had a long rat-like tail that ended in a tuft of black hair.

"This is fairy stuff!" the little creature squealed. He clutched the piece of her skirt close to his chest, and looked around the shadows. His ears twitched. "Soooooo light. So shiny!" He rubbed it against his cheek. Then he swung a small sack off his back, and tucked the piece of fairy cloth inside. "How did fairy things get here?" he said, hopping around the clearing on his springy legs. "There are no fairies in the dark woods." He found a black feather and picked it up, pulling it under his long nose. "The feathered one?"

Wynn felt a rush of joy. She knew this creature! His

name was Hob. He had greeted them when they first came to this land. Elric said he wanted to steal things from them. But Wynn liked him. He was nice, and he had tried to help them.

But what if this wasn't really Hob? She'd already met a Mildred that wasn't really Mildred.

Hob hopped around, sniffing suspiciously. "Feathery Otherworldsy cluck, cluck? Are you here, yes?" he asked. Mildred cooed her happy greeting. She stretched her neck out toward Hob. He bounded toward the sound of her clucking.

The little man-beast almost landed in Wynn's lap before he saw her behind the tree. He screamed, then Wynn screamed. She accidentally dropped Mildred into the leaves.

"You!" Hob shouted. "Wynn Otherworldsy girl, why are you in the woods? You are dressed in fairy things."

"Hob?" she asked. "Are you a snake?"

Hob looked down and splayed his long fingers over his thin chest. Then he looked up at her and shook his head, his ears flopping from side to side. "I am Hob."

Wynn grabbed a nearby stick and held it, ready to hit Hob if he changed form. "Mildred was Mildred, then she was not Mildred."

Hearing her name, Mildred strutted straight up to Hob and gave him a sharp peck on the top of his head. He covered his head with his hands and hissed at her.

Wynn leaped up and scrambled away, expecting Hob to change into another snake, but he just cocked his head as he looked at her. "Hob was Hob. Hob is Hob. I am Hob." He grinned, baring his sharp teeth. He clapped his hands together. "I know! Look!" He pulled his little sack off his shoulder and opened it. "I liked your strap-bag. I made one! So Hob could carry this." He reached into the tiny sack and drew out an old cork that had once been a part of a small honey bottle. It had been a gift that Elric had given the little creature when they first came through the Silver Gate.

"Hob!" Wynn cried, and rushed forward. The creature tried to leap away, but Wynn grabbed him and gave him a big hug. "I'm so happy to see you again."

"Happy?" He braced his furry arms against her as he cocked his head to the side. His large ears twisted sideways. "No one is happy to see Hob." His voice dropped a pitch and he frowned. "Elvsies don't share their fruit. They chase Hob and try to catch him in their nasty traps. Darkling creatures try to eat him."

Wynn hugged him again. "I am so, so happy. You are my friend."

"Friend?" Hob's large eyes grew round and shiny. "Hob is a friend?"

Wynn smiled at him. Slowly Hob wrapped his long fuzzy arms around Wynn's neck and hugged her back. He sighed, and his long tail whipped from side to side.

"Yes, my friend." Wynn gently let go of him.

He climbed up on her shoulder and patted her head. "I am happy too. You are a nice Otherworld child. My friend. With nice things to give Hob the way friends do." He touched the silver band in her hair. She pushed his hand away.

"That's not yours, it's mine." She scowled at him.

He just smiled and tucked his precious cork back into his little sack. "What are you doing? It is far here in the Nightfell Woods, and very, very dangerous in this place. Nasty beasties will eat you, elvsies will catch you in cages, or worse things will come."

Wynn looked around the clearing. It was hard to believe there was a sun at all in this place. She shivered. "I'm lost."

"Then we must take you back." Hob bounced up and down, his tail whipping wildly behind him. "Because Hob is very nice. He is a very good friend. And the fairies will like him now and let him stay in the safe place where the bugs are so tasty." Hob bounded through the trees. Mildred trotted after him.

Wynn followed as fast as she could. The sticks and leaves poked the bottom of her bare foot. It was scratched and it hurt. Still she smiled. She didn't care if her foot hurt. She would be back soon. Hob would take her to the right place to go.

Then she remembered the shield. She stopped in her tracks. Hob glanced back at her. "I can't go through," she said.

Hob sat back on his long furry feet. He rubbed his chin. "Didn't think of that. You don't have fairy magic." He thought some more. Then he bounced up so high, he flipped. "I know a way, a secret place. There is a crack. The fairies have not found it. They did not fix it. It has been there a long time, yes. But only little creatures like Hob can fit through. I will go and find the boy Otherworld child. I can bring him to you. Follow me!"

They changed directions and marched through the trees. Now that she had a friend, things didn't seem so scary anymore. The trees were bigger here. The bark was very black. The leaves were heavy, too. But for a little bit, Wynn felt like she was walking through the woods back home. Those woods were very nice.

Wynn hummed a tune and marched along after her guide.

Hob stopped. Lifting his nose high in the air, he sniffed. Then his ear slowly twisted one way as his other ear turned a different way. He went very still.

Mildred ran over and perched on Wynn's foot again. Wynn lifted her and stroked her back. "What is wrong?" Wynn asked. The cold feeling came back in her body. She shivered as each space between the trees looked dark and deep to her.

Hob's amber eyes flashed. "Hob can smell it, yes. A reaper nearby. Very stinky," he said, his ears pressed low on his head.

"What is a reaper?" Wynn asked. She knew it was something scary. Raven said something about them.

Hob looked at her with huge eyes as he shook all over. "Grendel sends the reapers in the woods to do his nasty hunting. They catch creatures and bring them back to their master. Then the Grendel sucks the spirit out of them until they disappear." He whipped his head up and looked behind them. "Run." He hopped quickly down the path. "Run!"

Wynn grabbed Mildred and held her tight to her chest. The hen squawked. Wynn ran. She tried to run fast. Hob bounded ahead of her. With his bouncy legs he sprang over twisted roots and sharp rocks. Wynn had one shoe. Her bare foot hurt. The bushes caught her dress and ripped it. The skirt trailed under her foot. She stepped on it, and the jerk of the snag nearly made her fall onto Mildred.

She had to keep running. It was hard to run while she held Mildred, but she didn't want to let go. She had to keep Mildred safe. She had to get back home.

"Run, Wynn-friend!" Hob shouted, his tail whipping behind him. "Run fast. The shield is near."

A howl slid through the darkness. Wynn gasped as she turned to look behind her. It sounded so close. Hob jumped over to her and leaped up on her shoulder. "Too close. You must hide. I will draw it away. Then you go that way." He pointed. "Find the shield. The fairies will see you."

"Hob, no," Wynn said.

He yanked on her hair, and pointed. "In there." He motioned to a place where mud had washed out from between a tangle of roots forming a cage of roots at the bottom of the tree. Wynn tucked herself inside. Hob hopped around the roots, furiously kicking and scratching wet and slimy leaves over the tree roots, until he made a little den of leaves around her. Some fell on Wynn in cold clumps. The scratching continued as Hob gathered big bunches of leaves in his little arms and threw them over her until she was completely hidden by the pile of moldy leaves.

"It's okay, Mildred," Wynn whispered, stroking her hen's neck. Mildred didn't make a sound, but she pressed her neck against Wynn's cheek. Wynn peeked out of a tiny gap in the leaves. She saw one of Hob's shiny amber eyes.

"I will keep you safe, friend." His long finger came up to his lips. He gave her a short nod, then hopped into the clearing. A howl filled the air around them.

The reaper was here.

CHAPTER SIX

Elric

ELRIC RAN AS FAST AS he could back to the heart of the palace. The shadow of the great stone archways passed over him as he crossed into the courtyards. The archways towered hundreds of feet high, more magnificent than any structure man had ever made, a perfect ring that old druids attempted to mimic with their own circles of stone in the Otherworld. Swirling runes shimmered in the enormous towers, set off by the light of the great shield that protected this place.

In the center of the circle, the great tree grew, its

high branches reaching out over the stones. Patterns of circles upon circles in endless woven druid knots had been set in colorful stones paving the way to the palace. He ran toward the steps that led up the large roots of the tree, and passed through the doorway carved in the center of the enormous trunk.

As he entered the great throne room, a glowing crystal floating in the center of the cathedral-like chamber, pulsed with a soothing white light. Like a heartbeat, it set a calm rhythm. The magic flowed through the chamber, unseen, but as present as the air around him. It settled over him with the warm feeling of sunlight on his shoulders. Normally it both awed and calmed him, but it couldn't help him now. He was in too much of a panic. His heart skipped and raced with terror. They didn't have any time to lose.

He stopped at the edge of the great magic seal on the floor. The queen's symbol, an iris blossom imposed over a star, took up most of the chamber. A small crowd of fairies were gathered there, drawing magic from the crystal. It flowed to them in waves of colored light.

"Where is the queen?" Elric shouted. His voice echoed through the chamber and carried up through the trunk of the great tree. All the fairies stilled and looked at him in shock. He'd never caused a stir before.

A tall, very thin fairy with narrow eyes and a pointed chin turned to him. It was Lord Raven, the queen's adviser. He wore dark indigo robes and a haughty air that always floated around him along with the overpowering scent of lilies. He looked down his long nose at Elric. "You are supposed to be practicing fighting techniques with Master Elk. Why are you shirking your duties?"

"Wynn is missing!" Elric shouted at him. A loud gasp and a couple of worried cries followed his words as the fairies gathered around him. "She's wandered into the Nightfell Wood."

"That's impossible. I left her in her room not that long ago," Raven said. "A child like her cannot sneak away unnoticed. She must be in the palace." He waved an imperial hand toward the fairies near the crystal. "You there. Search the rooms in the eastern branch."

At his words, several of the fairies broke away, flying through the hall and out the doors and high windows to search.

Elric held out the ribbon from Wynn's dress. "Zephyr found this on the other side of the barrier. She's trapped out there. We have to find her; there's a reaper in the woods. It already attacked Master Elk."

The voices rose around him, filled with terror.

Fairies rushed this way and that, disappearing into thin beams of light or streams of mist and smoke. The frantic motion was like standing near a beehive that had just been struck with a stick.

Elk and Fox entered the chamber. Their color looked diminished, as if a part of what made them solid and real had disappeared, and now they were something like a reflection. Elric ran to his master.

"Wynn is missing," Elric said. "I left her safe in the garden when the reaper attacked. I didn't want her to cross any bridges on her own. Now she's gone."

Elric choked on his words. This was his fault. He never should have left her alone. He should have found someone to watch over her first. But he had no reason to believe she would do something dangerous. If he hadn't been at the battle . . .

Elk placed a hand on his shoulder. It steadied him, but it didn't make him feel any less guilty. Wynn was gone.

"Are you certain she didn't return to her chambers on her own?" Elk asked, his voice weak. "She found you by herself. She could have returned."

At Elk's words, what little color that was left in Raven's cheeks fled. "You saw her outside? How close was she to the shield? Could the elf spies have seen her?"

A chilling wind blew through the chamber and the air filled with the crackling sound of delicate ice forming on the walls. The queen appeared, a blizzard of snowflakes swirling around her. Her eyes flashed fire as she floated toward Elric. "Where is she?" Her deep voice carried through the room like thunder. She gripped a silk slipper tightly in her hand.

Elric swallowed. His eyes stung and he blinked hard. He had never been this scared, not even when he had faced mad dogs or fallen off a crumbling cliff. This fear was like a monster gripping his heart and threatening to rip it straight from his chest. He saw the same fear in the queen's face.

Elk strode forward. The queen turned to her captain. He bowed low, dropping to his knee, then was slow to rise. "My queen, while I was training Elric as Lord Raven instructed, near the shield, the princess appeared, looking for her brother. She seemed distraught. I covered her with my cloak and sent Elric to return her to the palace. But then the reaper that has been lurking nearby found a weak place in the shield. Remembering the plan, I sent

Zephyr to call Prince Elric back. But the reaper nearly broke through. Fox and I were forced to battle it outside the shield. It fought to kill. Prince Elric appeared and distracted the beast long enough for us to escape. Then the creature ran off into the woods."

The queen towered over him, and Elric felt as if he were shrinking. "You left your sister alone."

Elric wished he could hide. She was right. He should have never left Wynn's side.

"Yes," he admitted. "I believed she was safe where she was."

He watched as the queen's expression turned to despair. Her magic snow melted around her as her face fell. "How could you leave her? She is too frail and delicate to ever leave alone. Where was she last?"

Elric stepped forward and answered. "I left her in the garden for not more than half of an hour. She promised she would stay and wait until I came back for her. She was safe there. But when Zephyr and I returned, there was no sign of her. We found her tracks. It looks like she ran toward the shield. Something drove her straight into the Nightfell Wood."

"What?" The queen stared at him in disbelief. "What could have possibly frightened her enough to make her do that? She knows the forest is dangerous. The shield keeps the monsters out." Her voice cracked.

A fairy with spiked pink hair came forward. "My queen, only an hour ago, Mildred was pecking at scraps in the kitchens. Suddenly she lifted her head and then ran straight out into the gardens. We didn't know what was wrong with her."

"We found her feathers near the shield," Zephyr said.

If something had attacked Mildred, Wynn would do anything to save her hen, even brave the wood. But it didn't make any sense. If Mildred was eating scraps in the kitchens, she wouldn't have left that for anything. There was only one thing that chicken loved more than eating, and that was Wynn. There was no reason for the hen to leave the kitchens except for Wynn, and no reason for Wynn to leave the gardens except for Mildred. Something strange happened.

"My queen." Master Elk stepped forward. "We have to consider that the timing of the reaper attack on the shield was not a coincidence. It was meant to be a distraction. This was a planned attack, just like the last one that claimed your child. Someone within the dome knew of Wynn, and set out to claim her for the Grendel. The only question is, who has betrayed us this time?"

The queen covered her mouth with her fingertips and slowly sank to the floor. "She's gone. My winter baby." The wind picked up around them, chilling Elric's blood. The sound matched the wail of his own heart.

The queen clutched Wynn's slipper to her heart, and let out a sob.

The floor beneath them began to rumble and shake. Elric nearly lost his balance as the light flickered in the chamber. A sound split the air like lightning striking at Elric's feet. Light flashed, and for a moment he was blinded. He blinked his eyes, but strange colors lingered in his vision before he could see the room again.

The chamber fell silent as everyone in the room gasped in horror. A deep crack sliced through the heart of the crystal. Silvery mist streamed out of it. It looked like fairy blood.

Beneath the crystal, the queen lay motionless in a soft drift of snow.

CHAPTER SEVEN

Wynn

WYNN CLUNG TO MILDRED WHERE Hob had hidden her at the base of the tree. The wet leaves covering the tangled roots felt like a soggy blanket that dripped water on her hunched head and neck. She remembered hiding under a thorn bush with Elric and wished he was next to her with his arm wrapped tightly around her. She didn't know what to do. Hold still. Be quiet. That's what Elric said to do under the thorn bush.

The horrible howl from the wood faded into a low rumble. Wynn felt it shiver down her back. It made her tummy feel sick. She couldn't see anything from beneath the thick pile of leaves. She shifted so she could peek out through a small gap between a root and a large spiky leaf. Suddenly she could see the form of an animal out there as it passed by her hiding place. It came so close, its shaggy gray hide blocked everything she could see out of the hole, before it circled around to the center of the clearing.

She had never seen anything so big. It was twice as tall as her father was. The monster had a thick bare chest and scraggly, mottled light gray hair that matched the pale color of its leathery skin. It dropped to all four feet like a true beast and sniffed the ground. With its long snout and sharp teeth, it reminded her of the mad dogs that had chased her once.

A voice filled the woods. It didn't sound like it came from the monster. It didn't move its mouth. The voice sounded like it came from inside her own head.

"Where is the girl?"

Hob bounded to the far side of the clearing only a dozen feet from the beast. "Please! Please don't take me to the Dark One!" Hob begged, flopping over on the ground, then scrambling back up. "I know Hob knows many things that the dark master wants. He will take me and suck the thoughts from my head to know them."

Hob's words came out in frightful squeaks. What was he doing? Her friend was so tiny. He was almost the same size as Mildred. The monster was huge. Hob couldn't fight a beast like that.

Wynn bit her lip until it hurt. Her eyes stung, but she held very still.

"I know she's here. I can smell the sweetness of her flesh."

Hob lifted his arm and took a big sniff beneath it. "That is just me."

The monster roared.

Hob took off, speeding through the woods on his rabbit legs. He was very small and quick. The beast followed after him, loping through the trees on all fours.

Wynn shook all over. She had trouble bringing her thoughts together. Mildred struggled out of her arms and broke through the leaves. She ran in the direction Hob had pointed before he hid her.

"Mildred, no!" She pulled herself through the roots, the sticky leaves still clinging to her. They couldn't hide now.

They had to run. Run!

Wynn scrambled through the woods, keeping sight

of Mildred just ahead of her. The hen's white legs flashed through the shadows as the chicken raced for the stormy gray shield. Wynn could see it through the leaves now. She could make it, she had to.

Wynn ran. Her foot hurt. Her breathing hurt. Mildred was just ahead of her, clucking encouraging noises.

Then Wynn heard a huffing behind her. She screamed and leaped forward, not daring to look behind her. She stumbled over a rock and fell on the hard ground.

Wynn rolled on her back and brought her arms up over her head as the monster bore down on her.

"Leave her be!" Hob yelled as he flew out of the brush. He caught the beast's ear and chomped viciously until the black gooey ooze dripped down the beast's face. Wynn bolted upright and backed away toward the shield. The monster shook its head, but Hob clung tight, still chewing on the reaper's ear even though his body was thrown to one side of the monster's skull, then the other.

"Enough!" It was the voice again. The terrible in-her-head voice.

The monster grabbed Hob around the middle and ripped him from its ear. Wynn watched in horror as the beast threw him as hard as he could.

Hob's wiry body hit a tree trunk with a sickening smack, and fell down into the bushes.

"Hob!" Wynn screamed, and ran toward where he fell.

Strong, hairy gray arms gripped her around the middle and pulled her away.

"Hob!" she cried, her tears streaking down her cheeks as the monster's claws dug into her sides.

"Scream all you want. You belong to the Grendel now."

A dark and evil laugh sounded in Wynn's mind. She felt the weight of it press down on her spirit. The beast dragged her away. Its arm wrapped tight around her middle, and she couldn't breathe. It made her dizzy as she grabbed fistfuls of the monster's hair. It was so coarse it cut through her hands like rough twine. Its claws dug into her sides, a stinging pain she couldn't escape.

Wynn screamed and screamed. Tears streaked down her face. She pulled and pushed. Tugged on the monster's shaggy hair until her palms were on fire from rope burns. Scratched, bit, kicked. She fought. Her other shoe came off. Her crown fell.

The monster ran and ran deep into the woods. Wynn

couldn't see. She couldn't open her eyes. The claws digging into her side hurt. She tried to pull them out.

"I have her at last, Master."

Wynn heard the laughing in her head. She screamed louder so she wouldn't hear it. She pulled on its matted fur. It didn't help. It didn't stop running.

The reaper had her. It would take her to the Grendel and she would disappear. Elric wasn't here. Hob was gone. She was scared. She hurt all over.

She felt dizzy. It was hard to breathe. The reaper held her too tightly around her middle. She couldn't close her eyes. She had to fight.

She ripped a chunk of hair out of the beast's side.

The creature snarled and winced. She was doing it. She had to hurt it. Wynn ripped harder at its hide.

The monster pulled her under its body, so her head was near its chin. She couldn't reach its long hair on its shoulders and sides. Its skin was smooth and tough under its bare belly. It didn't stop running. She kicked hard against its chest, ramming her head up under its chin. Her head hit its wolf-like jaw. Her teeth cracked together and a sharp burst of pain exploded in her head.

The monster flung its head up away from her blow. She heard a loud crack. Everything tumbled and fell.

The monster collapsed on top of her. It smelled like rotting meat. She choked, unable to breathe.

Pushing hard against its matted fur, she wriggled out from under it. She gasped as she struggled to her feet. The forest air smelled like moldy leaves, but that was much better than the stinky monster.

Wynn stumbled away from it. A low limb of a tree hung overhead. It must have hit its face on the wood.

Good.

Wynn kicked it and hurt her toes, that pain felt good. She turned and ran back the way the monster had come—at least, she thought she did. She had to get far away. Her heart pounded. She could hear the heavy *thump, thump, thump* in her ears. She could taste blood in her throat.

Behind her, she heard a growl.

The monster was waking up.

Wynn scrambled over a large tree branch. There was a deep ditch on the other side. She had to jump. She swung her hands back and leaned forward, but she just couldn't make herself jump. She didn't want to fall. The monster howled. Wynn flung herself forward, but she didn't jump far enough.

She landed hard in the ditch.

Trapped.

She saw the beast's long clawed fingers first, then its horrible monster face with its wolf snout and big ugly bat ears. She looked up at it from the bottom of the ditch as it loomed over her. Its slimy drool dripped from its sharp fangs.

It reached down for her.

"I have you now. You cannot escape."

She tucked herself down into the ditch so it couldn't reach her, but its claw scraped across her cheek.

Wynn screamed again. This time it was answered with a roar. Wynn felt it roll over her like thunder.

A flash of shimmering light and dark stripes crashed into the monster, knocking it back. Wynn turned to the side of the ditch. Using the roots and rocks, she climbed out.

On the other side of the ditch, a furious and beautiful creature was fighting with the monster. It looked like a cat, but bigger, so much bigger. It was nearly the size of the reaper. Its long, striped tail lashed at the ground as it slashed at the creature with fearsome claws. Dark stripes covered its coat, but the light stripes between them changed color, shifting from blue to green to white.

Both beasts had reared up on their hind legs. The big

cat moved so quickly Wynn could barely see its paws as it struck the other beast. They fell back to the ground and circled each other. The cat kept its enormous fangs bared as the monster's eyes glowed red. The cat's coat changed to the same fiery red. The cat arched its back and tucked its strong hips low.

Suddenly it exploded from the ground, leaping on the reaper's back.

The reaper tried to shake the cat off. The cat slipped to the side but held on, its hooked claws cutting through the thick gray ruff of the reaper and staining its pale fur with its murky black blood. With an angry snarl, the cat grabbed the underside of the reaper's throat.

The cat held fast, pushing the reaper's head and shoulders to the ground until no more sound came out of the horrible monster and it lay still. Slowly the big striped cat let go of the monster and hissed, baring its knife-like teeth. It turned to Wynn. Its eyes glowed in the darkness, a pure shimmering gold.

It stalked forward. Wynn liked cats, but this one had paws the size of her head. She backed up, holding her hands out as the big cat stared at her. It never blinked.

A low rumble sounded in its throat. It was both beautiful and terrifying.

The light stripes changed color again, fading to a deep violet-blue like the night sky just after the sun set. Wynn could barely see the darker stripes. The glowing yellow eyes seemed to float in the air, stalking toward her.

Wynn backed up. She didn't like these monsters. She wanted to go home.

Her heel hit a rock and she stumbled backward. Wynn screamed as the great striped cat charged forward.

"Hold!" a voice called from the shadows between two tall trees.

Wynn turned, hoping it was someone that could help.

She screamed again as she looked up at a tall silhouette surrounded by billowing curls of thick black smoke.

CHAPTER EIGHT

Elric

ELRIC RUSHED TO THE FALLEN queen's side.

She looked lifeless. He lifted her hand and his fingers looked ghostly against hers, taking on a bluish tinge as the temperature in the room plummeted. The other fairies rushed forward. He hadn't ever seen his birth mother ill. He never saw her dying. This terrified him. The crystal above him continued to bleed and there was nothing he could do to stop it.

"My queen," he said. "Wake up." He shook her gently as snow fell. It settled on the curls of her snow-white hair and didn't melt.

Lord Raven drew Elric back with a firm hand. Elric fought against Raven's grip. He didn't know what he could do, but he felt like he had to do something. Lord Raven conjured a bed of mist beneath the queen. She lay on it, blanketed in a soft fog. He didn't even try to wake her.

The crystal above them glowed with a cold blue light that made the cracked scars within it seem that much more pronounced. The largest one was so deep it cut through the very center of the stone. It continued to bleed even as a group of fairies poured their magic into the crystal's wounds. It didn't help.

Raven stood. "The queen is dying," he declared. His words boomed through the chamber. "We must make her comfortable and do all we can to strengthen the shield on our own."

"No!" Elric shouted. "We just need to find Wynn. If we can find Wynn, she can heal the queen. She did it before. Send everyone out into the woods at once. We will find her." Each minute lost was another moment the reaper could find his sister. "She's out there somewhere, alone and scared."

Raven looked at him with pity, and Elric hated it. His black eyes reflected the light of the bleeding crystal as he said, "You have no idea the dangers of the wood. She couldn't survive without protection, not for a moment."

Elric glared at him. "You don't know my sister. None of you do. Wynn is strong. She never gives up. I won't give up either, not yet." His voice broke. "You have to help me save her."

Raven swept his hand over the queen, thickening the veil of fog over her until it looked like a shroud.

"Wynn is still out there!" Elric shouted. He turned around to the crowd of dumbstruck fairies. "Doesn't anyone care that she is in danger?"

Fox came forward and tried to place a hand on his shoulder. "It's not that we don't care," she said. "It's just that this has happened before. The first princess was stolen from her bed by someone that we all trusted. She was only a baby. Her body was still flesh and blood, like your kind. Her magic hadn't come in yet. The queen nearly died of her broken heart then. She survived with her grief for decades as the crystal slowly bled. She traveled to the Otherworld to die, to ensure the Grendel could never find her diminished form. But while wandering the woods, she found her first changeling son and took him into her heart. Her health was restored, though it didn't return completely."

Master Elk nodded. "Unfortunately the last prince

was much like you. He wanted to be a warrior, to fight the darkness. One night he disappeared. The queen tried to use the amulet she gave him to call him back, but he was gone without a trace. The amulet went dark, and we knew he was no longer a part of this world."

Fox placed a hand on Elk's arm and supported him as he swayed on his feet. "The queen used all the magic she had to return to the Otherworld. That's when she found Wynn. She immediately bonded with the baby, but your mother found the queen before she could bring Wynn here. The queen let your mother keep your sister, but the tie to her heart remained, and a strange magic formed between them linking the Otherworld and Between. Now the queen has lost everyone she has ever loved. Her heart will never be whole. Sidian, Oberon, Estaria, Osmund, and now Princess Wynn."

"Osmund?" Elric repeated. They had met a man named Osmund on their journey to find the Silver Gate. He seemed to know things about the Between that were more than just legend. He had been kind to them, though he discouraged Elric from seeking the gate. "Was he this tall, shaggy brown hair?" Elric indicated Osmund's height with his hand at mid-chest, and a hushed but frantic murmur swept around the room.

Osmund's uncommon stature made it difficult to mistake him for another of that name.

"This cannot be." Raven looked at him, confused. "He disappeared twelve years ago. How could you possibly know of him? Did someone tell you about him?"

"He's alive!" Elric said. "He is in the Otherworld. He lives in a hut near the fairy circle where Wynn healed my wounds after we met trouble in the village. He took us in. He knew the way to the Silver Gate." Elric looked down at the enormous seal at his feet. "He didn't think I would be able to make it through. He knew I didn't really believe." Elric swallowed the lump in his throat. "Wynn had to teach me how. She taught me how to hope. I'm holding on to that now." Wynn never gave up, and neither would he. "There is always hope."

Raven stepped forward. "Prove what you say is true."

Elric thought for a moment, trying to remember every detail he could about the man. "Osmund wore a medallion around his neck. A medallion with this seal on it." Elric pointed at the floor, surprised he had never made that connection before. He had only caught a glimpse of the medallion, but now that he'd made the connection, the memory of the brief second he saw it felt like it had burned into his mind. He knew he was not mistaken in this. "He's alive, and Wynn could be too."

"There is one way to tell if what you say is true." Raven threw his cloak around himself and transformed into his bird form. He flew up through the tree and returned a minute later with a medallion in his beak. In a flash he became a man again. A gust of wind swirled over the seal, scattering the flurries off the great mark. Silver light from the crystal showered down on the seal and spread out like mist. He nodded to the fairies around him and they encircled the seal on the floor and held out their hands. A silver ring of light formed between them, then a narrow band of glowing light rose up from the edges of the seal.

Raven motioned to Elric. "Take the medallion and stand in the center of the seal." Elric stepped over to him and gently took the medallion from Lord Raven's hand. His stomach churned with nerves as he crossed over the edge of the seal and stood directly in the center.

The medallion glowed bright gold in his hand. Elric didn't know what it meant, but he held it up for all the fairies to see. He heard their murmuring voices, but he didn't turn from Raven.

"Bring Osmund back, and there may be a chance to save us all. We cannot hold the portal open for long, not with the queen so ill. You must return before the medallion stops glowing or you will not make it back." Raven swept his hands up, his robes looking like enormous violet wings. "Good luck."

Elric felt the floor drop out from under him. He shouted as his stomach rose up into his throat and he fell. He landed with a thud on soft mossy ground. Elric blinked and shook his head. A flock of birds took to wing from the branches of an ordinary tree. A creek bubbled nearby. Set around him in a perfect ring were several mossy stones.

He was back in the Otherworld, and he knew this place.

He had been terribly injured when Wynn had carried him to this clearing. She had started a fire all on her own, cleaned and dressed his wounds, and cared for him through the night. He repaid her care by lashing out at her in frustration over his pain. And still she had forgiven him and tried to make things right between them, when he was the one who should have gone to her and begged for her forgiveness.

Osmund helped him see that.

He had to find Osmund.

Elric looked down at the glowing amulet in his hand.

It was already beginning to fade. He didn't have much time. Looping it over his neck, he turned around in the circle, unsure of which way to go. Last time, Mildred had led him through the woods. He closed his eyes and tried to remember the moment exactly. She had hopped over a stone with a cracked top. He found the stone and set off at a run through the woods.

His feet seemed to fly over the ground as his desperation drove him through the forest. He came to a bank and climbed it. There he found the felled tree where he had met Osmund in these woods. There was significantly less of it than the last time he had seen it. Osmund's woodcutter's ax was lodged firmly in the heavy trunk.

Elric followed a narrow path to a squat little hut. Its walls were made of stacked logs with mud filling the cracks, and the earthen roof was overgrown. Where was Osmund's goat, Burghild?

"Osmund!" Elric called. He ran to the door of the hut and swung open the door. He thrust his head in the low doorway, knocking his forehead on the low log. Elric winced and backed up, holding his forehead. No fire crackled in the hearth, and the small house felt dead inside. Sinking dread filled him.

"Elric, is that you?" a familiar, gruff voice said from behind him. Elric spun around, knocking the top of his head on the overhanging roof. He fell on his backside in front of the door and sat there holding the stinging knot forming under his scalp.

Osmund stepped forward carrying turnips in a woven net. His hair was overgrown, and his face looked haggard.

"Osmund!" Elric jumped up again, this time more carefully. "Osmund, I'm so glad you are here. We found it. Wynn and I found the gate. You have to come with me, quickly." Elric reached out and grabbed Osmund by the shoulder to drag him forward.

Osmund slapped his hand away. "You found it?" He looked at Elric in shock. Then he reached into his shirt and drew out his medallion. It, too, glowed bright gold. He blinked as he looked up again. "I can't believe you found it."

"We have to go back. They can't keep the fairy ring open very long." Elric took two long half-running steps back toward the felled tree.

"No," Osmund said.

Elric stopped and turned. "What?"

"I don't want to go back," he said. "I have my life

here. I prefer it this way."

"Alone in these miserable woods?" Elric said in disbelief.

"It's better than a gilded cage." Osmund turned toward the door. "Why don't you stay here with me? No one is looking for you anymore. You will be safe. It's been too quiet since Burghild . . ." His face fell, but then he managed a smile. "Where is your sister? Is she inside? Wynn!" he called.

"Wynn is lost in the Nightfell Wood," Elric said, and pulled out his fading medallion. "And I need you to help me save her."

Osmund stared at him. Elric watched an internal war play out on Osmund's face.

"The Grendel is after her. There are reapers in the woods, hunting," Elric said. "Please," he begged. "Don't abandon her, too."

Muttering a curse, Osmund strode forward, tossing the turnips into Elric's arms. "I swore if I ever had the chance, I would never go back!" he shouted. "I'm only doing this for Wynn."

Elric dropped the turnips and hurried after him as Osmund dislodged his short-handled ax. "Thank you," Elric said under his breath even though he knew

Osmund couldn't hear him. He lifted the medallion at his neck. Its glow was nearly gone.

They rushed through the woods, Osmund leading the way, but he paused at the edge of the stones. Elric charged through to the center of the mossy ring. Looking like a man at the gallows, Osmund stepped over the threshold. "No matter what I say, play along," he warned.

Elric didn't have time to ponder what Osmund meant by that. "We're here!" Elric called, holding his medallion high, and the ground dropped away.

CHAPTER NINE

Wynn

WYNN BACKED UP FROM THE smoke and shadows in front of her. Then she remembered the fearsome cat was behind her. She stopped. She couldn't move, and her thoughts muddled in her head.

Shadows were bad. The fairies said the Grendel dressed in shadows.

The curling smoke and darkness spilled down, spreading across the forest floor.

A girl emerged from the cloak of shadow. Long, softly curling hair the color of midnight surrounded her. She held a worn and knotty staff. A dress formed of black smoke trailed behind her as she approached. She had scars on her face, like she had been attacked by an animal once. She stared ahead, somewhere between Wynn and the cat behind her. Her eyes were very dark brown and half hidden by thick lashes.

"Go back to your little stick city, elf," the girl said, crossing her long staff in front of her. "Before I change my mind about sparing you."

Wynn was so scared, she barely understood the words the girl had said. "I don't know," Wynn mumbled, because she had no other words that her mind could put together quickly.

The girl took a step forward, and Wynn had to take a step back. She almost slipped into the ditch.

"What do you mean, you don't know?" she demanded.

Wynn didn't have the words; they wouldn't come.

The girl charged forward with her staff. She hit Wynn in the arm, and Wynn fell on her side. The girl reached down, grasping for her, and touched her hair. She let go like Wynn was on fire. With her forehead furrowed, she backed away. She touched her own hair and frowned. "What are you?"

"My name is Wynn." She said each word carefully. "What is your name?"

The girl didn't answer; instead she peered over Wynn's shoulder at the other side of the ditch.

The enormous striped cat leaped over the ditch and circled around the girl. It pushed its head under the girl's outstretched hand and closed its eyes for a moment. The girl stroked the cat's head, then let her hand rest on the beast's striped shoulder.

"I'm not in the habit of talking. You have one last chance. What are you?" she asked. The cat's large yellow eyes fixed on her. "Shadow doesn't recognize your kind."

Wynn thought about her answer. "I'm a girl," she said, carefully forming her words.

The big cat stepped forward. It huffed, sniffing at Wynn's shredded skirt. Wynn reached out and patted it on the head.

It backed up, coming down on its haunches until it sat awkwardly with its back feet splayed out. It blinked its big eyes. Just then it looked very much like a large, confused kitty.

Wynn laughed.

The girl peered at her, her eyes staring. "What was that sound?" she asked. Her voice sounded strange, like she was surprised.

Wynn looked around. "What sound?" A howl rose deep, deep in the woods. Another reaper. Wynn covered her ears and ducked.

The girl turned her head, and the big cat made the rumbling noise again. "There's another reaper somewhere in the wood. You had better find your way home, girl."

Wynn hiccupped. "I am lost," she said. She missed Elric. "I don't know where to go."

The girl tilted her head toward the big cat, and the cat looked up at her and raised its striped brows. Both the girl and the cat let out a huff at the same time. The cat's stripes faded to white as it stood and resumed its position at the girl's side. Her hand returned to the cat's shoulder.

Together they turned their backs to Wynn, and the cat flicked the pale tip of its tail. Finally the girl said, "Come with us, and you might survive the coming night."

Wynn did her best to follow the girl and the big striped cat. It was hard. The light was fading quickly, but the girl didn't slow down at all. She walked with one hand on the cat's shoulder, and prodded the roots and branches around her with her staff.

Wynn had to climb over the roots and rocks. Sometimes she fell behind. She wasn't as good at crawling through the forest. This wasn't like the woods she had grown up in. There, the trees gave each other room to grow. These trees grew close together and were bigger and more twisty than the trees in the Otherworld. Every time Wynn stared into the shadows, she thought she saw eyes staring back. The big cat flicked the white tip of its tail, and Wynn hurried to catch up.

They reached a hill, where the roots of the trees became like the rungs of a ladder. It was hard for Wynn to climb in her dress. Shredded bits kept tangling around her legs, and getting under her toes. She wished she had smoke clothes like the girl. Her legs moved freely through the smoky dress. On her back, there was a strange mark. Wynn caught a glimpse of it every time the thick curls of the girl's hair swung to the side. It was a circle, paler than the rest of her tawny brown skin, with a star in the center, and what looked like flames. It reminded Wynn of the seal in the palace, but it was different. The flower seal was calming. This looked fierce.

"What is that?" Wynn asked.

The girl paused. She turned slowly back to Wynn, but not all the way, only enough to tilt an ear toward her. "What is what?"

"The mark on your back?" she asked. "It's pretty."

The girl moved away again. "I don't know what you're talking about." The girl's hair fell over the mark and hid it from her.

Still, Wynn was glad she wasn't alone. The forest wasn't as dark here. She could see the sky through gaps in the twisted branches. The light was fading. There was no color in the sun setting, the way there usually was when she looked through the shield that protected the fairy lands. Here the pale gray sky slowly turned to black. Still, the trees didn't look as angry in this part of the woods. They seemed more like the ones in the groves she used to play in.

Enormous mushrooms grew in clusters. They had red and orange caps sprinkled with white splotches. Ferns also curled up from the forest floor, giving the woods a soft and feathery look. It felt better here. It felt less sad, less scary. The woods were almost pretty. As the girl passed, the ferns uncurled their long fronds toward her. As Wynn reached them, they recoiled as if they were sad the girl had passed.

The girl paused on the crest of the hill, turned, and sat on a rock. She crossed her staff in front of her and stared at Wynn.

"Well, why don't you answer Shadow's question?" The girl gave her an expression that reminded her of Elric when he got impatient because she forgot something.

Wynn clung to the root she had been climbing and blinked at the girl. "I don't know." She didn't remember a question. "Shadow can talk?"

"Of course she can." The girl let out a huff that almost sounded like a laugh. But it wasn't really a laugh.

"I don't hear." Wynn reached the top of the roots and sat on the ground. She rubbed the bits of dirt and small rocks from the bottoms of her bare feet. "I don't hear animals talking." That was something fairies could do. But only if they were very old like Elk, or royal like the queen. Even then, they couldn't talk to every animal. No one ever knew what Mildred was saying. It drove most of the fairies batty. Wynn looked at Shadow. "She growls."

"Oh." The girl looked confused. "How awful for you. I'm sorry. I haven't met a girl before."

"I haven't met a Shadow before. I haven't met a you before," Wynn said.

"Shadow is a tigereon, the last of her kind in the Nightfell Wood," the girl said.

"I don't know the wood," Wynn said. "There are elves here. Are you an elf?"

The girl gave her a sour look. "Absolutely not. The elves would kill Shadow, like they did the rest of her kind. We stay to ourselves."

"You are all alone?" That didn't sound very nice. This was a scary place to be alone.

Shadow rubbed her thick head against the girl's side. The girl scratched the tigereon's rounded ear. "We like it that way."

Wynn didn't like to be alone. She missed Mildred. She hoped Mildred was safe. She was worried about Hob, too. He hit the tree so hard when the reaper threw him. What if he was dead? The reaper dragged her too far away for her to find him again. She couldn't help.

Wynn wiped her eye. She felt very sad and didn't want to climb through the forest anymore. She crossed her legs under her ripped and muddy skirt. It didn't glow the way it used to. She pressed a hand to her side. It was bleeding, and she had no honey to put on it to help it heal.

The smoke-and-shadow girl stood and took a step

closer to her. The warm scent of a campfire surrounded Wynn and made her feel a little better. She tapped Wynn on the knee with her staff, then held out a hand. "Come on. My home is not far. It's a safe place to sleep."

Wynn took the other girl's hand. She pulled Wynn to her feet.

Wynn's tummy growled. Shadow made a huffing noise and walked away into the ferns. Her stripes turned a dark green. The tigereon crouched low, slinking through the underbrush, until she disappeared. Wynn moved to follow her white-tipped tail.

The shadow girl crossed her staff in front of Wynn. "Stay back," she warned.

"Is it something dangerous?" Wynn asked. She hated the reaper, and she didn't want to meet another one.

"No," the girl said. "It's dinner."

Dinner! Wynn was excited. She was really hungry. But then she heard something that made her feel sick in her middle.

Awwwwk . . . bok . . . bok . . . bok.

"Mildred!" Wynn cried. She ran forward, leaping over roots and rocks as she scrambled through the ferns toward the crouching cat. Shadow pressed low to the forest floor, the colors changing in her stripes. Her hips shifted from side to side as she prepared to pounce.

Wynn threw herself toward the creature. She grabbed the tigereon's twitchy tail and pulled.

Shadow whipped around and snarled at her. Her thick muzzle drew back from enormous white fangs as her iridescent whiskers pressed flat against the sides of her head.

"Leave her alone!" Wynn shouted. She pulled hard on Shadow's tail. The cat took a half-hearted swipe at her with her paw. Wynn jumped on her back and clung to the fur on her sides.

The tigereon spun in a circle, trying to reach Wynn.

"Mildred is not for eating!" Wynn shouted.

Mildred leaped up with a panicked squawk. She flapped her wings furiously as the beast stretched and snapped. Mildred landed on the cat's head and pecked her.

"Mildred! No, bad chicken!" Wynn called, even as she clung to the cat's back. "Get away."

Mildred never ran from a fight. She was the bravest chicken Wynn had ever known. Wynn had to save her before she was gobbled up.

She reached out and grabbed one of Mildred's legs. Then she threw herself off the back of the squirming cat and rolled through the dirt, holding Mildred close to her heart. She would run if she had to. She didn't care if she got lost in the woods again. Mildred was worth it.

"You find something else to hunt," Wynn said, kicking dirt at the large cat. "Mildred is mine."

Shadow roared at her, so Wynn slapped her on the nose. The cat's eyes went wide, and she snorted and shook her head.

"That's enough of this," the girl said, tapping Shadow with her staff. "Shadow, leave it be." The girl turned her dark eyes to Wynn. "What is this thing to you?"

"Mildred is mine. I love her."

Wynn tucked the chicken under her chin, and Mildred let out a soft coo. Shadow hung her head. She looked angry. Her ears pressed back on her neck and her tail thrashed behind her. The girl stroked Shadow's flank, and the big cat hissed.

"I know you're disappointed, and I'm sure the strange creature is tasty, but I think this one is not for eating," the girl said to the cat. "Leave it be." The girl gave the beast a pat on the side of its strong neck. It growled at her. "You should probably apologize for slapping Shadow and pulling her tail," the girl said to Wynn.

"Thank you," Wynn said to the girl, then turned to

Shadow. "I'm sorry. Mildred is my friend and I love her."

"Whatever that thing is, keep it close," the girl said as she turned away from Wynn. "Love is a rare thing in these woods." Her hand stroked the tigereon's back.

Wynn cuddled Mildred and pet her neck. Everything that felt empty and achy in her body felt full and better now. She was so happy to see her hen again. The girl set off down a narrow path through the woods, using her staff and keeping her fingertips on the shoulder of the tiger. Wynn followed, carrying Mildred and snuggling her close.

Night was falling quickly, but somehow there seemed to be light. Small white flowers grew along the path. Like the ferns, they glowed as the smoke-and-shadow girl passed by. Their little spots of light shone brightly against the dark forest floor. Strange bugs floated around, dancing through the curls of smoke and darkness trailing off the girl's shoulders like a cloak; they flapped their wings like butterflies but gave off a faint blue glow. Wynn heard the splashing water of a creek nearby.

All around them were large boulders. Some of them were square. Boulders shouldn't be square. These were stone blocks someone had shaped long ago. Moss clung to their sides, hiding patterns that had been carved into them. The thick coating of moss grew in a squishy layer over the flat stones under their feet. Wynn turned around and stared into the fading light of the wood. Crumbling stone towers from a ruined city reached up higher than the tops of the trees that grew between them. The forest had taken the city back. Ahead was a crack between two boulders. No, it was a doorway.

The girl motioned for them to come inside.

Wynn ducked through the doorway, and placed Mildred on the floor. The hen stayed close to her ankle as the big cat slid past them and melted into the dark. Mildred gave Shadow an angry tut. She wasn't ready to be friends with Shadow. To be honest, Wynn wasn't sure what she thought of Shadow, either. Sometimes she seemed nice, but she had tried to eat Mildred. Wynn didn't want to have a friend that had tried to eat her other friend.

Wynn entered the doorway, and it was like stepping into a very dark cave.

Inside, she couldn't see a thing.

"It's dark," she said, and kept her body pressed against the stones to the right.

"Does that matter?" the girl asked.

"I don't like it," Wynn said.

The girl sighed. A fire sprang to life in the center of the room within a small circle of stones. The girl didn't seem surprised, but Wynn was. The fire didn't burn sticks or grass. Instead it licked over a pile of ordinary-looking rocks.

"Is this better?" the girl asked. Bright tongues of flame danced through her curls for a moment, then faded.

"Yes," Wynn murmured as she looked around. They were in an old room. On one side a wall had collapsed and was now a pile of rubble. The roots of a tree gripped the chunks of stone and held them. On the other wall was a faded mural of hunters holding fearsome contraptions and firing arrows into a dying tigereon that was caught in a trap. Shadow blinked her large gold eyes at the mural, then turned back to Wynn. Wynn frowned.

Poor Shadow. That was a terrible picture. Maybe if she had something to draw with, she could fix it for her. Wynn eyed the fire. Charcoal would work, but there was no wood in the fire, only rocks. The rest of the chamber was cramped, but relatively comfortable, with a pile of soft mosses and springy ferns in the corner. Wynn sat on a rock with a flat top, one of the blocks of stone that had fallen from the old wall.

"This is your house?" Wynn asked.

"At the moment," she answered with a shrug. "It's nice to have some company. You may stay as long as you want. The reapers won't find you here. The smell of smoke that lingers in this part of the wood masks our scent, and the reapers are afraid of fire."

Wynn was confused. The smoky smell came from the girl herself.

"I need to go back to the fairy palace," Wynn said. Mildred strutted over to Shadow and gave her paw a peck before jumping on the tigereon's hip and settling down to roost. Shadow growled at her and twitched her tail, but didn't try to eat her. Wynn turned to the other girl. "Can you take me?"

"No," the girl answered. "You don't want to go back there. You can never trust the fairies."

"The fairies are nice!" Wynn said. Mildred clucked in agreement.

The girl didn't blink. Her dark eyes caught the flickering light. "I'm sure they are very kind as they sit in their protected little bubble and let the rest of the world around them rot under the stench of the Dark One."

Wynn didn't know what to say. She had to concentrate

hard on the girl's words. Shadow curled up behind the girl. She lounged back against the cat's striped side. "If you think the fairies are going to risk their precious safety to save you, you're going to be waiting for a long time. They will never set foot in this wood. This is your world now."

CHAPTER TEN

Elric

ELRIC BRACED HIMSELF AS HE fell through the fairy portal. Now that he knew what to expect from the fall, he was determined not to lose his balance this time when he landed. His feet hit the floor hard, but he managed to stay upright, even though he stumbled a little to the left. Osmund took a quick step back, but used his woodcutter's ax to steady himself.

Elric blinked. The woods had disappeared and now he was back within the fairy palace. A circle of fairies surrounded them, all gaping at Osmund.

"Prince Osmund," Raven said in a reverent voice. He fell to one knee and bowed. "You return in our hour of most dire need."

Osmund handed Elric his ax. He walked past Raven without a word. He strode straight for the queen on her bed of frozen mist.

With gentle care, he lifted his medallion from his neck and placed it on the queen's chest, then took her hand and laid it over the pendant. He rested his hands over hers.

"Mother, I'm home," he said softly.

A thread of golden light reached down from one of the deep cracks in the crystal. It connected to the center of Osmund's back, then pierced through his heart and reached the heart of the frozen queen.

Osmund cried out as he let his hands fall. He grimaced as the light grew brighter, and one of the deep cracks in the crystal slowly fused together. The light bleeding out of the cracks slowed, though it did not stop completely. Elric watched as the blue light of the crystal pulsed again, dim but steady. The heartbeat returned to the great tree. But three deep cracks remained in the fragile heart of the palace.

The queen's eyes blinked open. She stared up at him

without saying a word as the golden thread connected them. She reached out her hand and cupped the side of his haggard face. "Osmund?"

A great cheer went up in the hall.

Elric ran forward, but the queen didn't look at him.

"Can it really be you?" she asked Osmund as the light glowing between them faded. She propped herself up, then leaned forward and drew him into a loving embrace. "I thought you were dead. What happened?"

"I don't know," Osmund said. There was a hitch in his voice and Elric wondered if he was telling the truth. Before he came through the portal, Osmund seemed pretty clear about what had happened. Elric listened carefully as Osmund spoke, wondering what he was hiding. "I found myself in the Nightfell Wood. I couldn't get back through the shield. But I discovered the old elf city and the fairy ring there. The Grendel came for me in a cloud of smoke. The portal activated, and I fell through to the Otherworld. I have been there ever since, waiting for the day I could return."

Now Elric knew that was a lie. Osmund had claimed he never wanted to return. He had also told Elric to go along with whatever he said, so Elric bit his tongue.

Raven rushed forward and offered the queen a hand.

"Your Majesty, we should get you to your quarters so you can rest. It has been a terrible, terrible day. But the return of Prince Osmund gives us hope." He pointed to the fractured crystal. "A piece of the crystal has mended."

The queen nodded, looking dazed and still ill. "Yes, yes, that would be wise." She allowed Raven to pull her to her feet.

"But what about Wynn?" Elric said. "We have to send a rescue. I will gladly lead it."

The queen faltered and Raven caught her. "Do not upset the queen. She is in a fragile state."

Elric stared at Lord Raven in shock. "And my sister is in danger!" he shouted. "We have to go and find her."

Osmund gave him a warning glance, but then stilled his expression.

"No, we don't," Raven said in a hard voice. It fell as heavy as an executioner's ax.

Elric's heart pounded as he shook with rage. "Are you just going to throw her away, like she didn't even matter to you?" He clenched his fists. "When I was a shepherd, I protected all of my sheep. If one was lost, I searched for it."

Lord Raven handed the queen over to her attendants.

He approached Elric. "And how many more of the flock would we lose in the effort?" he asked. The air turned cold and a biting wind blew across Elric's face. "The Grendel will destroy our world if he can, and it won't be enough. How many should we sacrifice?"

Elric didn't have an answer right away. It was hard to think of facing danger and the reality that some might not make it home. But it was each person's choice to fight. And there were some things worth fighting for. Fighting to save a loved one was worth the risk. That's what love meant.

Elric looked around the room at the faces of all the fairies crowded around the circle. "Don't you love Wynn too?" he asked. "Aren't you willing to fight for her?"

One by one they looked down at the floor. Not one would meet his eyes but Zephyr, who looked stricken and worried.

"She's out there. Wynn is out there. Your princess, your friend. She needs you," he said as he paced in front of the crowd trying to meet the downcast eyes of the fairies. "Are you going to hide forever? How many children like Wynn will you sacrifice?"

Now they looked away.

"Fine." Elric ground his teeth together. "If you are all

too much of cowards to help me, I'll go find her myself."
At least Osmund said he would help.

Elric turned to leave the room. One of the royal
guards grabbed him by the arm. He spun around and
tried to pull free, but the stronger man held him fast.

"I know you are grieving," the queen said. "As deeply
as I am. But I cannot allow you to leave. No matter what,
I have taken you in as my son, and I will protect you.
Your loss would put this entire realm at risk of the darkness. I will send Lord Raven to fly over the wood in the
morning. Take him to his room. Be sure the door is
sealed."

"No!" Elric screamed as he dropped his weight and
tried to pull out of the guard's grip. He wrenched his
shoulder. He wouldn't let them drag him from this room
like a disobedient child. Lord Raven wouldn't risk himself. He'd fly high over the trees. He wouldn't see her.
"She's my sister! She needs my help. Please!"

The queen said nothing as the guard pulled him forward. "Osmund!" he cried. "Wynn needs us. Help me!"
The words tore out of his aching throat.

Osmund's face gave away nothing. He glanced down
for a moment, then back up to Elric. "The queen is right.
I've waited a long time for a chance to come back to this

place. We cannot risk the shield breaking. I'm sorry. There's nothing I can do."

Elric's shock made his muscles go numb. In that moment, the guards dragged him toward the spiral stair that climbed up the trunk of the tree to the rooms in the branches above. They were just about to pull him from the throne room when he regained control of himself and fought against the grip holding his arms so tightly.

"You're her friend!" Elric screamed at Osmund. "I thought you cared for her. You protected her. She trusted you!"

He tried to twist his arm free, but it was no use. "She'll die without our help." Elric watched as Osmund lowered his gaze, looking ashamed of himself. "Her death will be on your head." His voice filled the chamber. "Her blood is on your hands. All of you!"

No one met his gaze as the guard dragged him from the room.

Elric pulled against the fairy holding him the entire way up the staircase. With every step he shifted and twisted. He threw his weight down like a sack of rocks, only to have the fairy guardsmen haul him back up by the armpits. He tried to throw his arms out and hold on to the door frames in the hall, but the fairies dragged him along until his shoulders felt like they would be torn from their sockets. With every turn of the staircase, he felt like he was being torn away from his sister. He fought. With fists, scratching nails, and more than a few curse words, he fought.

He used all the tricks and leverage Master Elk had taught him. It didn't do any good. Master Elk had trained these guards too. When they pulled, he used his heavier mortal body against them. Wynn's life was at stake. That gave him enough strength to yank his arm away from his captors and run back down the staircase.

He had only one thought in his mind. He didn't know what had driven Wynn through the shield, but he was determined to follow her. He wouldn't rest until he found her again.

He charged down the stairs and glanced behind him. When he turned back around, the knife-like points of a rack of silver antlers were only a half a foot in front of him. Elric skidded to a stop, throwing his weight back from the stag in front of him. He lost his balance and fell onto the stairs.

The snow-white stag snorted through his black nose as he stared up at Elric from under the branching silver antlers he carried like a crown. In a clouded mist of silver light, Master Elk transformed. The antlers melted away, and instead of a snowy stag, his teacher stood before him in his impressive white robes with his long braids falling over his shoulders. He held his sword like a barrier between them.

"She is gone," he said in his low melodious voice. "I understand that you are hurt."

"No." Elric shook his head. "You cannot know that she's dead."

"I can." Elk took a step forward, and it forced Elric further up the stairs. "The reaper almost made me diminish today. Wynn is a mortal child and frail in both body and mind. What you saw at the shield was a trap. Think. The second part of that trap is yet to be sprung. The Grendel knows about you. His reaper saw you. He knows you will follow your sister to whatever end. I cannot allow that."

"She is not frail, she's strong. I won't abandon her." Elric rose to his feet and faced his teacher. He didn't have a weapon. He didn't have thousands of years of experience with fighting. But he did love his sister.

"You are young." Elk gave him a sad smile. "And a mortal creature. I commend the strength of your feelings." He gave Elric a slight bow. "You saved my life today, and I will repay that debt."

Elk's eyes turned pure white, and a flash of silver light was the last thing that Elric remembered.

When Elric woke, he found himself in his room. The walls formed from the inner wood of the living tree and surrounded his soft bed. He threw the down-stuffed blankets off his body feeling hot with rage. The roof of his room glittered with the white light of the stones embedded in the ceiling. He grabbed the edge of the chest next to his bed and overturned it. His clothing spilled out onto the floor as the chest rolled to the center of the room with a satisfying crash. He crossed the soft woven rug to the door and pounded on it.

"Let me out!" he shouted. He beat at the door until his hands felt raw. He shouted until his voice felt hoarse. And when he could finally say no more, when the strength of his arms failed him, he stumbled over to the window.

"She's my baby sister." The words tore from his throat, clawing their way from his broken heart. "I promised to protect her."

He stared out through the enormous leaves of the tree to the shield that arched over him. When they first came to the Between, he found the shield beautiful. It had made him feel safe, like nothing in the world beyond it really mattered. Darkness and pain couldn't touch him as long as the shield remained above him. Now it felt like a wall—a stone wall as high and impenetrable as a fortress.

His sister was lost on the other side, and he was under siege. The problem with fortresses and walls was that the armies beyond them would always find a way to cause suffering within. The safety of a wall was an illusion as shifting and beautiful as the colors swirling through the shield overhead. There was nothing more terrible than a siege. The army outside could hold their ground until the people in the fortress slowly starved. The fairies weren't really safe here. They were trapped.

Wynn was in danger and there was nothing he could do about it, because he was trapped with them. His throat felt painfully tight. He kept trying to swallow to relieve the soreness there, but it didn't help. His jaw ached from clenching his teeth, and his heart hurt. He pressed a fist against his chest.

The dark woods beyond the shield stretched on forever. Wynn seemed so small in comparison when he stared out at it. He had to believe she was strong enough to survive. He had to believe she was smart enough to make it on her own. But that was so hard to do. Things were difficult for Wynn, and surviving in a magical wood filled with dangerous creatures was even worse. It would be a challenge for someone who had magic at their fingertips. Wynn had nothing but a single shoe and a fat black hen. Or at least he hoped she did. It made him feel better to think that Mildred was with her and she wasn't alone.

Wynn had spent too much of her life alone.

He could hear her voice in his head, hear the words she had said to him when all hope was lost: Believing is easy. Making fires is hard, and you can do that.

He needed to believe in her. But she couldn't even start a fire on her own.

No. That wasn't true. She had started a fire on her own when she needed to save his life. She wasn't help-less. He had to trust in her abilities.

Why was that so difficult to do? He knew why. No matter how brave, bright, and loyal Wynn was, the world held dangers for her that no one else seemed to have to face. He thought they would escape those dangers when they passed through the Silver Gate. But the dangers didn't go away. They just changed.

He leaned against the wall, then slid to the floor, hugging his legs as he cried. Each sob felt as if it had to be pulled from him. His heart was broken.

Wynn was gone. His sister. His funny, sunny, irritating, and loving sister was gone.

"I'm sorry, Wynn. I promised I would come back for you," he whispered into the shelter of his own curled body.

Elric didn't know how long he sat against the door. It didn't matter. Every minute wasted was another moment where he had to accept the reality that Wynn wouldn't survive.

CHAPTER ELEVEN

Wynn

WYNN DIDN'T WANT TO LIVE in this wood forever. It wasn't a nice place to be, or pretty, or warm, or comfortable. There were dangerous creatures here. She missed the fairies. She missed the Fairy Queen. And if she stayed here forever, she would never see her brother again. She missed him most of all.

"I don't want to live here," Wynn said, crossing her arms. "Elric will come find me."

"Who is Elric?" the smoke-and-shadow girl asked.

"Elric is a prince," Wynn answered. *Prince* sounded

more important than *brother*. "He is very brave."

The girl scratched her tigereon under her chin. "We'll see. It's easy to be brave when you live behind a wall." The girl rubbed her thumb along a groove in her staff. "The fairies save only themselves. It's what they have done for ages."

Wynn didn't think that was right. The queen saved her from the snow. She used magic to help Wynn find the Silver Gate. But now she wasn't sure what to think. Something else was bothering her.

"How old are you?" Wynn asked. The girl knew old things. She looked the same age as Elric, but some fairies were very old and they still looked young, like Zephyr.

The girl shrugged. "Don't know. Does it matter?"

"What is your name?" Wynn asked.

The girl tilted her staff against her shoulder and crossed her arms over it. "That doesn't matter either."

"What is your name?" Wynn repeated. Names were very important.

"I don't know!" she shouted. "No one ever gave me one." She looked down and to the side, peering at the dark corner of the room. "The elves have a name for me, but I don't like it."

"What does she call you?" Wynn asked, pointing at Shadow.

The girl stared at Wynn. She squinted, then stroked the beast behind her. "Shadow? She calls me 'cub,' 'wee one,' 'little thing,' 'stripeless,' 'two-legs' . . . actually I'm not that fond of those last two." The girl stroked the side of the cat's face. "She found me in the wood and helped me survive for as long as I can remember. She is my only friend."

Shadow closed her eyes and her cheeks relaxed into a contented smile. Her pale stripes shimmered with shifting colors as she let the girl pet her. "She's very beautiful," Wynn said.

The girl smiled. "Yes, she is. The fur here beneath her ears is so soft, it is hard to tell you are really touching it." The girl slid her spread fingers into the deep fur behind Shadow's ears. They completely disappeared in the thick color-shifting fur.

The girl leaned over and let her head rest on Shadow's strong shoulder. "And when you press your ear to her side, she growls a low, soothing sound that can reach you in your bones." She took in a deep breath, then lifted her head and continued. "Shadow told me that in the days when there were more tigereons like her, the rumble of their growls filled the wood and helped other creatures sleep peacefully through the night."

The girl crawled over the beast and tucked herself into the shelter of the larger animal's body. "When it is cold, she wraps around you, warm and strong. You know you can sleep and be safe. She is very beautiful."

Wynn didn't think about it like that. She just liked the creature's pretty colors. She lifted her hen from her lap. "Mildred is beautiful too."

The girl smiled. "What is she?"

"She's a chicken," Wynn stated as she pushed her chest forward with pride. Mildred didn't change colors, but she was warm and soft, too.

"You said that before. What is a chicken?" the girl asked.

Wynn wasn't sure how to answer that. "A bird?"

"She's a bird?" The girl sat straight up. Her expression completely changed. She looked like Elric used to when Mother said she had baked fresh bread. "Can I touch her?"

Wynn lifted Mildred and scooted forward over the stone floor. "Here." Mildred squawked and kicked her legs in protest. She managed to pull her wings out of Wynn's hold and flap them.

The girl let out a delighted noise. She reached forward and touched the feathers near Mildred's neck.

After one touch, she pulled her hand back. Then she reached forward again and moved her hands all over Mildred's body. Mildred decided she liked the petting, and stopped flapping. "She's smooth, but soft, and this isn't like fur. It's springy," the girl said. "I've heard birds in the canopy, Shadow told me what they were, but I've never touched one. What strange creatures they are. And how is it that they can fly? Is it magic?"

"Mildred can't fly. She's too heavy." Wynn shook her head. The girl didn't lose any of her wonder as she continued to pet Mildred. The hen closed her eyes and cooed in contentment. Sometimes the girl buried her fingers in Mildred's fluffy feathers. Other times she stroked carefully over the bird's smooth wings. Finally she smiled. It was a pretty smile, even though her scars reached down to her lip on one side. Wynn didn't think she used it often, but she should.

"Thank you. I've always wondered." The girl handed the hen back to Wynn. She took Mildred gratefully, and settled the hen in her lap.

They sat in silence for a while. Wynn thought carefully about everything she said. "Your name is Stripeless?" she asked.

"That seems silly." The girl gave her another smile, this one was more like Zephyr.

"What is your name?" Wynn asked again, more insistently this time. She didn't like not knowing what to call the girl.

"I call myself 'I.' Or sometimes 'me.' I have never needed more than that. You are the one who needs something to call me. What would you choose?" She leaned forward over the fire she had made in the rocks. The light flickered over her skin, lighting the warm brown tones with soft golden light. Wynn remembered the mark on her back, flames in the shape of a star. Fairies were always named for the magic they could do. She had fire in her hair, and smoke for a dress.

"Flame," Wynn said. She wished she could make rocks catch on fire. That would be easier than lighting tinder with flint.

The girl closed her eyes a minute. Shadow rumbled a low growl and squinted. Finally the girl smiled again. "Shadow likes it. I think I do too. You may call me Flame if you want. I'll do my best to answer if you call it."

Just then Wynn's stomach growled as loud as Shadow.

"Hungry?" Flame smiled again, and for a second she seemed very familiar. She pushed herself up, leaning on her staff. "I'll go out and get us something to eat. Stay here with Shadow where you are safe."

"It's dark." Wynn stood and looked out the doorway. It was pitch-black beyond the crumbling room.

Flame tipped her head to the side. The scars across her face stood out in the dim light. "Don't worry. I'll get along fine. I'll be right back."

Wynn watched as Flame strode past her and out the door. Wynn followed her out, keeping a hand on the door frame. Flame swept her staff in front of her, then climbed up the crumbling ruins like a cat.

Now she was very alone. Except for Shadow. Wynn noticed a white rock at her feet. She picked it up and rubbed it. It was soft and sandy for a rock. Wynn liked it. It felt good in her hand so she kept it. Wynn came back inside as Shadow rose and circled around her. Mildred hopped up on a branch of the tree root. She looked happy as she tucked her beak in her feathers and fell asleep.

Wynn sat by the fire and tried to wait. She didn't like waiting. The rock warmed in her palm, and she passed it from hand to hand. Softly she sang a song under her breath. It was her favorite song. The one that told the way to the Silver Gate. She and Elric had battled many scary things to reach the gate. She knew he would come for her.

But she was far from him. She had to get closer to where he could find her. She needed help. She didn't think Flame would help her. She was nice, but she liked it here in the woods. Wynn needed to go home.

Wynn tapped the rock on the stone floor. It left little white marks where she tapped. She looked at the stone again, then pulled it slowly against the floor. It left a dull white line.

She could draw! She would fix the picture on the wall. That would keep her busy.

Wynn found a smooth, dark part of the wall and scratched the stone against it. Shadow made a funny noise in her throat and came forward. She sat next to Wynn, watching Wynn draw a new picture.

Wynn continued to sing, and Shadow flopped her tail back and forth. Each soft thump landed in time with the song. Wynn rubbed Shadow's ear and sang louder, before turning back to her picture. She had to do a good job.

Wynn worked a long time. She was very focused on her picture when she drew the last little part.

"Why are you over there?" Flame's voice filled the

room. Wynn had gotten used to the quiet. She jumped up and dropped her drawing rock on the ground. It clattered at her feet. She stepped away from the wall.

"You're back!" Wynn was very glad Flame was safe and didn't get lost in the dark or eaten by a monster. She gave her a big hug. Flame seemed surprised, and held her arms stiffly down, without wrapping them around Wynn's shoulders. Wynn let go. Maybe Flame didn't know hugging. Wynn smiled anyway. "I made a picture for you," Wynn said.

Flame dropped a clump of bulbous fruits by the fire. She squinted again, coming very close to the wall. Her nose almost touched it as she looked at Wynn's drawing. Then she reached out and touched the wall, drawing her finger over it.

"What is it?" she asked.

Wynn felt sad. She wasn't very good at drawing. The people looked like sticks, and Mildred was a blob with two legs poking out of her sides. Shadow's stripes didn't stay in her lines. "It's you and me and Mildred and Shadow. We are all together. We are friends."

Shadow pressed her enormous head against Wynn's side. She almost fell over as the cat rubbed against her. Flame turned away from the wall. "Thank you," she said. Her voice sounded different. "Shadow likes it very much. She says it is wonderful."

Wynn wrapped her arms around Shadow's neck and gave the tigereon a tight squeeze. "You're welcome."

"Come, sit by the fire and eat." Flame used a stone knife to slice off a chunk of the dark purple fruit. Its insides were bright yellow and a little bit stringy. She handed a piece to Wynn. Wynn took a bite, and immediately shoved as much as she could in her mouth. It was sweet!

She smiled, but then the flavor changed. It turned bitter. Wynn swallowed it quickly.

"Do you like it?" Flame asked. She took her own bite, and chewed it without flinching.

"I like the sweet part," she said. She took another piece. She knew how it felt to be so hungry it was dangerous. She wouldn't turn down food, even if it did taste bitter at the end.

"The fruit nearby is better here than any other place in the wood." She wiped her chin with the back of her hand. "Fruit in the rest of the wood only tastes bitter."

"Thank you," Wynn said, helping herself to more.

"It's a blessing and a curse. The elves come around here to pick the sweet fruit sometimes. That's when we have to hide." Shadow settled down between them, and curled her long tail around Wynn. "Shadow and I used to live near the rock ledges. The sweet fruit grew there, too. The elves came around so often to gather them, we had move to a new part of the forest, a hollow near the stream. After a while, the fruit there turned sweet as well. We came here not long ago. Now the sweet fruit is growing here. It seems to be spreading. We'll have to move again before long."

"Are the elves mean?" Wynn asked. The fairies always said they were bad.

"They aren't mean. They're very desperate. They do what they must to survive. As long as you stay away from them, they aren't a bother. It's the fairies they are really after." Flame used her staff to prod the fiery rocks. Sparks flew up and drifted toward the ceiling. "There is something about you I don't understand."

Wynn knew what that was like. She didn't say anything, just tucked her ruined dress around her legs.

Flame didn't really look at her, but stared past her out the door. "If you were safe underneath that shield, why did you come into the wood? You were protected there."

"A snake tricked me," Wynn said. She felt heat rising

in her face. She was very angry at that snake. "It looked like Mildred. She was hurt. I needed to help."

Flame brought her pale gaze back toward Wynn. "You risked your own safety for your bird?" Her hand stroked Shadow's neck.

"She is my friend," Wynn said. "Friends do nice things."

Flame's forehead wrinkled. She looked like she was thinking hard. The fire danced over the rocks, sometimes growing bright, and other times dimming to a soft glow. "I will help you find your way back," she said. "You don't belong in these woods. If you are my friend, I'll get you home."

In the distance, a reaper howled.

CHAPTER TWELVE

Elric

ELRIC SPENT MOST OF THE night awake, sitting on the floor near his window staring out at the wood and praying for his sister. The night sky was unbearably bright underneath the glowing dome. He could see the darkness beyond it, and imagined Wynn lost or hurt somewhere in those shadows.

He paced until exhaustion forced him to sit again. He didn't want to go anywhere near his bed. He knew he would fall asleep, and that would feel like giving up. The hours slowly passed, with Elric only feeling more and more sick with his situation. He could see no way out.

Then he felt a cool breeze against his cheek.

Zephyr appeared next to him. "Hello, Prince."

"Zeph!" Elric shot to his feet. It was such a relief not to be alone, locked in his room with his grief. He really needed a friend. "I'm so glad you're here. What time is it?" He had lost track of the hours in the quiet part of the night.

"Not yet morning. It is still dark beyond the dome." Zephyr's feet left the floor as he peered through the window.

"I can't leave her out there, Zeph," he said. "I have to get out of here and find her. If there's any chance at all that she's alive, I can't give up."

Zephyr looked down and nodded. "I know. That's why I brought help."

With a wave of his hand, a sparkling mist covered the door, then faded to nothing. It slowly opened to reveal Osmund standing on the other side holding his woodcutter's ax.

"So, are we going into the Nightfell Wood or not?" he asked with his usual ambivalence. But Elric could see the light in the man's eye.

Elric stared at the man in his doorway in shock. His

mind was reeling. He thought that Osmund had sided with the Fairy Queen. Osmund stepped through the door and softly shut it behind him as if nothing were amiss.

"But—but you betrayed us," Elric stammered as he stared down the man. "You told the queen to lock me up!"

Osmund shrugged. "The Otherworld has taught me a thing or two," he said. "Including how to say one thing and mean another. Masking intentions can come in handy, especially when you need to get away with something dangerous and you don't want your mother to know. If I hadn't said what I said, the queen would have locked me up too, and then where would we be?" Osmund glanced around Elric's room. "I told you to play along before we left the Otherworld, but like always, you have trouble listening."

Elric stared at him with his mouth agape.

"So, are we going to save Wynn or what?" Osmund asked. He held out his hand. Elric hesitated only a moment, then took it. Osmund helped him to his feet. "We need to be sneaky to get out of here. There aren't many fairies around at this time in the morning, but the ones who are walking around are almost all guards. We have to take care or we'll be spotted."

"I can help with that," Zephyr stated. "I've been working on something."

He pressed his palms together. A strange blue-gray shadow formed around his fingers. Slowly he drew them apart and made a motion similar to shaking out a blanket. The shadow grew and stretched. It filled the air above their heads, then settled down over them. Elric felt the weight of it, like the cool, moist air of a summer night lingering on his skin.

He looked up at Osmund, and all the color was gone from the man. His normally green tunic looked shadowy gray, and his dark brown hair was now black. Elric looked down at his own hands, and his skin was the color of bleached wool. Zephyr floated in the air, an enormous grin spread across his face. "I can't believe that really worked!"

"What did you do?" Elric asked, still looking at his ghostly gray hands.

"I gathered twilight," he said. "I've cloaked you with it. As long as you aren't moving, you will disappear from sight. The magic should be stronger in the shadows, but I'm not sure how long it will last. It's a new magic for me."

"It's brilliant," Elric said. "We still might need a

distraction to get out of the palace, though. The fewer eyes on us, the better."

Zephyr nodded. "I can take care of that. I'm good at distraction. Listen, once you pass through the shield, there is no way to get back inside unless a fairy lets you through. I will stay by the twisted oak near the shield to the north of the gardens. That's the place where Wynn disappeared. I will stand there for the next hundred years if I have to, so you'd better come back quickly, because it is going to be terribly boring waiting around for you that long."

Elric clapped Zephyr on the back. "You're a true friend."

Zephyr turned to Osmund. "I know what you think, but I won't let you down."

Elric got the impression something was amiss between the fairy and the former prince as Osmund glared at him. "You'd better not," Osmund warned. "Or I'll have your head."

Zephyr turned. "Elric, am I not reliable?"

Elric gave the fairy a sidelong look. He didn't know Zephyr to be reliable, but he chose to trust him now. Elric gathered the contents of a bowl of fruit near his window and dropped them into his old traveling sack.

"I'm glad to have you at my back. We will find you at the oak when the time comes."

Zephyr's smile faded, and suddenly he looked more serious than Elric had ever seen him. He nodded. "Go, and good luck."

Osmund gripped his ax with both hands, and Elric looked around his room. The handle of the silver sword the queen had given him glinted from its mounting on the wall. He climbed on his bed to pull the hilt from the hooks. The blade gleamed like moonlight and the blue heart of fire.

Elric rifled through his overturned things to find his belt and a scabbard. He looked at the sword again and had a sinking feeling. "This sword is a relic. It's full of fairy magic. It was never meant for me."

Osmund hitched his ax over his shoulder, "That's the nature of being a changeling. You never quite fit in. The only question that matters is, is it sharp and pointy?"

Elric let out a snort and put the sword in the scabbard.

Osmund tucked his short ax into the strap of his sack. Let's go."

The three of them crept through the door. Zephyr disappeared and Osmund and Elric pressed against the wall. Elric watched in amazement as the details of

Osmund's hands, then his arms and shoulders, slowly blurred and melted until he couldn't make out Osmund at all.

"The way is clear," Zephyr's voice whispered as a soft breeze blew through the hall. Elric pushed forward and hurried down the stairs with Osmund behind him. The steps seemed to fly under his feet. He felt as if he were sliding down the stairs, his shoes barely touching the ground as he raced downward.

A stiff wind hit him, harsh and cold.

"Back," Osmund whispered, and he pressed himself into a nook. Elric followed and held perfectly still. Once more, he watched his body melt into the wall as if he didn't exist. It was like being in a dream, floating through the air, but he was awake. He could still feel his body even though he couldn't see it. He wondered if this is what Zephyr felt like every time he became the air.

A fairy climbed the stair, carrying a heavy dark cloth. Mourning chimes rang from the bells he had tied around his waist and ankles.

Once the fairy had passed, Osmund nudged Elric. It was eerie watching Osmund's hand appear as he moved it, to tap Elric on his invisible arm. No matter how long he lived in this world, he wasn't sure he would ever get used to magic.

They came to the entrance of the throne room. Now was the time they needed a distraction. Four guards lingered in the chamber, including Lord Raven. He was talking to a fairy in the form of a large owl perched near the fractured crystal. They both inspected the thin lines of silvery mist still leaking from it.

A metallic clang echoed just beyond the main chamber door. Shouts rang out as the sound of water splashing on stone rang through the chamber. All the fairies turned their heads. The guards twisted and disappeared, only to reappear as a badger, hawk, boar, and wolf. Raven didn't change form, instead he ran toward the door muttering under his breath. The owl flew after him.

"Zephyr, get back here! You are to set this right!" Raven's voice called out.

Whatever Zephyr had done, it had worked.

Cloaked in shadow, Elric and Osmund ran toward the halls that led to the kitchens and the gardens beyond.

Once in the darkness of the abandoned kitchens, Zephyr's spell seemed to pull night from the air around them, and hid them even as they ran. They snuck right past two fairies running toward whatever mess Zephyr had made. Once they reached the fields of flowers, Elric finally felt free. He wanted to run as fast as he could, but kept his pace measured to stay with Osmund.

They became one with the shadows of the early dawn as they finally reached the shield. Elric knew at least one of the dangers that lurked in the darkness of the wood. The reapers were terrifying, and he didn't know what other monsters awaited him. He reached out, then hesitated to touch the shield. He could get lost out there. He could be trapped in the wood, too. Would he know enough to find his way? Did he have the courage to find his sister?

Osmund stepped forward. "Wynn has the heart of a dragon," Osmund reminded him. "She's out there somewhere. Let's go get her back."

Together they stepped through the shield and into the darkness beyond.

CHAPTER THIRTEEN

Wynn

WYNN WOKE TO A GENTLE tap on her shoulder.

"It's morning," Flame said.

It took a minute for Wynn to remember where she was. She rubbed her eyes and blinked up at Flame. It didn't seem like morning. It was still very dark. Wynn got to her feet. Mildred pecked at one of the bulby fruits near the fire. Wynn motioned for her to follow, and the hen trotted to her heel. As Wynn came to the door, she saw the heavy dark clouds hanging over the trees.

"The air is too cool. You can feel the charge of

lightning in the air. A storm is coming," Flame said as she leaned on her staff. "We have to get you home."

Flame crept down the path that led out of the ruins. She hunched over low, swinging her long staff in front of her. Shadow joined her with long strides. Flame reached out to grip Shadow's thick ruff. Together they climbed down the hill. Wynn did her best to follow. Mildred flapped and clucked along. She pecked at several fluttery bugs along the way.

Flame stayed silent, and Wynn did the same. Flame knew these woods, so what she did was probably wise. As they wandered farther from Flame's home, the woods grew heavy. The forest felt dark and bitterly cold and damp. The trees became twisted and ugly. The bark on the trunks was as black as the crackled husks of old logs that had burned through the night.

There were no more colorful mushrooms here with pretty white spots. The mushrooms that grew here looked like dripping trenchers of moldy stew, sickly and brown. No white flowers shone in the dim light. Wynn didn't see a single flower at all. The sweet purple fruit was different. Wynn saw the fruit hanging from the trees. It was black and wrinkly, and looked as bitter as it probably tasted.

Whatever beauty she found in the Nightfell Wood faded with every step they took away from the ruins. And yet, as they walked, the forest seemed to be trying to be pretty. Wynn spotted tiny sprouts pushing up through the leaves in Flame's footsteps. But they wouldn't last long in the dim light of this part of the Nightfell Wood. The cold, wet air clung to Wynn's face and neck, chilling her. Every once in a while, a heavy droplet of water would hit her on the top of the head.

Wynn followed Flame as she marched through the woods. Her smoke-and-shadow dress billowed around her, and Shadow stayed close to her side. Mildred hopped up on Shadow's hindquarters and settled down to roost on the tigereon's backside, but Shadow turned around and hissed at her. The hen jumped off, flapping her wings in a very insulted sort of way.

Every once in a while, Shadow lifted her head and sniffed, then swung her tail and let out a low growl. Flame dropped down next to the tigereon, and Wynn tucked herself down too. Even Mildred would hunch down over her feet and coo softly. They would wait for a moment or two, before Shadow would twitch the tip of her tail and lead the way forward again.

"What is out there?" Wynn asked.

"There are elves nearby," Flame whispered. "Stay close and be careful. They are cunning creatures."

The path twisted through the gnarled trees. Wynn couldn't see the shield. It blended with the stormy sky through the gaps in the leaves. Mildred came close to her ankle, and pecked at her bare foot. Wynn picked the hen up.

"What is wrong?" Wynn asked the hen. Mildred looked back over Wynn's shoulder and let out a cautious clucking sound.

Shadow stopped too. The tigereon lifted her head and sniffed the air. Flame prodded the ground with her staff. She took a cautious step, testing the ground before shifting her weight forward. Shadow crouched low and crept up beside her. Her tail slashed through the darkness, the white spot on the end of it looked like a warning flag.

"Flame?" Wynn had a bad feeling. She could feel it crawling on her skin, like an oily slime oozing over her.

"There's something here," Flame said, letting go of Shadow and taking a few careful steps forward. "The ground doesn't feel right."

Wynn placed Mildred down. Thick, dry leaves crunched beneath her bare feet. They weren't wet and slimy here like the rest of the trail. She didn't like this.

Flame jabbed at the ground again with her staff. Something cracked. It sounded like an old branch. The ground beneath Flame gave way, and she sank down several inches. "Wynn, stay back!" Flame shouted.

Shadow snarled and leaped forward to reach Flame.

"Shadow, stay!" Flame called. But the tigereon didn't listen.

Shadow landed in front of Flame. The ground beneath them buckled. Wynn ran as fast as she could and grabbed Flame's outstretched arm. She pulled them both backward toward the roots of a thick tree.

Flame landed on top of Wynn, knocking her down on the solid ground, but Shadow wasn't fast enough. The ground fell away from beneath the tigereon. She jumped, her enormous claws outstretched, and caught the twisted roots near Wynn's feet.

The great cat screamed as she clawed at the ground, desperate to pull herself out of the pit that had opened up beneath her. A vine pulled taut, shaking several broad leaves away from a large bell. It sounded above them, tolling with a dark and grim sound.

"What just happened?" Flame asked, pushing away from Wynn. "Where's Shadow?"

"Oh!" Wynn crawled forward, reaching the edge

of a great pit. Sharp wooden pikes had been buried in the bottom of the trap, but the tigereon had managed to avoid falling on them. Her claws still clung to the tree's roots, while her tail thrashed over the sharp pikes. "Shadow fell!"

Flame prodded the ground with her staff, but as soon as she came to the pit, she fell to her knees. "Shadow!" she called. She clung to her staff. "Is she hurt?" she cried.

"No," Wynn answered. But Shadow was in danger. The spikes were very sharp. They would hurt her. The tigereon needed something to climb out with. Wynn looked around. There had to be something she could use to help.

A part of the top of the trap hung on the far side of the pit. It had caught on the vine that rang the bell. It looked like a lattice of branches tied with ropes. It didn't look very strong.

"Do something!" Flame screamed. She reached down the pit with her hand, and Shadow tried to claw up toward her. "Please!"

Wynn grabbed the piece of lattice and dragged it over to the side of the trap where Shadow clung to the wall of the pit. She had to use her whole body to drag it. Flame stayed on the edge of the pit. She knelt along the side, reaching down into it with her staff a few feet away from Shadow.

Wynn pulled the lattice over to the tigereon by herself. "Help me," she called to Flame. She looped a section of the lattice over a thick root. It swung deeper into the pit, but didn't fall.

Shadow's enormous claws caught on the lattice. They sliced through a piece of rope, and part of the lattice crumbled. Shadow hissed.

"Help!" Wynn called as she clung to the lattice and fell back, bracing her feet on the curled root holding the lattice. Flame slapped Wynn on the shoulder, then felt along her arm until she too grabbed the lattice and braced.

Shadow tried again, reaching with her large paws. This time the lattice didn't break. Slowly the tigereon dragged herself out of the pit. Her paw reached the top of the trap and Wynn grabbed it. Shadow's eyes blazed with amber fire and she snarled. Flame grabbed the cat's ruff and pulled. Finally Shadow dragged herself to the top.

Flame wrapped her arms around Shadow's thick neck and cried into her fur. Shadow panted, then looked toward Wynn and squeezed her eyes shut.

"You saved her, Wynn," Flame said. "You saved her."

Wynn came forward and stroked the cat's shoulder. Mildred trotted over and sat on the tigereon's paw. Her stripes shimmered with pretty lavenders and yellows. Wynn knew, even though she couldn't hear Shadow talking, that she was grateful.

A whistle floated over the air somewhere behind her. Wynn turned. That was a strange-sounding bird.

Shadow stopped panting and her stripes immediately faded to dark green and brown, until she nearly disappeared into the forest floor. Another whistle answered it.

Flame's eyes went wide. "The elves. They're here."

Flame swung herself over Shadow's back. The cat got to her feet. Flame reached back for Wynn to help her climb up on Shadow's back too. "Come on!" she shouted. Wynn tried to swing her leg over Shadow's hip. But then Shadow bounded forward, and Wynn tipped backward. She rolled off Shadow's back and hit the ground hard.

"Wynn!" Flame cried. But Shadow did not stop. "Wynn, run! Hurry!"

Wynn scrambled to her feet and chased after the tigereon, but it was too late. Shadow charged forward with Flame riding her. The two of them disappeared into the woods.

Wynn bent down, panting. Mildred had disappeared. She had to find her. She straightened and began calling for her, but Mildred didn't come out from under any of the bushes. Wynn was alone again. She lay down and curled into a little ball as the woods teemed with movement.

Suddenly an enormous boar emerged from the underbrush with a loud squeal. It had been harnessed to the strangest wagon that had been camouflaged with thick leaves and branches. The wheels had pegs jutting out around the tread that looked like severed boar's feet. They left boar prints on the trail instead of wagon tracks.

The driver of the wagon rode high on a crafted seat. He wore a simple brown robe with a heavy hood. He pulled on the reins, tied through a ring in the boar's nose, and his hood fell away from his face.

His skin was a vivid green, with patches of lighter green skin that swirled in complex patterns over his bald head and cheeks. The same curling patterns covered his hands. He had a narrow nose, tall pointed ears, and deep-set eyes that glowed orange.

Another wagon approached. The man in front of her tipped a contraption with a sharp spear point toward

Wynn's throat. She batted it to the side, but he frowned at her, and pointed it even closer to her neck.

"*Quis es?*" he said.

She looked at him, puzzled. "I don't know," she said. She had never heard those words before.

The other fearsome green man murmured more of the strange words in confused whispers as they attempted to rein in the restless boars. The beasts swung their heads and squealed. The second man pointed a terrifying contraption with an arrow toward her. She recognized it from the scary picture on Flame's wall.

"You speak the Saxon language of the Otherworld?" one of the strange boar riders asked. He said the words funny. They sounded very different. He peered at her with those burning orange eyes. "What is your name?"

"My name is Wynn," she said. "I need to go home."

More murmurs in strange words.

"You are to come with us." An elf motioned behind him. Two more green men, and one green woman jumped out of the strange wagons. They rushed to Wynn's sides. They hurt her as they bent her arms together and tied her wrists tightly with a rope.

"No!" she cried. "I don't like that." She couldn't say anything else before her throat closed up and her thoughts didn't come to her mouth anymore. She wanted to go home.

The man in the front leaned very close to her. She saw his orange eyes flash as his mouth set in a grim line. "You belong to us now."

CHAPTER FOURTEEN

Elric

TWISTED TREES LOOMED OVER ELRIC on the edge of the Nightfell Wood. Cold mist rose from the damp ground. He could feel the wetness of the air on his face and couldn't fight the urge to shudder. It was still very early, and not yet fully light. Elric wasn't sure bright light ever made it through the thick canopy of leaves above them. It felt very strange here, like the trees could reach down and steal any happy thought from his head. He tried to imagine Wynn laughing and singing in this place as she chased after Mildred. It didn't seem possible.

He peered through the shield. On this side, the surface of it looked like a storm of dark clouds that washed everything within the shield with bleak gray. It was as if the light, magic, and vibrant colors of the fairy realm simply didn't exist at all. He could see the great tree in the distance, but it appeared as dark and lifeless as the trees around him. No blue lights shone in the stone towers surrounding it. The fields of colorful flowers looked like barren winter fields.

Osmund brushed his shoulders, as if shaking spiders off his vest. "Well, this is awful." He gave Elric a hard pat on the shoulder. "Let's get moving."

Elric shook his foggy head. "Right," he said. "You're right. Are you any good at tracking?"

Osmund made a wobbly motion with his hand. "I didn't really have a need back home."

Elric nodded. "Then I'll lead the way." He'd often had to track lost sheep through the woods, or hunt down the predators that stalked his flock. He tried to push the bad feeling out of his mind as he looked to the ground for clues. The dirt was soft, which was good for tracking, and the soil held a lot of clay. Tracks would be deep and clear, and they would hold their form.

He immediately found several footprints. One a

muffled shape of a foot, and the other distinct with toes. He also found chicken prints. But there seemed to be two sets of them, and they scrambled all over. He also found the long, twisting whiplike marks of the belly of a snake.

It looked like Wynn had found trouble almost immediately. His heart sped up. He couldn't let his imagination run away with him. Too much was at stake. He had to look only at what was in front of him and follow the clues she left him. Her footprints crisscrossed the clearing, but then led into the woods. "This way." Elric pointed through a gap in the trees. He couldn't really call it a path.

Osmund swung his ax and lopped off a branch. He pulled a crystal out of his pocket and set it in a split in the wood. It glowed with a soft light.

"That's one of the starlight crystals." Elric came closer. He had several of them embedded in the wood of the tree above his bed. "How did you get it out from the wall?"

"When you live in a tree"—Osmund gave a half shrug—"an ax comes in handy."

"You didn't!" Elric stared at Osmund.

"Let's not worry about that now." Osmund lowered

the stick to the ground to better illuminate the tracks. "I'm sure it will grow back. . . ." He took a couple of steps forward, concentrating on the tracks. "Eventually," he added. "I knew we would need a light under the canopy."

"How?" Elric asked.

Osmund looked up at him and grimaced before inspecting the ground again. "Because I've been here before."

"What happened?" Elric asked in shock.

Osmund bent to pick up one of Mildred's dark feathers. "It was foolish, and Zephyr's fault." Osmund sighed. "No, it was my fault."

He searched the ground for another clue, twirling Mildred's feather between his fingers. "When I was about your age, Zephyr and I were stealing pies from the kitchen. I told him I wanted to see what was on the other side of the shield. He was livid. He said he wouldn't help me. I threatened to tell Lord Raven about some terrible prank he had pulled. He still insisted he wouldn't help, said it was too dangerous. I called him a coward. I'm sorry for that.

"That night Zephyr woke me up. He stayed silent and motioned me to follow. He led me out to the shield and I stepped through, thinking he would be there to help me back. But he disappeared, and I was trapped." Osmund tossed the feather to the ground and peered more intently at the path.

"Zephyr just abandoned you?" Elric couldn't believe his friend would do such a thing.

"I confronted him about it when he caught me trying to undo the spell on your door. He swears he never saw me that night. He claims he never knew what happened. I'm sure he doesn't want to be held responsible for my disappearance, but it bothers me that he won't admit he made a mistake." Osmund faced Elric. "I hope he'll be there when we need him."

"He will be," Elric insisted. He couldn't believe Zeph would leave Osmund in the Nightfell Wood alone. Something wasn't adding up.

"How did you end up in the Otherworld?" Elric asked. Maybe Wynn could find a similar way to escape this place.

"There was a reaper in the woods. I hid in the ruins of the lost elf city, but was chased by the Grendel." Osmund rubbed the back of his neck. "He surrounded himself with shadow and smoke and kept a fearsome striped beast at his side. I came upon the old portal that had been used by the elves. As soon as the Grendel stepped on the seal, it glowed, and I fell through to the Other-world. It was a narrow escape."

"Why would you want to see the other side of the shield?" Elric asked. "This place is terrible."

"You wouldn't understand," Osmund insisted.

"Of course I wouldn't. The shield is there for a reason. It keeps everyone safe." Sure, he had felt trapped while he was locked in his room, but now that he was beyond the shield, he wanted to run back inside it. Elric didn't like feeling so exposed. There was a reaper somewhere in these woods. He had seen it.

"Yet here we are," Osmund said, motioning around. "Wonderfully unsafe."

"I had no choice," Elric protested. "The queen forbade me from finding Wynn."

"Well, maybe I didn't have a choice either." Osmund's voice was tinged with a very old anger and frustration. He let out a sigh and shrugged. "I was a foolish kid, what can I say?"

"It had to be hard, when you discovered what the Otherworld was like." Elric remembered how difficult it was to survive on his own with Wynn, with no one to look out for them. "The Otherworld has so many bad things."

Osmund gave him that disbelieving look that he had given Elric when they first met, and Elric under-estimated the man. "You can be truly terrible as seeing past your own nose." He motioned to the woods with his glowing rock. "I liked the Otherworld. I had a home that I built with my own two hands that suited me, the woods gave me what I needed, and for the most part I endeared myself to people."

Elric gave him a skeptical look.

Osmund bent to examine a broken stick. "What? No one can resist my sunny personality."

If they were anywhere else, Elric might have chuck-led. Here, he didn't have the spirit to give Osmund anything more than an exasperated shake of the head. Osmund walked ahead. "When I lived here, I knew I was growing older, but I wasn't sure if I was growing up. Make no mistake, I'm not glad to be back."

He thought he knew what Osmund meant. Zephyr was over four hundred years old, and yet he seemed like any other young boy Elric's age. He wasn't changing.

No matter how Osmund felt about being here, Elric was sure of one thing. "I'm glad you're back," he said.

Osmund gave him a warm smile, then contin-ued down what could barely be called a path. There was a pride in Osmund's bearing. Elric thought about Osmund's hut and how comfortable he had seemed in it. He had made himself his own world. "Will you return to the Otherworld when all this is over?" Elric asked.

Osmund bent to inspect a footprint and didn't answer. "Let's find your sister." He took another step forward and pushed aside some brush with the handle of his ax. "Look at this."

Elric ran forward, but when he saw that Osmund had found, he immediately took a step back. Lying on the ground in the small clearing was a large snake-like creature. Its enormous eyes had been clouded over by death. Stiff spines ran the length of the creature's back. "What is it?"

"I don't know," Osmund admitted. "I don't know much about the creatures of this wood. I'm only familiar with the elves, and trust me, we don't want to run into them."

Elric knelt, picked up a twig from the ground nearby and poked at the dead snake. "It looks like its head was bashed in."

"And the scales are ripped," Osmund noted. "Claws, perhaps?"

More bird prints dotted the mud around the carcass;

they were the right size and shape for an odd-toed hen. "Wait a minute," Osmund said, inspecting one of the slashes in the snake's skin. There was a distinctive wound to the eye as well, as if it had been pecked. "Did Mildred do this?"

A tiny flame of hope lit in Elric's heart. He looked around and found a blunted stick sitting on top of a thick thornbush as if it had been hastily thrown there. There was a dark stain of dried blood on one end. "I think she did. I think they both did." He glanced behind him and saw more prints leading away. Hope and the swell of pride mixed with his worry. Wynn had faced a darkling creature and she defeated it on her own.

Elric followed the tracks, with Osmund close behind. They came to a dry creek bed. Some branches of a nearby bush were broken. Elric took a closer look, and found a glittering thread caught on one of the thorns. Elric pulled the thread free; it glowed in the dim light. It must have come from Wynn's dress.

"What are these prints?" Osmund was bent low near a thick tree trunk. Elric came to his side and saw long, thin rabbit-like prints in the shape of a V. Very different marks had been pressed in the mud where a rabbit's front legs should be. They looked like miniature hands with long, bony fingers. Elric felt a jolt through his whole body. He knew a creature with rabbit legs and long, bony hands.

"Hob!" Elric said. He couldn't contain his excitement. "Hob found her."

"Who is Hob?" Osmund asked. "Or should I ask, what is Hob?"

"I don't know what he is," Elric admitted. "He's a mix of a man, a rabbit, a fox, and a rat, I suppose."

Osmund gave him a blank stare. "How does that work?"

"He's the strangest creature I've ever seen, of that there is no doubt, but he helped us when we first came through the gate. He led us to the palace, even though the guards chased him back into the wood." If Hob had found Wynn, Elric thought, then she had help. She was with someone who knew what it took to survive in these woods— someone who he trusted would not hurt her but help her find her way back to safety. Sure enough, the tracks turned and led back in the direction of the shield. Elric pointed down the path. "He knows how to lead her home."

But Hob couldn't get her through the shield. Elric didn't know how old the prints were. At the moment he didn't care. "We're going to find her! Hurry."

"Elric, wait!" Osmund called as Elric tore ahead. The shadows thickened as he ran forward, leaving Osmund's light behind. Yet with what little light there was, he could see the tracks. Hob's strange rabbit-like tracks, Wynn's muffled shoe print, her bare footprint, and Mildred's angular prints trotting along beside.

He could almost picture the happy troop as they marched back home. Mildred would be bobbing her head, her bright comb jiggling and her tail held high. Wynn would be singing, happy to be with Hob as the darkling creature bounced out front with the twitchy energy that reminded Elric of a squirrel.

Wynn would be hungry and tired. He couldn't wait to get her home and safe in the castle where nothing could hurt her again. Then he would sleep for a week. He was beginning to feel the effects of staying up worrying about her all night.

The path suddenly veered in another direction, farther away from the place where Zephyr was waiting to help them back through the shield. It didn't matter. Once they found Wynn, they could follow the edge of the shield until Zephyr caught sight of them. Then they would be safe. He'd make sure Wynn never set foot outside of the palace again.

"Elric, wait!" Osmund called again. Elric paused his stride to make sure Osmund could follow down the sudden turn in the path. Osmund jogged up to him, sweat beading on his high forehead. "You can't just go charging through the wood like that. This forest is dangerous."

"All the more reason we should find Wynn, and quickly." Elric turned to set out again.

Osmund blocked him with the flat side of the head of his ax. "We're no good to Wynn dead. There are elves in these wood who will shoot you with one of their mechanized bows as soon as they look at you. They create elaborate traps, and you would never see them until you were caught in one. That's not to mention the creatures here. There's a reaper in the woods, and if it finds us, we're worse than dead."

Elric nodded, and tried to contain his restless energy. Osmund was right. They had to be careful. They came to a small clearing where the roots of a tree formed into a twisted cage where the dirt had washed out from underneath them. Leaves littered the ground everywhere. Osmund lifted his stone torch.

There on the ground was another one of Mildred's dark feathers, nestled in the roots of the tree.

"It looks like the rabbit creature went this way, and Wynn ran that way," Osmund said, pointing with his light.

"Why would they split apart?" Elric asked with a sinking feeling.

Osmund lowered the glowing rock to an enormous, deep print at their feet. The pit of the print was the size of Elric's head, and there was no mistaking it. It looked half man and half beast.

The reaper had found Wynn.

CHAPTER FIFTEEN

Wynn

WYNN SAT IN THE BACK of the elves' terrible wagon. The pig-foot wheels bumped over the uneven trails and Wynn felt every hard jolt. The rope tied around her wrists hurt. She yanked and tugged on it, but it only got tighter. Her fingers felt tingly.

She was so angry. One of the elves sat next to her with his arrow shooter across his knees. She kicked him in the elbow.

He shouted as the arrow shooter fired, nearly hitting the driver of the wagon. The driver pulled on the reins and turned the wagon too quickly. The stumpy, pig-foot wheels tipped, and the whole wagon turned over. Wynn tumbled to the forest floor. She got up and ran away from the boars and the nasty elves. Her skirt twisted and tangled around her legs as the sharp rocks and roots of the forest floor cut into her bare feet. But she was free!

She had to get away. She had to find a place to hide. She had to find Mildred and go back to Shadow and Flame. Her skirt tangled around her legs again. She tried to hold it up, but it was hard with her hands tied together. The ropes dug into her wrists and made them ache. She pulled at them as she ran. She needed her hands to run right. It was hard to balance.

Run! It was all she could think about, her only hope. She had to get home.

Suddenly a net flew over the top of her, and she fell, hopelessly tangled.

"I got you!" an elf shouted behind her. Her heart flew into her throat. She rolled over and tried to kick at him.

The elf pulled at the net, when a furious black hen charged out of the shadows. She leaped off a high bank and flapped and scratched at the elf's face. He let out a terrified cry, and Wynn struggled from under the net.

A boar wagon charged toward them, and a second net flew from a wooden arm that whipped out from the side of the wagon. It fell over Mildred.

"Mildred!" Wynn screeched. She struggled from under her net, and ran toward her trapped bird. An elf leaped from the wagon and balled up the net around Mildred. Her feathers stuck out in ruffled tufts between the ropes. One of her white legs poked out, and her clawed toes curled.

"This creature means something to you?" the elf asked.

"She's mine. Give her back!" Wynn lunged for the net, but the elf pulled it away from her with a swing of his long arms.

"I'm taking it. If you ever want to see it again, you will follow orders. Do you understand?" He held the bundle and Mildred let out a desperate squawk.

Wynn wasn't sure about all of his words, but she knew she had to behave. She nodded. Quietly she followed the elves, and sat glumly in the back of the wagon.

They rode a long time. Wynn wasn't sure how late in the day it was, but her stomach growled and she was very tired and thirsty. As they traveled, the woods seemed less tangled. Wynn noticed certain branches had been cut. The circles left on the trunks from the severed branches shone white where the soft inner wood was exposed. There were a lot of large boulders here too. Some of them had clean edges, as if they had been shaped by a stone cutter. The black fruit hung from several trees along the path. It probably wasn't sweet at all.

This part of the woods looked angry. So did the elves. Not one of them had smiled.

The band of elves stretched out down a narrow path before they came to a large wall of thick tangled vines. One of them put his fingers to his mouth and whistled. It was the same strange whistle she had heard earlier, but she thought it was a bird.

Wynn heard a great wrenching sound, and the clattering of a chain. Something groaned, the way a tree does when it is about to fall.

An enormous door opened up in the vines, slowly pushing toward them. The elves whipped their reins over the backs of the large boars. Wynn peered around as she passed through the gate. The vines covered the front of an enormous wooden wall made of sharpened poles. From the outside, the vines covering the face of it made it disappear into the forest. Behind the wall stood a bustling village teeming with more green-faced bald people.

They all wore long tunics made of woven cloth in drab browns and grays. They were simple and functional clothes that made it difficult to tell the girls from the boys. They reminded Wynn of the clothes she used to wear in the Otherworld. Most of the elves wore hoods over their bare heads, though some of them wore strange contraptions on their faces with glass over their orange eyes.

"Take her to the Headmind," one of the wagon drivers said as he slid off the seat of his wagon and handed the reins over to another elf. "And keep this with you." He shoved the net with Mildred in it into another elf's arms. Mildred squawked and wriggled.

"Give her to me," Wynn said. She reached out for the net. "I will be good." She wanted Mildred safe in her arms, and not wrapped up in the net.

The elf looked her up and down. His grim expression didn't change. "You'll be good, or else."

Wynn didn't wish to test the elf. He was already very angry. The new elf grabbed her by the elbow and pulled her through a series of strange houses. They were tall, and made from neat mud bricks in interlocking patterns. Large wheels paddled running water to the tops of the houses. It flowed through hollow reed gutters linking the houses together. The wheels also turned heavy rope belts that powered several other machines Wynn didn't understand.

The elf led her to a large brick and wood building in the center of the village.

Inside, stone steps led up to a large room with a throne at the back. Fires burned in stone pits to either side of it, fanned by billows that pumped themselves.

They warmed the room, but did not make the room feel lighter. An elf sat on a very old-looking stone throne. The back of it was enormous, and had pictures carved into it. The pictures looked a lot like the one in Flame's house in the ruins. Carved elves stood holding hunting trophies. The arms of the throne were carved to look like the heads of tigereons. The seat was covered with a striped animal skin that looked like the one the Fairy Queen had on her wall.

Around the room, woven panels showed more elves. Some of the elves in the tapestries looked at the stars through strange devices. They mixed potions, and worked with tools. There was even one picture of an elf posed in a mutual bow with a man with a beard, an Otherworld man.

The leader rose from the throne. He wore very fancy clothes with fine stitching that seemed very old, but well cared for; they piled on his shoulders in heavy layers that made him look bigger than all the other elves. Shaggy boar hide lined the collar of his dark brown outer robe. It glittered with embroidered threads that looked golden. A tarnished crown sat upon his bald head. It too seemed very old and was set with large pieces of amber.

He didn't seem very happy.

He said several things to her guards. They answered him in words she couldn't understand. It was very rude to talk in a language she didn't know. When they stopped talking, he turned his glowing eyes to her.

"Who are you, and what do you seek in our woods?" he asked. His words were very clear.

"I am Wynnfrith," she said. "I want my chicken back." She tried to tug her hands apart, but couldn't free them.

"That tells me nothing," he said. "You were found near a trap in the Witch's Wood. And the carcass of a reaper is rotting on our doorstep."

Lots of elves came into the room from the doors behind her. They stood around the edges, giving her plenty of clear space. Only the guard who held Mildred in the net stood near her. He looked angry.

Well, she was angry too. She wanted to cross her

arms, but couldn't with her hands tied.

"I don't like this," she said, holding her wrists up.

The leader looked down on her. "I am Axis, Head-mind of the darkling elves. You have trespassed in our wood. We are not a merciless people. But I will have answers."

"I don't like you." She dropped to the floor and crossed her legs beneath her. She was tired of standing. She didn't like the elves. The fairies were right. They were very mean.

"Wynn!" a familiar voice squealed.

She turned to look over her shoulder. Hob darted between the feet of those standing in front of the door and barreled toward her. She fell to the side as Hob leaped up onto her shoulder. "You are safe! Hob is so pleased, yes." He threw his thin arms around her neck, and she noticed the bandages tied around his narrow ribs.

"Hob!" She was so happy to see him. "You're back." She knew that wasn't the right thing to say, but it was the first thing that came into her mind, and he didn't seem to care. She was so, so happy!

He let go of her neck and bounded around her. "I thought the reaper had taken you far away. That Hob would never, ever, ever, ever see you again."

"You were hurt." She looked him over. He seemed well. The Headmind crossed his arms and listened to their conversation with cool interest.

"The elvsies found me and healed me. They are good with medicine." His large eyes blinked at her. "Not so good at magic."

"I don't like them." Wynn crossed her arms.

"And we don't like being treated with disdain," the Headmind growled as he hovered over her. "I should toss you in with the pigs."

Wynn let out a cry of fright. She didn't want to go in a pen with pigs. A horrible memory came back to her, of cruel laughter and mud in her hair. She started to cry. She couldn't help it.

"Do not speak to the princess that way," Hob shouted. His tail lashed the ground like a whip. "She is very kind. I won't let you hurt her." He stuck out his bandaged chest.

"Princess?" The light green swirl above the Headmind's eye rose as he peered down at Hob. "What do you mean by this?"

Hob slapped his long fingers over his mouth.

The Headmind turned to Wynn and peered carefully at her. He knelt down and touched the hem of Wynn's dress. She scooted back from him. "This is fairy-made," he said. "But you are not a fairy. You are an Otherworld girl. That can mean only one thing." Axis rose and looked around the crowd. "It seems the Fairy Queen is stealing human children again."

"No!" Wynn shouted. "She did not steal. I found the Silver Gate. Now I am a princess!"

Hob jumped forward and slapped his hands over Wynn's mouth this time. "Shhhh." He shook his head, and his large ears flopped from side to side. "Elvsies are very nice when they want to be, and they are not accusing you of stealing their fruit, as long as you are *not a fairy.*"

The elves in the room broke into restless chatter. Hoods leaned together, pressing green-striped faces close in huddled whispers. Several of the elves near the door slipped out into the village. Wynn could hear them shouting. Hands covered mouths, as if they could hide the sound of excited words. It was so noisy that Wynn clapped her hands over her ears.

Headmind Axis threw his hands up. His embroidered sleeves fell down to his elbows like sweeping waves. "Pax!" he shouted at all of them. They took longer to settle this time. Words escaped them in urgent whispers.

"Well, this changes things." He reached down and untied her wrists, then offered her a hand. She crossed her arms and remained sitting on the floor. He scowled at her, then folded his hands back into his fancy sleeves. "Very well," he said, turning away from her. "If you are the queen's new Otherworld pet, you may stay here as my guest."

He smiled at her, but it wasn't a friendly smile. It was a not happy smile but a pretending one. It reminded her of her father, and she didn't trust her father. "Show her to one of the healing house chambers. Keep the bird to ensure her obedience." He spared a downward glance at Hob. "Toss that one in the pit until we're sure he's not the gob who's been stealing from our fruit cellar."

The two elves nearest her lunged for her. She couldn't escape them because she was sitting. Strong hands gripped Wynn by the shoulders and hauled her to her feet. Wynn shouted and kicked out, hitting one in the shin. He stumbled to the side. Hob bounded through the room as another elf chased after him.

"Run, Hob!" she cried. Hob dashed about, bouncing as quick as lightning. His red fur looked like blurred streaks as he darted through the legs of the confused elves. The elves wrenched her arms back. Wynn stomped on the foot of the one to her right, and he let go enough for her to yank one hand free. She lunged forward and grabbed the net wrapped around Mildred.

She pulled it away from the elf holding it, and it loosened enough for Mildred to push her way out.

Elves scrambled around the hall as the hen darted between their legs and managed to slip out the door.

"Run!" Wynn screamed at both of them, before strong arms wrestled her away from the hall. Mildred was free! She was a clever hen. She'd find a way out of their nasty village. Wynn wanted to follow, but the elves holding her dragged her down a narrow hallway and through a doorway to a courtyard in the back of the throne hall. A pen of snorting boars grunted and squealed as they passed. She couldn't see Hob or Mildred. She hoped they would escape. Hob could find help.

"Get on, you troublesome creature!" the elf dragging her shouted as he kicked open the wooden door to another building partially built down into the ground like a cellar. They carried her down a narrow and dark hallway with crossed timber beams overhead. An elf in a simple brown hooded robe used a key to unlock a narrow door. The elves holding her tossed her in a dark room, and shut the heavy door.

Wynn struggled to her feet. Her arms burned where they had held her. She pounded on the door and screamed at it. It wasn't any use. It didn't matter. She pounded and screamed at it some more because she wanted to. She was angry. She carried on until her throat felt raw and her fist burned with pain and splinters.

Finally she collapsed on a framed rope bed in the corner. Wynn hugged herself as she sat on the lumpy mattress. The ropes creaked beneath her as she rocked herself to soothe her fear and her anger. Mildred and Hob were gone. That was good. She didn't want them trapped too.

It was very dark in the room. There was no window. Just bits of streaky light shining in between the planks of the heavy wooden walls. She was completely alone, and she didn't see any way out.

CHAPTER SIXTEEN

Elric

ELRIC PUSHED ASIDE A SMALL pile of leaves on the trail he had been following most of the day. He couldn't afford to make a mistake, even if it meant the hunt for the reaper lasted until they lost the light of day. He would search all night if that was what it took. Each moment that ticked by was another moment that his stomach twisted into knots and the bile rose in his throat. Wynn was in danger, and he couldn't find her.

They had tracked the reaper back toward the stormy shield. "Elric! Over here!" Osmund called as he stood on the root of a large tree and stretched upward to get a closer look at something on the trunk. Elric ran to him. There was a dark stain above the bushes. He reached up and touched it. His finger came away smeared with old blood. Small red hairs had caught in the bark.

Hob.

He was wounded.

Elric searched the bush below. He saw broken leaves and twigs, but he didn't find Hob's body. He couldn't locate Hob's tracks, either. Blood stained some leaves beneath the bush, but Elric detected no signs that he was still alive. Elric's heart pounded harder as he searched for signs of Wynn. Footprints, bits of cloth, anything.

"Over here," Osmund called. He held up Wynn's crown.

The dangers of the wood faded away. He took the circlet in his hands. It was a simple crown, a silver band engraved with stars, where his had leaves. It was bent in on one side, like it had been stepped on. Now it was nothing more than a fragile broken circle that had once sat on his sister's head. Words didn't come. Thoughts wouldn't come. Even his feelings seemed pressed under a weight so thick and terrible it seemed like he could drown in it.

The terrifying monster had his sweet sister. He had only had the courage to face one through the safety of the shield. There was no safety here. Those claws, those teeth, those burning eyes.

A creature like that could kill Wynn in a second. It had no mercy.

Elric gritted his teeth. And Master Elk said that a reaper would drag him back to the Grendel. They didn't kill outright.

"He's taking her to the Grendel," Elric said. "We have to stop him. Follow me." Elric ran down the narrow path.

"Elric, wait!" Osmund demanded.

He clutched Wynn's crown, following the path of the reaper like a hound on the scent of a wolf. His rage drove him forward as he climbed over the twisted roots of the trees, and leaped over ditches filled with slimy leaves.

Osmund did his best to catch up, but an unnatural determination had come over Elric. He wanted to destroy the foul beast for daring to touch his sister. He had to find and stop the creature before he could deliver her to the evil fairy who waited in the shadows.

The Grendel had caused the fairy realm endless misery. No more.

Elric blazed forward, but the trail was becoming harder and harder to follow. The ground was firmer here, the tracks less evident. Under a bush he found a piece of bright silk, Wynn's slipper. He was going the right way.

Just as he was about to run forward again, Osmund caught him and spun him around. He fought to catch his breath, but his expression looked as if he were about to breathe fire.

"You have to slow down," he panted. "We are going to lose the trail, and then we will be turned around in these infernal woods."

Elric paused enough to take a quick glance around. The trees had grown thicker, their branches hanging with heavy vines, turning the forest into a maze beneath the dark canopy. Cold water dripped on his shoulders from the edges of serrated leaves. Every feature of the woods looked the same until he had a hard time distinguishing the direction they just came from.

"We can't let him get away," Elric said. His throat burned, and he, too, struggled for breath. "She might still be alive."

Osmund put a hand on Elric's shoulder. "I know. But now is not the time to lose your wits. Your sister needs you, and the queen needs all of us."

"I don't care about the queen," Elric said.

Osmund took a step up the path. "Yes, you do. And you care about the people beneath that shield. They would be in terrible danger if the queen died. The best thing you can do right now is keep your head."

"The queen doesn't care about me," Elric said. "It's Wynn she loves. She wanted to use me as bait for the Grendel to keep the reapers away from Wynn."

Osmund's eyes widened. "That can't be true."

"Look, I don't mind," Elric said, starting off down the path again, knowing each step brought him closer to battle with a terrifying monster. "Wynn needs to stay safe, and if I have to sacrifice myself, then so be it."

Osmund grabbed him by the sleeve. "Listen to yourself," he said. "What would Wynn think about what you are saying right now?"

"Wynn wouldn't understand." Elric hung his head. "Back in the Otherworld, Mother kept her. I had to go with Father."

It wasn't exactly a pleasant life. Father hardly ever talked to him growing up. When he did, it was to complain about the weather, or the fact that Elric smelled like wet sheep. Mostly he just barked at Elric to do chores and accept his lot in life. He knew his father cared for him in some way, but he was only focused on their survival.

Mother, on the other hand . . . their mother was different. Elric wished sometimes that he could have stayed with his mother all the time the way Wynn did. It was no use thinking this way. Elric sighed. "Wynn had to be cared for. I was fine on my own. I didn't need that love. I could get by."

And yet, the times in his childhood when he had been the most happy were the ones when he could sneak away from his responsibilities and spend a few carefree hours with his mother and sister singing songs and playing silly games that Wynn made up using sticks and rocks.

Osmund rested his hands on his ax handle. "You don't give Wynn enough credit," he said. "Or your mother." He used the ax to push himself up an embankment. "Or the queen, for that matter. She may have been overprotective, but I never doubted that she loved me."

"She barely knows me," Elric complained. They had only been living in the Between for a few months.

"She has watched you from afar for over ten years," Osmund stated. "She gave you her silver branch and showed you the gate. Don't take those actions lightly. It means she believed in you." Osmund let out a sardonic huff. "I sure didn't."

"She showed Wynn the gate," he said. "Wynn was the one who knew where to go."

"Did she?" Osmund asked. Now that Elric thought about it, when the gate appeared, Wynn was unconscious. Osmund took a cautious step forward toward a deep ditch. Something caught his attention in the bottom of it. "Come look at this." Osmund got down on his belly and reached into the ditch with his ax. He hooked something with the curve of his blade, and lifted it up.

It was the sash from Wynn's dress. A dried brown stain marred most of the material.

Elric's hands shook as he lifted it off Osmund's blade. "She's bleeding."

"It's dried," he said. "This probably happened not long after she entered the wood."

Elric bit his lip to keep his emotions from overwhelming him. He needed a clear mind. He inhaled deeply to calm himself, but the scent of rotting meat entered his lungs. "Do you smell something?"

Osmund got to his feet and lifted his nose to the air. "Faintly, but I never had a very good sense of smell."

Now that Elric could smell it, the scent nearly

overwhelmed him. It reminded him of the animal carcass pit on the edge of the town near where Osmund
lived, but there was a fouler scent that clung to the rotting odor, something oily and acrid.

Elric followed the scent under a low-hanging branch.
He nearly got sick again, hoping against all hope that
he wouldn't see what he thought he might see when
he ducked under the branch. In his mind he pictured a
crumpled body in a ripped and dirty white dress.

When he looked up, he saw something else entirely.

The body of a pale gray reaper lay on the ground
in a pool of sticky black blood. Its tongue lolled out of
its mouth between its fangs as large dark flies buzzed
around its dead eyes.

Osmund stepped up next to Elric and caught sight
of the beast. He made to say something, but ended up
gaping at the dead creature. "I don't think Mildred did
that," he finally said.

Elric cautiously stepped forward. He poked at the
creature with the tip of his sword. "Its throat has been
ripped out. What could have done this?"

Osmund approached with cautious steps. "I don't
know. This is definitely not the handiwork of elves. They
use much cleaner and more sophisticated weapons."

He looked at the claw marks raking the reaper's side. "Whatever creature attacked him, it had to be enormous, at least as large as the reaper itself."

Elric had watched the finest warrior in the queen's guard battle this monster, and he nearly lost his life in the struggle. The only wounds he had been able to inflict had been in his animal form. "Could it have been a fairy, one who was in the form of a large animal, like a bear?"

Osmund rubbed his scruffy chin. "I'm not sure how much has changed since I left. Do fairies enter the woods now?" he asked.

"No," Elric answered. "Never. It is forbidden." For a brief moment he hoped against hope that the fairies had changed their minds and sent their fiercest warriors into the wood in search of Wynn and killed the reaper. But judging by the smell, the reaper had been dead at least a full day, and there was no possible way a fairy rescue party could have stumbled upon this place before him.

Osmund pinched his nose closed and looked around. "Let's keep searching for Wynn," he said, his voice sounding funny with his nose closed.

Elric bent and took a closer look at the creature. "This isn't the reaper I saw attack the shield. The one at the shield had black fur and a black mane. This one is gray all over."

Osmund stilled, dropping his hand. "If this isn't the same reaper you saw, there must be more than one in these woods. It will seek to do its master's bidding." Osmund gripped his ax. The fading light was masked by heavy clouds. A storm was on the horizon. "We're being hunted."

CHAPTER SEVENTEEN

Wynn

WYNN FELT HER WAY TO the corner of her prison and sat in it. Sometimes she could hear voices from the elves passing by on the other side of the wall. Sometimes she heard voices through the door. When she did, she pounded on it and told them to let her out. But they spoke in strange words and ignored her.

The light streaking in through the planks of the wall lit up little bits of dust floating in the air. They reminded her of the fairies, and she desperately missed the palace. She was sad. She needed a hug, so Wynn cried. She cried loudly. It made her face wet and nose runny. She started to hiccup between sobs, and her body felt out of her control. She didn't care if the elves could hear. Her heart felt broken.

The light from outside faded, and she was left in the complete dark. She didn't think that she'd ever been in a place so dark. When her eyes were open, it looked like they were closed. Wynn wasn't sure if she had them open or closed anymore. The noises died down. The elves went to go eat supper or sleep. She should be sleeping too. She was very tired, but she was cold, and it was hard to sleep without Mildred.

Wynn hugged her aching knees. Just then, she thought she saw something strange. She blinked, then she saw it again. It was a light, but it was underneath the floor? Wynn crawled forward, placing her hands on the planks of wood beneath her. She leaned all the way down so she could peek with her eye through the crack. Her forehead pressed against the grainy wood. She heard something. Something whirred beneath her, and softly clanked.

The light flickered. Then Wynn saw a hand reach up and cover the crack right where she was peeking. Wynn pulled her head up. Someone grumbled something in another language below her. That's when she felt something beneath her hand wiggle. One of the planks pushed up into her palm, then collapsed back down. Wynn pulled her hand up, and backed away.

Slowly the plank rose and slid to the side. She saw small hands push another plank, then a third. The hand appeared again, lifting a small lantern into the room. Wynn had to blink because the lantern light seemed very bright. Wynn had never seen anything like it. Light was trapped in a glass globe, but it didn't look like it was on fire. It wasn't a glowing magic rock, either. It was very strange. Green hands reached up, bracing on the floor. An elf in a long black robe pushed up through the hole and sat on the edge.

Wynn scurried backward like an upset garden spider until she felt her shoulders thump into the wall. What did this elf want? They weren't very nice. She didn't know if this one would be nice, either. She didn't want to be alone with one.

"Hello?" The elf lowered the dark hood, and Wynn stared at her. She was young. A child just like her. She had a bald head like the other elves, and a soft, round face with long eyelashes framing her eyes. The lighter green marks on her skin made looping patterns that reminded Wynn of flowers, and she wore a necklace with a large amber pendant. A spider was caught inside. She dragged up a sack after her. "I thought you might want this," she said in a high, sweet voice. The way she spoke was a little clearer than the man elves, like she said her words carefully.

The elf girl opened the top of the sack, and a leathery red chicken comb popped out, followed by a rumpled hen.

"Mildred!" Wynn scooped her chicken up and gave her the biggest hug. Mildred cooed at her, and rested her head on Wynn's shoulder. Wynn's body shook, overcome with her happiness.

"They caught her in the village. She couldn't jump over the wall. She led everyone on a big chase for over an hour. Father put her in a cage and told me to feed her. She looked sad to me, so I brought her to you." The girl looked down and twisted her fingers. "The elders don't understand about pets. I have a turtle. I call him Turtle. It's not a very good name."

"Thank you," Wynn said. It was hard to say the words even though she knew them so well. She had been wrong. This elf was very nice. "Thank you so much."

The girl brightened. She scooted forward on her

knees, pulling the sack into her lap. She smiled. It was a nice smile. The light caught in her eyes and they looked gold, like her amber necklace. "I brought you some food. I thought you might be hungry." The girl pulled a couple of the dark fruits out of her long robe. They were purple, and looked tasty. "Here, take them."

Wynn took one and bit into it. She enjoyed the sweet taste of the spongy fruit, and even liked the bitter taste that followed this time. She was so hungry. She ate the fruit quickly, shoving as much of it into her mouth as she could. The elf girl giggled, and covered her smile with her hand.

As Wynn swallowed the fruit, she thought hard. "You're nice," she said.

"I'm sorry." The elf girl's face fell. "I'm not supposed to be here. Please don't tell." She looked back down and tugged on the hem of her robe.

Wynn didn't say anything. She felt very confused. Finally the girl looked her in the eye. "You live with the fairies, don't you?" the girl blurted out.

Wynn nodded.

The girl stared at the torn skirt of Wynn's dress. "Are you magic? There isn't much about magic people in the Otherworld in my books." She reached into her sack and pulled out a strange object. It looked like a small box with a leather wrap around most of it.

Mildred gently scratched at Wynn's skirt with her feet, then settled down in Wynn's lap with a contented flip of one wing. Wynn stroked her as she thought about the question. "The queen said we all have magic."

"Elves don't." The girl sounded very sad. "We have nothing. We hide, we hunt, we die."

"What is that?" Wynn pointed to the thing in her hands.

The elf looked surprised. "This?" She held it up. "It's just a book. Haven't you ever seen one? I know men in the Otherworld have them. Elves shared the idea for books with men long ago. I have seen pictures."

Wynn shook her head. She had lived her whole life in the Otherworld with her mother. Her mother didn't have a thing like that in her hut. The elf opened it up, and delicate squares of leaf-like material arched in a beautiful fan. On the leaves were pretty drawings and lots of squiggled patterns that made Wynn dizzy to look at them.

"You read it. These are pictures of words. When you write words down or draw pictures, you can keep them forever and you don't have to remember them. Then when you die, those thoughts stay in the book, and you can give them to someone else. That way nothing is lost, even if you are gone." The elf girl scooted beside her and brought the book in front of Wynn. Wynn turned the pages, looking at the beautiful pictures painted with such vibrant colors. They were of fairies.

"You like fairies?" Wynn asked. She didn't think the elves liked fairies at all. The elf leader didn't like her. He was very mean.

The girl got a dreamy look in her golden eyes. "Oh yes. They are very beautiful, and magical."

"But you are very beautiful," Wynn said.

The girl raised one eyebrow. "I have green skin and no hair."

"And that is very beautiful," Wynn insisted. "Your skin looks like my garden. And it has flowers on it. That is good for hiding. What is your name?"

"In your language, my name is Lexicon," she smiled at Wynn. She had a very nice smile. "You can call me Lexi."

"I am Wynn." Wynn said each word as clearly as she could. She reached out a hand, and Lexi took it.

The pretty light flickered in the room. Mildred felt warm in her lap. Wynn was happy again. Lexi was wrong. She was magic. Wynn smiled at her.

"I need your help," her new friend said. Her eyes were very shiny, and she blinked them, then looked away.

"I can help," Wynn said. She was happy to help.

Lexi gave her a strange look. Her nose scrunched up. "You don't even know what I was going to ask."

"I don't understand," Wynn said. She hated those words. But none of this made sense to her. If Lexi needed help, she would help. Lexi was very nice.

Lexi sighed and closed her book. "How do you know if you can help me, when I haven't even told you what the problem is?"

Wynn blinked at her. "You need help."

Lexi nodded. "That's right."

"I will help." This didn't seem very difficult to Wynn.

"And you ask for nothing in return?" Lexi's forehead wrinkled.

"I will help," Wynn insisted.

It took a long time for Lexi to answer. Wynn knew how it felt to search for words, so she waited.

"My brother is dying," she said. "And it's all my fault."

CHAPTER EIGHTEEN

Elric

ELRIC THREW A STICK DOWN in frustration as he watched what little light they had slowly die. They had been searching for a new trail all day, but it was no use. Night was upon them, and he was exhausted. He could barely stand without swaying. They would have to find shelter, and quickly.

No matter how hard he had searched, he couldn't find any sign of Wynn, only the tracks of a band of wild pigs. They were strange, though. The space between the tracks seemed very regular, and the beasts had lined up in perfect rows.

Elric rubbed his neck as Osmund came closer with the stone in his branch glowing brightly. One reaper was dead, and he was glad for that. But, there was another reaper somewhere in the woods. And the fact that Wynn had met with a monster even more powerful and deadly than the reaper filled him with fear.

"Elric," Osmund called. Elric found his way back to him with his heart in his throat. He still feared the worst at every moment. Osmund looked up at the canopy, secured his ax in a strap across his back, and then tucked his glowstone torch beside it. "We have to climb up a tree and wait out the night. Otherwise anything could sneak up on us in the dark, including whatever killed that reaper."

Elric sheathed his sword and laced his fingers together to give Osmund a hand up. He boosted Osmund to the first branch and watched as the woodcutter expertly climbed to the topmost branches of the tree.

Reaching over his head to pull himself up on the first branch, Elric climbed more cautiously. He was never comfortable with being off the ground. He struggled higher and higher into the upper branches of the tree, to a place where he could peek through the highest layer of the leaves. Osmund reclined in a crook of a branch, as if he were in a hammock. "Not a bad view," he said.

Elric found a sturdy branch to lean against and glanced up at the sky. He lost his breath and nearly fell out of the tree. He had seen the night sky many times, but he had never seen anything as magical as this.

The stars opened up in a great blanket above his head. They formed thick bands of light mixed with distant stardust that looked like clouds. They painted the sky with deep blues, pinks, and purples exploding in great billowing storms of color in the deepest depths of the sky. He could see distant bodies of light, swirling like spirals or great twisting pools of light in the distance. All the while, stars streaked through the endless sky—falling notes from silent music that was no longer allowed to be heard. They reminded him of Wynn, and another magical night they had spent under a broken oak tree that looked like great hands holding the moon aloft.

He hadn't seen the stars since he had come to the Between. The shield prevented it. The light from the shield never faded, and it remained bright under the dome, even in the night. Elric had forgotten what the stars looked like, how they made him feel. As he stared out at the infinite sky, he wondered what else the fairies had sacrificed for their safety when they had closed the shield around their kingdom.

"It's beautiful, isn't it," Osmund said.

"Yes," Elric said. "It really is." He wondered if these woods were once beautiful in the time before the Grendel. As he stared up at the depths of the sky, large orbs of swirling colors rose on the horizon like great and beautiful moons. One had vast striped rings as it sailed through the endless sea of stars.

"On the night when I slipped through the shield, I did it to see the stars," Osmund said, his voice soft, and less gruff than Elric had ever heard it. "The queen named her lost daughter after the stars, and I wanted to know what was so special about them. I didn't get a chance to see them here, but when I got to the Otherworld, I finally understood. I've never seen the stars like this."

Elric nodded. It was like they were both adrift in the heavens on a dark boat of leaves. "How did the queen's daughter die?" he asked. "I thought fairies were immortal."

"In a sense, they are. Experience ages them, not time. And they never die from growing old, but they aren't born that way," Osmund said, crossing his arms and resting his head in the crook of the branches. "When fairies are born, they are very much like us. They bleed, they scar, they can be killed if their magic has not come in yet. Sadly they are very fragile. Not many survive."

Osmund gripped the branch over his shoulder and leaned back, peering up at the wonders above them. "The fairies' magic wasn't always as strong as it is now. The elves discovered a way to refine certain crystals to hone and amplify magic. They gifted a staff to the royal court. The Grendel took it for his own, and became obsessed with its power."

Osmund looked out over the woods. "He wanted to rid the woods of the monsters from the Shadowfields, but the staff made him believe that power and strength gave him the right to rule. The fairy court didn't agree, and they gave the crown to the queen."

"And he didn't take that well, did he?" Elric said. He had heard parts of this story.

"The queen wed a bold knight. He went to battle the Grendel to protect what was left of the fairy kingdom. He managed to steal the staff and give it to the queen, reducing the Grendel's terrible power. The battle raged into the Shadowfields. He drove the Grendel off, but the Summer King, the queen's one love, never returned."

"That's awful," Elric said. The queen must have been heartbroken.

"She was, but then the queen realized she was going

to have a baby. All the love she felt for the Summer King, she poured into the new child. The princess was born, and fairies and elves rejoiced. They vowed to fight the Grendel together, but the elves betrayed us."

"What happened?" Elric asked.

"The Headmind of the elves, a woman named Reason, came to the queen to give the fairies a new crystal, infinitely more powerful than the one in the staff. It had the power to unite the magic of all good fairies and channel it as one force through the heart of the queen. It seemed like the perfect weapon to use against the Grendel to defeat him once and for all. But it was all a ruse. The elves were still loyal to the fairy who had once protected them from the monsters of the Shadowfields. In the night, Lord Raven saw Headmind Reason with the baby. She carried it into the Nightfell Wood."

"Why would she do such a thing? It doesn't make any sense." Elric felt his stomach twisting.

"I don't know." Osmund shook his head. "Lord Raven believes that the elves knew the crystal had a weakness, that it was only as powerful as the strength of the queen's heart. If the queen's heart broke, so did the crystal. I don't know why the elves wanted to destroy the fairies, but by linking all of the kingdom's magic, the fairies became powerful, but fragile. For the first time, the magic of all the fairies could be used as one single force."

"But that force is dependent on the strength of the queen," Elric said.

"Exactly. The next day, the Grendel appeared in the Nightfell Wood carrying the baby's blood-soaked blanket. He thanked the elves for their loyalty and said they would be rewarded. You know the rest. The queen used the crystal to create the shield, locking the Grendel out of the kingdom and the elves with him. The queen nearly diminished as the crystal bled for decades, but then she found me and some of the crystal's power was restored, and now she has you."

Elric tried to comprehend the tragedy of the entire situation. He didn't blame the fairies for their hatred of the elves. The queen was right to shut them out from the shield. Why should she protect someone who hurt her? But one thing still confused him. "You mentioned that she had nearly diminished. What does that mean?" Elric shifted to sit more securely in the braches.

"Once a fairy has magic, they cannot die the way a mortal does. Instead of blood, they bleed light," Osmund said.

Elric remembered the silvery light spilling from Fox and Elk during the battle with the reaper.

Osmund continued. "If they lose enough of that light, their life as we know it is gone."

"I'm not sure I understand," Elric said, plucking off a leaf of the tree that was tickling his neck.

Osmund thought about the question for a moment. "Take Zephyr, for example. The first form of his magic that he was able to control is the air around him. In the future, he will master other forms of magic and add to his name. That twilight trick shows promise."

"I'm with you," Elric said, slowly peeling the fleshy parts of the leaf away from the center vein.

"If fairies lose enough of their magical light, they are reduced to becoming the form of their simplest magic," Osmund explained.

Elric thought about what he just said. Then the true horror of it finally struck him. "So if Zephyr were badly wounded, he would turn into air?"

Osmund nodded grimly. "Others become a rock, or a shadow, or mist, or a flower somewhere. They retain a consciousness, but lose control over their simplified form. There's no way for them to come back again and become what they were. Not without powerful magic, and they would be beholden to the one who brought them back."

Elric looked up at the stars, trying to imagine living for an eternity stuck in a form of a rock or a twig. It was worse than death. "The crystal is linked to the queen, so the cracks—that's her blood spilling from it, isn't it?"

Osmund closed his eyes. "Yes. If she diminishes completely, the Grendel will come to claim his staff and whatever power he can steal from the lives around him. Make no mistake. If the Grendel takes over the fairy kingdom, he will drain each and every living thing of their power and reduce them all to nothing. Only then will he have collected enough of the light magic to be able to use the portals again. He will fully come to the Otherworld, not just as a storm or a shadow. He will feed his dark magic with misery and pain. He will cause death and destruction, the likes of which I cannot imagine, to increase his power. Not a living soul will survive."

Elric looked beyond the masses of stars to the storm clouds building over the Shadowfields. They seemed so far away. The woods stretched on forever, and Wynn was lost somewhere within it. The reaper howled, a long, deep sound that seemed to carry the promise of the pain and destruction of the Grendel on the wind. "Then we must defeat him," Elric said.

They had to find Wynn before that reaper did, or it would be too late.

CHAPTER NINETEEN

Wynn

WYNN WATCHED THE ELF GIRL wipe her eyes with the hem of her robe. She hadn't talked for a while, but Wynn waited for her to speak. She was very upset. Finally she sighed and looked back up at Wynn.

"What happened?" Wynn asked. Now it felt even more important to help her friend. She knew what it was like to have a brother in trouble. It was terrible.

Lexi dried her nose with her sleeve. "The Grendel put him under a spell. Now he is very sick. Come with me. I'll show you."

Lexi picked up the lantern, but left the sack. Wynn gently lifted her sleeping hen and placed her on the bed. "Stay here, Mildred," she whispered.

The elf girl pushed aside the loose floorboards and swung her feet down into the hole in the floor. She stood up, and the floor only came to her waist, but didn't fall quickly. Instead she slowly drifted down through the floor like a feather. It was very strange.

Wynn peered through the floor. "Drop your feet down. I'll help you," Lexi said as she stood next to a strange contraption made of long boards and gears looped with ropes.

Wynn did as she was told and slid her legs down. She felt Lexi's palms on the bottoms of her bare feet and slid down farther. Lexi steadied her, and placed her feet on a narrow board. Wynn tried to balance, but she wasn't very good at balancing. The gears whirred, and the board under her feet slowly lowered, but Wynn couldn't keep her balance. She tipped backward, and landed with a soft thump on the lumpy sacks. A puff of dust came up out of them.

"I'm so sorry," Lexi whispered. "Are you hurt?"

Wynn shook her head and stood, slapping the dust off her tattered skirt.

"My invention isn't the best, but I had to put it together with whatever I could find," Lexi said as she lifted her lantern. "It's all storage down here. I had to break open the lock. Don't worry, I can fix it."

They wandered through a maze of old stone walls, tall woven baskets filled with ropes and wheels, old crates, and several more sacks. It smelled dank and musty. In the shadows, Wynn could see larger wheels and billows. Moss grew in the spaces between the stones. Lexi's lantern flickered, making the shadows dance around them.

"I'm not good at following rules," Lexi said. "I don't know why. I just get an idea in my head and I do it without thinking."

Something creaked above them, and they stopped. Lexi shielded her light with the edge of her robe. They heard a soft snore, and Lexi motioned them forward again.

"I like books. I was named for words." Lexi peered around, then carefully stepped over a fallen broomstick. "Before the Grendel destroyed the old city, we had a great library. The books are still there, all the thoughts of everyone who is gone now. I'm obsessed with those lost books.

"When there was peace with the fairies, they gave

us a great gift, a portal near that library. On the full moon, they used to come and use their magic to light the portal. We would go to the Otherworld and listen to the people there—hear their stories and write them in the books. In return we developed the stones that help amplify the fairies' magic." Lexi let out a sigh. "That didn't turn out so well. The fairies used our gift against us. Dark times came, and then the shield. The Grendel realized there was still a portal in our city. He wanted to use it to go to the Otherworld, but he can't make it work now. His magic is too dark and unfocused. He destroyed the city in his rage. Now it is all gone; we live in this patched-together town while the fairies use the crystal we gave them to protect themselves and not us."

"That is sad," Wynn said. She didn't like it when things got broken. She thought about what Lexi said, and brightened. "Mother told elf stories," Wynn said. "She said elves borrow people things. They get lost. I lost my shoes in the garden once. I didn't see elves take them." Wynn looked down at her bare feet. She had lost her shoes again. She knew the elves hadn't taken them this time, either.

"We haven't been to the Otherworld in a long time. When we do go, you can't see us. We turn invisible." Lexi giggled. "And we do like to investigate interesting things, sometimes borrowing them for a while." She held the light higher and it shone on the shimmering strands of a spiderweb. "We always give everything back, though, when we can. Not always in the same place. If we accidentally misplace something, we speak to people like you and tell you where you can find it. We also share our ideas, especially if you are dreaming. Then the people can invent things, and pass that knowledge on. That way elves create things in your world too, and our ideas grow like flowers. We don't have magic, but we had ideas once. All of that is lost now," Lexi said sadly.

A long millipede slowly snaked across the floor in front of them. Wynn liked to think of the elves as invisible friends. They must have very good ideas. She liked their inventions. Wynn carefully stepped over the crawling creature.

Lexi continued. "When I heard about the library in the old stone city, I had to find it. I had to save the books so they wouldn't be lost forever. There's a dark witch who lives in the ruins. She burns things with evil fire spells."

Wynn ducked under a spiderweb, and paused as they reached a flight of stairs. She wanted to say something but couldn't. Her thoughts were moving very fast, but wouldn't connect together.

Wynn didn't think that was right. Flame didn't seem interested in elf things. She liked to be alone, that was all. But she could start fire. Wynn started to speak as Lexi put a foot on the stair. The old wood creaked. "Be careful up the stairs," she whispered. "We're almost there."

Wynn held on to the half-rotted rail and forgot what she was going to say.

Lexi stopped on the step and Wynn almost ran into her. She spun around and closed her eyes as she balled her fists. "Three weeks ago I snuck out of the village so I could rescue the books from the burning witch." Her words came out in a rush. "It was dangerous and stupid. My brother followed me. He was trying to protect me. A reaper found us. My brother sacrificed himself so I could run." She placed her hands over her mouth and began to cry.

Wynn put her hands over her mouth too. That was terrible. That was something Elric would do. She remembered the night he had been beaten by the men who had tried to throw her in the pigpen. He saved her. He gave her a chance to run.

"I'm so sorry he's hurt," Lexi said. "Father chased down the reaper, but it was too late. We couldn't stop him, and he took my brother to the Grendel. When the Grendel was finished with him, he left my brother at the gate. He was alive, but barely. Father said it was a warning. Now everyone is afraid."

Lexi reached a door at the top of the stair and slowly opened it. She peeked through it with her lantern and motioned for Wynn to follow. They crossed a dark hall and entered another room, much like the one Wynn was supposed to be in.

"When we found Codex, he looked like this," Lexi motioned to a bed in the corner.

At first Wynn didn't see anything on the bed. The flickering light of the lamp didn't reveal anything, and the shadow of the top of the bed was perfectly flat.

Then she saw him. A young elf lay still on the bed, but Wynn could see right through him. He looked like he was made of smoke, thin and gray. Lexi put her lantern down and sat on the edge of the bed. She lifted the nearly invisible hand and held it in her own. "We know how to heal bodies. We're very good at it. His body is fine, but he is slowly disappearing. It's like his spirit is gone. This magic is beyond us. We don't know how to save him."

Wynn came forward. She could barely see the different markings on the boy's skin. His face looked much thinner than his sister's. His eyes were closed, but she could see his chest slowly rise and fall.

Lexi turned tear-filled eyes to Wynn. "I need fairy magic. I have to save him."

Wynn wrinkled her brow and thought hard. She couldn't make plants grow. But that magic wouldn't help anyway. She couldn't change into an animal. That fairy magic also wouldn't help. How could she help?

"My brother was hurt," she said, remembering how scary that night was. It was dark. Elric was dirty and bleeding. "He wouldn't wake up."

Lexi looked up at her, her golden eyes bright and filled with hope.

Wynn thought hard to remember, to pull the right thoughts forward. "I made him clean."

"Dex is already clean," Lexi interrupted.

Wynn was used to people not waiting for all of her thoughts. She ignored Lexi's interruption but she had to find the words in her mind again, and that was frustrating. "I put honey on his bleeding."

"What is honey?" Lexi asked. Her nose scrunched up. "Is it magic?"

Wynn shook her head.

Lexi huffed and looked frustrated. "That won't do any good, either. Codex isn't bleeding anywhere." She ran a hand over her smooth head. "I need something magical."

"And I sang," Wynn said, finally finishing her thought.

Lexi stared at her, her long ears twitching. "What is sang?"

Wynn wasn't sure she understood the question. "Music."

Lexi looked very confused. "I have never heard of this thing. Is it magic?"

Wynn remembered what the Fairy Queen had said in her room of secret things. She nodded. "It is magic. It helped lead me here. It opened the Silver Gate. The queen said it was strong magic."

Lexi's eyes went wide. She reached forward and gripped Wynn on her forearm. "You have to teach me. Please. I'll do whatever it takes." Something clattered in a different room. Lexi jumped to her feet. "Only not here. We have to go back. If Father catches me with you, he'll feed me to the pigs."

That would be a terrible thing for him to do. Wynn understood about angry fathers, so she jumped up and followed Lexi out of the room. She paused at the door to give one last look at Codex, then slowly shut him in the darkness. Together they crept down the stairs. "You need windows," Wynn said. She didn't like the dark.

"Windows let in stinging bugs and creatures the Grendel uses to torment us. The closed rooms keep us safe," Lexi whispered as they wove through the old crates and sacks. "In the old city we had glass windows, but we don't have the right sands to make glass here. We can't risk traveling to the crystal desert anymore. Give me your foot. I'll hold on to you as you go up, so you don't fall again."

Wynn stepped up on Lexi's machine, and felt the other girl's hands on her ankles. Before she knew it, she rose up through the hole. She flopped her upper body onto the planks, and dragged her feet up after her. The room was completely dark. It didn't feel safe. In Wynn's opinion, all of the woods needed more light.

Lexi rode up on the machine until she appeared through the hole. The light from her lantern filled the room. Mildred looked like a black ball of fluff on the corner of the bed, and the world didn't seem so scary anymore. Lexi crossed her legs under her robes and leaned forward. "So how do you make this sang?"

Wynn laughed. That didn't sound right. "You sing," she said. "Like this." She quietly began to sing the song of the Silver Gate as best she could. She didn't want Lexi to be in trouble. Lexi listened without moving. Her amber eyes glowed as she listened. Wynn finished a verse and said, "You try."

"How do you make your voice do that?" Lexi said.

"You do it," Wynn said. "You sing." She patted Lexi on the knee several times, because she was excited and couldn't help herself.

Lexi tried. She let out a rough sound, then another just like it. "That's not right," she said. "Elves can't do this. We don't have magic."

"You can do this." Wynn knew she could. She patted her friend on the knee again. "You try."

Lexi let out a sound. It was much better. It didn't sound so much like a frog. Wynn clapped. "Go up." She sang a higher note to demonstrate. Lexi followed, and Wynn clapped again. "Now go down." Again Lexi followed. It wasn't exactly right, but it was different than the first sound, and that was all that mattered. Wynn clapped harder. "You're doing it!"

Lexi stopped. "How do you know when to go up, and when to go down? What words do you sing?" she asked. "Do you have to get the spell exactly right for it to work?"

Wynn thought about it. It was a hard thing to think about. She didn't know how she knew what to do. She just sang. Lexi waited patiently for her to answer this time. "You know. You find the right things. Those are the best songs."

Wynn listened to what was in her heart and sang.

> *"Lexi is my friend.*
> *She brought me my hen.*
> *And she has a light*
> *When it is the night."*

Lexi clapped her hands over her mouth and giggled. She tapped Wynn on the knee this time. "Let me try."

> *"I like my friend Wynn.*
> *She has a pretty grin.*
> *And a shiny dress*
> *That is such a mess."*

Lexi smiled the biggest, most beautiful smile. The light in the lantern glowed brighter. "How was that?"

"That was amazing." Wynn threw her body forward and hugged her new friend. "I knew you could do it."

The two girls sang into the deep of night. Wynn taught her all the songs she knew and together they made up more of their own. Finally Lexi had to leave. She picked up Mildred to take her back to her cage, promising Wynn she would take very good care of her. Wynn hugged the elf, and waved good-bye before helping Lexi place the planks back down in the floor.

Wynn cuddled by herself on the bed. This time she wasn't frightened. She sang the tune she had made with Lexi under her breath, and the room didn't seem so dark anymore.

CHAPTER TWENTY

Elric

ELRIC HAD A HARD TIME falling asleep in spite of his exhaustion, then woke early when a gust of wind shook the branch beneath him. He watched the clouds on the horizon as they billowed upward into enormous thunderheads that flashed lightning from peak to peak. The reaper in the forest had stopped howling, but that only made Elric more wary. Even though the howl seemed to fill the woods, it had given Elric a sense of where the reaper was. Now that the monster was silent, he felt like he was being stalked.

Eventually the sun rose, lighting the tops of the trees. From high in the canopy, the light spilling over the forest gave him hope. Not far off he could see old stone towers crumbling into ruin as thick vines and trees grew over and around them.

Osmund let out a sudden loud snore, and Elric almost fell off his branch. It took a full minute for his heart to stop racing. Using his foot, he nudged Osmund awake.

He snorted, and blinked open his eyes. "Wait, what?" he grumbled. "Stubborn goat."

"Osmund, wake up!" Elric gave him a second gentle kick. "It's morning."

Osmund sat up and let go of the tree to rub his eyes. The sight made Elric's stomach do a little flip as he clung to the branches tighter. Osmund stretched and looked around.

"Any sign of the reaper we heard last night?" Osmund asked.

"Nothing." Elric peered down into the tree, but the ground below them still looked dark and forbidding. "But I doubt he has moved on. We have to be careful. Do you know what those ruins are?" he asked.

"Those are the remains of the great elf city, Merit. After the Grendel destroyed it, the remaining elves ran

off into the woods. I don't know where they are now."
Osmund started climbing down the tree. "And trust me,
we don't want to find out."

"But those ruins could be a good place to hide. There
has to be shelter there," Elric said. "Do you think Wynn
might have found them the way you did?"

Osmund held up one finger, and crinkled his brow
in a serious manner. "First rule of the forest: If there is
a hole, something will fill it. Those ruins are probably
crawling with dangerous darkling creatures and elves
who are thinking exactly the same thing." Osmund
swung onto a lower branch, and Elric inched down
after him. "When Wynn was lost in the woods near my
house, she insisted on staying in one spot. She said her
mother told her to do it. I had a hard time convincing her
to come with me back to my hut. If Wynn escaped the
reaper, she's likely hiding in place behind a tree nearby,
the way she did before."

Elric nodded. "That makes sense, and if it's true, that
means she is close." They hadn't wandered far from the
dead reaper before they lost their light and had to climb
the tree.

"Don't worry," Osmund said. "We'll find her."

"She's been in these woods for two full nights." Elric

carefully lowered himself to the lowest branch, then swung down to the ground. "How could she possibly survive out here that long?"

Osmund placed his hand on Elric's forearm and gave it a squeeze. "Don't give up. The darkness of these woods can steal your hope. But hope is the best weapon we have here. You don't really believe she is gone, do you?"

Elric closed his eyes and just let himself feel. Beneath the fear, and the twisting worry that stole his will to eat, there was still light and life in his heart. "She has to be alive," he said. "I believe it."

A warm feeling swelled in his heart. He had to find her. He opened his eyes. "This way."

For hours, they cut through the brush searching for any clue that Wynn, or any other living thing was nearby. The palms of Elric's hands burned with ripped-open blisters from pulling on vines and dead branches. His neck and shoulders ached so badly he hunched his back as he walked.

Elric wiped a hand over his exhausted eyes, and did his best to maintain his spirits, but it was difficult. It was as if the air of the wood itself had the ability to press all the good feelings from his heart, and steal them from his mind. He became cold inside, and focused on his task, which was useful in the moment. He could feel the storm in the air. The dry crackle of electricity had the hairs on the back of his hands standing up, as unpredictable gusts of wind made the forest sound alive.

"Elric," Osmund shouted from a thicket nearby. "Over here." By the tone of his voice, Elric knew he didn't want to see whatever Osmund had to show him. Still he hurried to his side. Osmund pointed down at a soft patch of dirt with the head of his ax.

It was only a partial print, but it was enough. There was no mistaking the enormous claw marks. It was the reaper, and the print was fresh. It broke a thin layer of dry mud into flakes around the edges of the imprint, unlike the tracks they had found from the slain beast. They had been made in wetter clay and the impressions in the mud looked smooth. The reaper that made this track had to be the one they had heard during the night, and it was very close.

Elric swallowed a lump of fear as it formed in his throat. He looked ahead and found another partial print, and another. They pattern was loose and erratic. "This one is searching," he reasoned. He could picture it with its long snout to the ground, wandering back and forth across the narrow trail looking for a scent.

Osmund nodded. "For Wynn." He gripped the handle of his ax. "Or us."

Elric looked at the direction the prints were pointing. "I think we should follow it."

"Have you lost your mind?" Osmund said with a dumbstruck look on his face.

"What if it's getting closer to Wynn?" Elric crept down the path.

Osmund caught the hem of his tunic and pulled him back. "What if it's getting closer to us?"

"Then I would rather have it in front of us, than behind," Elric said. "Come on. We'll be cautious. Keep your ax ready." Elric drew his sword.

There was a stillness in the air. The woods had been humming softly with the sound of insects, but now it was unnaturally silent. It was as if the woods held its breath.

They found a path, wide and unusually straight, but it only seemed to be used by wild pigs. Their tracks were everywhere, following in lines. There must be a lot of boars roaming in bands in the woods. Elric wished he were a better hunter. He was beginning to get hungry. But by the size of the tracks, the beasts were larger than the ones in the Otherworld. And a wild boar could be more dangerous than a wolf when confronted. It was probably best to avoid them, as well. The pig tracks diverted onto a branching path that swung around a large boulder.

Elric pressed on through a patch of thick fallen leaves. The ground felt strangely springy under his feet.

"Elric!" Osmund's sharp call sounded like the crack of a whip. "Don't move."

He froze, his sword at the ready. "What is it?" Elric's heart picked up, and he did his best to breathe like Master Elk had taught him and steady his hands. He had a sinking feeling, and thought he heard the brittle sound of a twig breaking. That was odd.

"Turn around. Place your feet very lightly," Osmund said in a calm voice, his hands outstretched as if he were balancing on something treacherous. "Don't make any sudden moves."

Elric placed his foot, and this time he definitely felt the ground sway underneath him. To his right, he noticed a peculiar twisted vine pulled taut between the ground and the thick branch of a tree above them. That twist didn't happen naturally; it was a rope. He traced the rope up over the branch to a cluster of leaves above him hiding a large bell.

A trap. And he was standing on it.

With a racing heart, Elric sheathed his sword and held his hands out wide for balance. He dug his feet under the leaves and felt a woven lattice of branches tied together with lumpy knots. The entire thing felt as if it would break at any moment. He stepped on the knots, hoping that they reinforced the strength of the branches at the joints. Every time he shifted his weight, the entire contraption shook under his feet, and the bell above him swayed even though it didn't ring just yet.

"Grab my hands!" Osmund said as he leaned forward as far as he could. Elric couldn't do it. If the trap did give way, he didn't want to pull Osmund in with him. He needed another plan. Stepping carefully to the edge of the scattered leaves, he used all his strength to leap as far as he could, landing with a thud on the path beside Osmund. His heart was still pounding, but he took a deep breath to calm his nerves.

"That was close," Osmund said as he helped Elric up. "This is elf handiwork. I have no doubt."

"From now on," Elric said, "we follow the pig tracks. They seem to recognize these things, and we'll avoid large patches of leaves."

"Good plan," Osmund agreed. "You're lucky you're still a boy. If you were any heavier, that trap would have collapsed."

They skirted around the edge of the leaves, testing the give of the ground to make sure they actually had dirt beneath their feet. They walked ahead a little ways before they saw a huge open pit farther up the path. Elric hurried forward, fighting the urge to call out Wynn's name, but he couldn't without the stalking reaper hearing him. What if she had wandered onto one of these terrible traps?

Elric reached the edge of the pit, out of breath. The pieces of the lattice that had covered the top of the pit hung down into it like broken sections of a rotting roof. Elric bent his knees and leaned his weight back before looking into the pit.

He let out the breath he was holding when he saw that the pit was empty. Well, it was not exactly empty. The pit was deep, at least twenty feet, and at the bottom, large sharpened pikes had been sunk into the ground so they would hold fast when some unfortunate creature fell into them. Now that he saw what was at the bottom of the trap, he felt a little sick. He was glad he didn't know what waited below him earlier.

Osmund came up beside him and let out a low whistle. "Whatever fell in here, it looks like it climbed out." He pointed to claw marks fiercely raking one side of the pit by a dangling portion of the lattice.

"Lucky for it." Elric backed away. He didn't want to remain near these traps any longer than necessary. They didn't know what other surprises the inventive elves laid in this area.

He heard a leaf crunch behind him. The hair stood up on the back of his neck and his ears tingled.

"Osmund?" A creeping sensation followed a chill running up and down his arms. "We should get out of here. Now."

A low rumble of thunder sounded somewhere on the horizon, but the sound didn't fade. Instead it melded into the distinct growl of the reaper.

"Where is it coming from?" Osmund said as he turned his back to Elric's. They readied their weapons and protected their backs, just as Master Elk had taught. Only then did Elric realize Osmund likely had the same lessons when he lived in the Between.

The reaper howled, and the sound seemed to come from everywhere at once. Elric gripped the hilt of his sword and focused on his breathing. Elk had faced this creature and nearly died. Elric wasn't a soldier. He was only a shepherd.

As the storm continued to rumble in the distance, only his darkest and most defeating thoughts surfaced in his mind. There was no way Wynn could be alive. He had failed to protect her. He had failed as her brother. He was entirely alone in the world now, and there was no one left who loved him.

This was a trick. As sure as fairy magic, this had to be a trick.

"Whatever you're thinking," Osmund said, "I know you will protect my back. I'll do the same for you."

Keeping his thoughts centered on Osmund helped. It gave him a clear goal and a focus.

"Right," Elric responded. The uneasy feeling was bearable enough to push aside as he braced for battle. "We fight for Wynn."

"For Wynn," Osmund echoed.

The reaper charged through the brush like a bull ox. Its fiery eye blazed in the dim light as glistening saliva dripped from its yellow fangs. The red eye that Elk had injured in the earlier battle was now swollen shut and crusted over. Its shaggy black hair clumped together with dried blood from the wound at its side. Yet, even wounded and half blind, the reaper moved with power. It didn't care if it suffered or not. It had one goal: to bring its prey to its master. The reaper opened its wide jaws and snarled at them.

It leaped at them. It was too big for them to stand and fight it.

"Jump!" Elric shouted, and he threw himself forward. Osmund ran in the opposite direction. The reaper charged between them, then spun around and stalked toward Elric.

The monster kept its head low as it paced forward, its constant growl rumbling in its long throat. Elric took a step back as the beast pressed closer. And another.

"Elric, the pit!" Osmund called.

Elric took one more step back, and his heel momentarily slipped on the loose dirt at the edge of the open trap. Heart racing, he steadied himself and charged forward with a feral yell. The shout strengthened his courage. Elric swung the sword down across the reaper's shoulder as hard as he could. Black blood poured out of the fresh wound and soaked the crusted-over gash that Elk had given the beast.

The reaper swung its arm out and knocked Elric into the brush. It hit the ground hard as the creature shook like a wet dog, its foul blood spraying into the air. Osmund powerfully swung his ax, and buried the weapon into the hip of the beast.

It let out a scream that felt like knives piercing through Elric's ears. His heart went cold and he let out a cry of pain as he tried to cover his head to protect against the noise. Osmund tried to pull out his ax, but it was stuck. The reaper grabbed the smaller man, sinking its claws into him. Osmund shouted in pain.

The monster bit down on Osmund's shoulder. Osmund cried out in agony. The reaper held him in his jaws and shook him, then flung Osmund toward the pit. He disappeared over the side.

"No!" Elric screamed. He scrambled toward the pit but the reaper grabbed his leg. He felt the claws sinking into his flesh like white-hot knives pulled from a forge. With all his strength, he shoved his sword up, and pierced the beast's chest. He felt his blade hit bone, and the beast screamed again. It pulled away from him, cradling its new wound.

"You will not find her, and you won't take me," Elric said as he fought his shaking knees to stand. He held his sword loose at his side.

"But I did find her. My master has her now. And soon he will have you."

The words sounded within his own mind as the

creature gave him the same snarled grin as when they had faced each other through the shield.

"The plan has worked perfectly."

"You lie." Elric shook his head, as if he could shake the beast's terrible voice from his consciousness. "Your reaper friend is dead, and soon you will be too."

And with those words he dropped his sword.

With his heart in his throat, he ran. He only had one shot at this. He'd outsmarted the beast once. He had to do it again. Elric gritted his teeth and ran faster even though his leg was on fire. He could hear the snorting breaths of the beast as it howled and limped behind him. He could smell the foul breath of the beast rolling over him, but it did not catch him.

Only a little bit farther. He prayed the ropes would hold.

Turning the slight bend in the path, he saw the patch of leaves ahead of him. Elric ran as fast as he could toward them. His foot met the lattice of branches hidden by the leaves. He coiled his body as he felt the branches sag under his weight, and when they sprang back he launched himself toward the braided rope.

He felt the reaper's claws rake his hip as he stretched forward to grasp the rope. His fingers wrapped around

it, and he clung on with all his might. He swung forward over the elf trap.

There was a shattering crash, and the reaper
screamed in fury.

Elric clung to the rope, swinging on the vine as he
watched the reaper fall into the pit below and land on
the pikes.

The terrifying scream fell silent for good.

CHAPTER TWENTY-ONE

Elric

THE BELL TOLLED, A LOW and mournful sound that resonated through the woods as Elric swung on the rope above the pit. Carefully he climbed down, using his momentum to reach the edge. He caught a branch of a nearby tree to steady himself as he landed, but almost fell backward as the pain in his wounded leg shot through him. With his stomach fluttering somewhere up near his throat, he pulled himself clear of the pit. He resisted the urge to look back over his shoulder at the grisly scene below. He wanted reassurance that the monster was really dead.

But there was no time for that. He had to get to Osmund.

Deep in his heart, he prayed Osmund hadn't met the same fate as the reaper. As he ran along the path, he picked up his sword and scrambled forward, toward the second pit where Osmund had fallen. "Osmund!" he called. He felt his whole body alive with terror as he neared the pit. "Please be alive," he whispered.

"Help me!" Osmund shouted, his voice breaking. Elric felt as if a fire had been lit directly beneath his feet.

He reached the pit, and his knees collapsed from under him. Gathering himself, he looked over the edge. Osmund hung by one hand from a piece of broken lattice over the deadly pikes.

"Hurry!" he shouted. "I can't hold on much longer!"

"I'll get you out." Elric grabbed the edge of the lattice and pulled. His arms felt weak. His whole body was shaking, but his efforts paid off as he dragged Osmund out of the trap. The edge of the lattice came out of the trap and Elric laid it down, then ran to Osmund. He grabbed Osmund's hand and hoisted him up out of the pit.

Osmund let out a pained cry. He grimaced as dark red stains soaked into his shirt from where the reaper bit him. "The reaper, what happened?" he asked, his forehead wrinkling in pain.

"Dead." Elric took off his own tunic and cut it into strips on the sharp edge of his blade. "I lured it into the other trap."

Osmund smiled, then winced. "Clever."

Elric used one of the strips of his tunic to tie off a wound at Osmund's shoulder and one to bandage his own wounded thigh. While his wounds seemed superficial, he couldn't say the same for Osmund's shoulder. The puncture wounds from the beast's long teeth seeped through his bandage. "Don't worry. We'll be fine now."

Osmund shook his head. "The reaper's fangs are poisonous. I can feel it like fire in my veins."

"What?" Elric felt the world spinning. No. This couldn't be. He couldn't lose Osmund. "No, you'll be fine. I'll get you back to the fairies. They can heal you."

Osmund placed his hand over Elric's. "Find your sister. Return to the queen. Keep the shield strong. It is the only hope."

"You can't die!" Elric shouted. Osmund was valiant and generous. He had saved both Wynn's and Elric's lives.

"I'm mortal," he said. "I assure you, I can die. The fairies aren't good at healing mortal wounds. They never have been. That's why they protect us so fiercely. It's why they would never risk us." He laughed, then coughed, and held his chest tighter. "Too bad I was never very good at living in a cage."

"You will not die," Elric swore. He'd find a way to get Osmund to safety. The queen would be able to do something.

"Don't make a promise that could crush you when you can't keep it." Osmund let his head fall back and closed his eyes. "Find your sister. She's a sweet girl. I like her, and I hardly like anyone. She needs you now."

Elric held Osmund, unsure of what to do. Wynn needed him. So did Zephyr, Elk, and all the others who were in danger should he fail. The queen needed him. Most of all, Osmund needed him now. The queen needed Osmund. Who knew how long the shield could stay standing? The queen was weakening every moment the crystal bled. It was only a matter of time before the Grendel took advantage of her state and the shield failed.

Elric didn't believe what the reaper had said. Wynn was still alive. She had to be. He wanted to save her, but he had to trust in her to save herself now. If she were here, she'd tell him to save Osmund.

The weight of his decision felt like a boulder on his

chest. Everything within him told him to find and protect his little sister. But Osmund was right here, and he deserved a chance. He had to get Osmund to help and safety.

If he were still a shepherd looking after his flock, and he came across a wounded lamb in his quest to find a lost one, he would tend to the wounded one first. Then again, Wynn was not a lost lamb. She was his only family.

He looked at Osmund. The other prince's normally dark bronzed skin paled before his eyes. He had to deal with the problem at hand. Even if it broke his heart to abandon his sister to the woods.

"Don't worry. Everything is going to be fine," Elric whispered. He went back to the pit and pulled over the piece of the lattice that he had hauled up onto the edge. With his sword, he hacked away the knots until he created a section that was just big enough for him to pull Osmund on a sort of sled. He tucked Osmund onto the sled, and secured him with the strips of his tunic, before lifting the sled and pulling it down the path. He turned them toward the great shield. His only hope was to get Osmund back to Zephyr, and quickly.

He prayed his navigational instincts didn't fail him as he set off through the dark woods.

Elric pulled the sled, but the going was slow with his

injured leg. The paths were steep and rocky. His whole body hurt from the battle with the reaper. Twice he had to stop and climb a tree just to make sure he was going in the right direction. The stormy shield seemed so far away, and he wasn't sure how far they had wandered from the point where he should meet Zephyr. No matter how difficult things got, he couldn't give up.

Osmund's life hung in the balance.

"Don't worry, we're almost there," Elric said, hoping it was true. He could see the shield through the canopy of leaves above him. He just needed to figure out which way to go to find Zephyr. Left or right? Never had a such a simple decision been life or death.

He dragged Osmund forward.

"Elric," he said, his voice sounding weak. "You shouldn't."

"Be quiet." Elric pulled him up the path. "This isn't up to you. I'm going to get you help. I won't let you die." He had to say something to keep Osmund with him. "If you think I'm going to explain all this to the queen without you taking the blame for this little adventure, you're sadly mistaken."

Osmund chuckled, then groaned with a fresh wave of pain. "But Wynn," he said.

"I have faith in her." And he did. If she had survived

this long, she could make it a little longer. "You taught me to."

"So now you listen," he grumbled.

Elric tried to peer through the thick brush get his bearings and figure out which direction to turn. But there was a rustling in the bushes.

He heard the snort of a hog. Slowly he lowered Osmund's sled to the ground and drew his sword. He'd finally caught up with the troop of wild pigs. After the reaper, they didn't seem nearly as scary.

A boar trotted out from around the thick trunk of a tree. He pulled a cart with strange wheels driven by a man with a dark green face. The elves had found them.

Elric braced himself as the elf pointed a fearsome contraption at him, loaded with the sharp point of an arrow. His eyes were orange and bright, a contrast to his skin, which was a deep green hue with lighter green patterns over his face and arms. He wore a cloak and hood adorned with bits of brush and bramble that camouflaged into the backdrop of the woods.

"Quid agis?" he shouted at Elric.

Shaking his head, Elric held still as more pig-carts slowly emerged from the woods. They were surrounded.

"I don't know what you want," Elric shouted at them.

"I can't understand you. I mean you no harm. I need to find help for my friend."

The leader snapped his reins and his boar moved forward. The creature squealed as the driver pulled on a chain attached to a loop in the beast's nose.

"You are not fairy, and not elf," the man said in Elric's own language. "You speak the old language of the North. What are you?" he asked.

"I'm in a hurry," he said, grateful to hear words he could understand. "My friend is badly wounded. He's been bitten by a reaper."

The elf man considered him. "He needs medicine, and quickly. Place him in the back of my cart. My people will help him."

"We need to get back to the fairies," Elric said, pointing in the direction of the shield.

"Do you want your friend to live?" the leader asked. Elric fell silent. "Then follow my instructions."

Elric turned back toward Osmund. *Don't trust them*, Osmund mouthed at him, though he didn't open his eyes. Elric tried to lag, to turn back onto the path toward the shield.

But when he did, he found five different weapons pointed at his neck.

"I don't have a choice, do I?" Elric asked.

The elf shook his head.

Elric was outnumbered. He didn't know enough about the elves to be able to tell if he was getting into deeper trouble or not. He had a bad feeling about this, but at the same time, they had promised him they would help. He intended to hold them at their word. He didn't know what he would do if they didn't. He'd just have to be clever, and careful.

"Don't worry," he said to Osmund, or maybe he said it to himself as he placed his friend in the cart and climbed in beside him. "We're going to get help."

"Not from elves," Osmund whispered, then coughed.

Elric kept a hand on Osmund's bleeding shoulder and prayed that Osmund was wrong as the cart rumbled through the woods. In the deep part of the forest where the shadows stretched so far that they all blended together into a murky twilight, they came to a stop in a small clearing. A mass of vines created a dark green wall in the heart of the woods. An enormous door opened in the solid vines, driven by large wooden gears and thick ropes. The guards let the party pass. Elric glanced down at Osmund beside him. He looked pale and sweaty.

As the cart passed through the gate, he realized

the wall of vines were growing over a thick wooden wall made of pikes formed from the trunks of young trees. Inside the wall was a village with wood and brick houses. All of the elves here had green skin with distinctive pale patterns. They wore long robes and woven belts that reminded him of the clothing from home.

The elves took Elric to a large building at the center of the town. More of the elves came out of the buildings to watch them.

A grand elf with a metal crown and long flowing robes stepped forward. His eyes contained the wisdom of the deepest part of night, glowing like the orange eyes of an owl. And yet, this elf gave him a look of controlled interest. He had to be the leader.

He addressed the crowd without really looking at Elric. "What is this?" the chief of the elves asked, his words clear and in Elric's language.

"Headmind Axis, we found a dead reaper in one of our traps. We followed some strange tracks, and found these two wandering in the woods, heading toward the fairy realm."

"You said you were bringing us to help!" Elric shouted at him. "My friend is desperately ill. He was attacked by the reaper." Elric raised his voice enough that it rang out over the crowd. "Please. He's dying."

The Headmind came closer and glanced at Osmund's wounds. "Aren't we all?"

"Can you help him?" Elric asked. "Or was that a lie?"

"We can. It is in our nature to help the injured, and we also keep our promises, despite what the fairies think. You, however, are not injured. Not seriously, anyway. Whatever will we do with you?" he said, fixing Elric with a steady gaze.

"Just help him. I am nothing to anyone," Elric said to the elf.

"Oh, I think you are," he said, "my prince."

CHAPTER TWENTY-TWO

Elric

ELRIC'S MIND RACED. LORD RAVEN'S plan had worked; the elves knew who he was. This was bad.

Axis's face was expressionless, and his orange eyes now seemed calculating. "Lock them in the infirmary," he said.

A guard scooped up Osmund's now-limp body and carried him toward a nearby building, but Elric fought.

"What do you want from me?" Elric shouted. He tried to make himself bigger, but he was still only a boy, and these were grown men. It was no use, they had him overpowered and surrounded. He stopped struggling and stood up straight.

Axis glanced down at the ground, then folded his hands behind his back, creasing the elaborately embroidered edges of his heavy robes. He paced away from Elric. "I want to right a terrible wrong," he said. "And fortune has smiled upon us. I have you now. The queen's power will weaken, and without you there, her precious shield will lose its strength. That is when we can finally mount our attack."

"Why would you do such a thing? The queen is only trying to defend her people," Elric said through gritted teeth. He felt a tightness in his chest, and he fought the stinging in his eyes.

Axis turned to him and stared him down. "So am I," he said.

"No," Elric said. "You're a selfish betrayer."

The Headmind's eyes widened as he stormed forward and grabbed Elric by the throat. Elric grasped his forearm and tried to pull away from him, but it was no use. "We betrayed no one!" he shouted.

He let go of Elric and turned away as Elric fought to find his feet.

"That shield is powered through the crystal that we

gave the queen in friendship," Axis said with a growl in his voice. "It has the power to defeat the Grendel, but instead of using it to rid the world of darkness, she has used it to keep her people safe while we suffer in this wood alone. The Grendel destroyed our great city, decimated our people, and does the queen care? No. When my mother, Headmind Reason, was murdered in our woods, did the fairies come to our aid? No."

The elf's gaze turned piercing. "The queen put up her precious shield using the power of our crystal, and left us to suffer and die alone in these woods. She has never cared about us. That changes today. We will break the shield and take our crystal back."

"Reason stole the queen's child and gave her to the enemy. The fairies saw what happened!" Elric argued.

"What?" Axis shouted. "Why would we do such a thing? We were friends to the fairies. Besides, we found my mother dead in the woods the night before the shield appeared."

Elric looked at him dumbfounded. He didn't know what to say. "How is that possible?" If what the elf said was true, the elves had nothing to do with the death of the fairy princess. And if they were innocent? But this could all be a trick. It was easy to lie. However, it wasn't easy to fake the shock and confusion he saw on the elf leader's face. Axis looked to Elric like an old king who was tired of war, but unable to escape a siege. And when he first met the elf, he struck Elric as the sort that never gave any hint of emotion away freely.

"Father!" A young elf in dark robes with a necklace made of amber skittered into the room. She carried a fat black hen under her arm. "Father! You have to come and see!"

"Not now, Lexicon," Axis growled.

"Mildred!" Elric shouted. She was alive! Elric pulled against the elf holding him.

Mildred let out a mighty squawk. She looked over toward him, then immediately struggled to free herself from the elf girl's grip. She flapped and twisted, leaving the elf girl awkwardly holding on to her legs as Mildred fought to go to him. Mildred fell forward, landing on her chest on the hard ground. The elf girl let go, then blinked up at him with big orange-yellow eyes so like the color of her necklace.

"You're Elric," she said with wonder in her high-pitched voice. Then she clapped her hands over her mouth. Elric didn't think it was possible, but her huge eyes widened even more.

Elric's heart jumped. Mildred was here. This girl knew his name. That could mean only one thing.

"Wynn is here!" he shouted. "You have my sister!"

Mildred ran to him. He pulled free of the guard's hold and scooped up the hen. She chattered and clucked, as if she were recounting her entire journey through the woods to him. "Where is Wynn?" Elric demanded of the Headmind.

"Lock him in the infirmary with the other one. Allow no one to speak with him," Axis insisted.

The elf girl took her father by the hand and pulled him forward. "Father, now is not the time. You have to come, quickly. You have to see."

"Lexicon, I will deal with you later," he said. "I have urgent business to attend to."

"Dex is awake!" She balled her fists, and the thick sleeves of her robe fell over them. "I went to Wynn in the night and asked her to use fairy magic on him, but she said she didn't know fairy magic, but she knew a different kind of magic and she taught it to me. She taught me to sing, so I did."

"Music is forbidden!" the Headmind shouted. "It gives the fairies power!"

The elf girl balled her fists. "Well, I sat up and sang

all night at Codex's bedside, and now he is opening his eyes."

The girl's words tumbled out in such a rush that Elric wasn't entirely sure he understood. He only really caught the bit about singing. That certainly sounded like Wynn's doing.

The Headmind's skin paled to a sickly green, and Elric watched as his face lit with a sudden fire. "My son? He's awake?"

Axis strode toward the building where they had taken Osmund. The elf girl gave Elric a look, then reached out and took his hand before pulling him forward. He dropped Mildred to the ground and the hen followed at his heels, clucking merrily.

They entered a dim building lit by the small fires of several strange lamps. There were no windows, only a long hall filled with doors. The elf girl pulled him forward to one of the last ones. Elric turned into the doorway and the elf girl stayed close by his side. Guards followed right behind them. She scooped up Mildred.

Elric watched as the terrifying elf leader who had given him so much grief knelt at the side of a simple bed and took up the hand of a young elf lying on it. The boy appeared to be sleeping.

"Codex?" Axis smoothed his hand over the boy's brow and bald head.

The boy blinked open his eyes, bright yellow eyes that glowed in the dim light. "Father?"

The Headmind pulled the boy into his arms and held him in a desperate embrace. The elf girl squeezed Elric's hand as she wiped her sleeve under her nose.

"He's saved. You saved him." Axis looked back at the girl.

She shook her head. "Wynn taught me how."

"She comes from the fairy realm. Fairies do not change. What great gift did she demand for this magic?" the Headmind asked. "Her freedom?"

"She asked for nothing," the girl said. "She said it was the right thing to do for a friend. She is still locked in her room."

He stood, though his fingertips remained on his son's shoulder. "Bring the girl to me."

CHAPTER TWENTY-THREE

Wynn

WYNN SAT ON THE BED in the corner and waited for it to be night again. Her back hurt from sitting in the corner all day, but she knew night would come soon, and then she could see her friend. She wanted to talk to Lexi. She also wanted to see Mildred again, but she knew Lexi was taking good care of her. Lexi was very nice. The rest of the elves ignored her. She was used to the fairies being busy and leaving her alone. But this was different. At least the fairies would wave or say hello. When the elves came into her room to give her some stale nuts to eat, they spoke in their language so Wynn couldn't understand, but she knew they were talking about her.

Wynn scratched at her bandages and wished she could take them off, but the elf who came in at dawn to treat her wounds told her not to pull on them. Headmind Axis wanted to make sure she was healthy.

The door opened with a creak. Wynn looked up. Maybe someone was bringing her lunch. She was hungry. A grumpy-looking elf with deep wrinkles in his forehead stepped inside.

"You are to come with me," he said in a gruff voice.

Wynn hugged her knees and shook her head. She didn't want to go anywhere. She liked this room. Lexi could pop up through the floor. She didn't want to go to a different one.

"The Headmind has need of you." The guard came forward and loomed over her. She looked at his thick leather shoes, then back up at the grumpy elf. The elves liked to threaten a lot. She crossed her arms and stared at him.

"I could drag you out of this room," he said, but he didn't actually do it. Maybe he didn't want to do it. Wynn just blinked at him.

"What do I have to do—"

"Smile?" she said. He was very grumpy. She didn't like that he looked so scary.

He looked at her, confused, and his brow got even more wrinkly. "What?"

Wynn smiled at him, showing off her teeth. She wasn't sure if he knew how to smile.

"That's all you want?" He looked even more confused.

She nodded. That would make things a little better.

He did his best to pull his lips back into a smile, but it made his eyes squinty, and his forehead more wrinkly. His nose crinkled up too. He looked funny, and it made Wynn want to laugh. That made her feel better. It would do, for a smile.

"I like your smile," she said, and took the elf's hand. He closed his hand gently around hers. Wynn decided he was very grumpy, but grumpy didn't always make someone mean. Osmund was grumpy, but Osmund was never mean.

The elf led her out the door and down the long hall to another room. She recognized it immediately. It was the room Lexi's brother was in. It was more crowded now.

Axis knelt by the bed. Wynn worried that Lexi's brother had died, but when she stepped forward, she saw that Lexi's brother wasn't turning invisible anymore.

He looked real again, or at least she couldn't see through him to the other side. That was wonderful. Maybe now he would get better.

"Wynn!"

She knew that voice. Everything in her body happened at the same time. Her heartbeat stopped and started, and she couldn't pull a new breath in. Her mind rushed with a hundred thoughts all at once. She couldn't control her hands. Her body shook, and she flapped her arms as she tried to say something. "El . . . Elric . . . you're here!"

Elric pushed forward, but a guard held him back from her. The guard who had smiled for her gripped her arm as she tried to pull it away from him.

Elric was here. She needed to give him a hug. She slapped the guard's hand, then twisted her arm the way that always made Elric release her when he was holding too hard. The guard let go with a surprised shout. Wynn ran forward. She didn't care if guards were holding him. She threw her arms around Elric's neck and held on to him as tightly as she could. She didn't want to let go of him ever again.

"Wynn, I can't breathe," he gasped. She stopped hugging him, but didn't fully let go.

"I . . . I don't believe it," she said. "You found me."

He had dark circles under his eyes, like he hadn't been sleeping in a long time, but he smiled at her like she was the best thing he had ever seen. Even better than a pot of honey. "I thought I had lost you forever. Are you hurt? How long have you been a prisoner?" he asked.

Wynn shrugged. "I'm . . . I'm well. I had a hurt, but they are fixed now. Want to go home?" She was ready to go back to the fairies.

Axis looked at her even as she took her brother's hand and squeezed it. Lexi put Mildred down on the floor and the hen ran to her. Wynn picked her up and hugged her. Her feathers tickled Wynn's nose. The Headmind came forward while scratching the back of his head. "Is it true you taught this singing magic to Lexi?"

Wynn nodded happily. Lexi was very good at singing.

"Why?" he asked.

She didn't think that was a very good question. "Lexi needed help. She is my friend. Singing can help."

"And you wanted nothing for yourself?" he asked.

"I already know how to sing," she said. "I am a very good singer."

Elric snorted beside her and squeezed her hand. "Yes, you are, and you are very kind."

Elric stared up at the Headmind. Her brother looked angry. Wynn could tell. It was Elric's quiet sort of angry, though. That was the most dangerous kind. "Kindness doesn't seem to matter much here. After all, these are people who would keep a child from her heartbroken mother in the name of revenge."

Everyone in the room went very still. Even Mildred stopped clucking. Wynn stroked her and pressed closer to Elric's side. Now that she had her brother, she didn't want to be away from him one inch.

The elf boy on the bed pushed himself up. Everyone in the room turned away from Elric and looked at the boy. They still didn't seem to breathe.

"Father?" he said in a weak voice that sounded very scratchy. "Where is Lexi? Did the reaper capture her?"

Lexi rushed to her brother's side. "No. I'm here," she said. "I'm here and I'm well." She sat on the edge of the bed, and her brother wrapped her in a tight hug. "And I saved you, with some help." Both of them looked up at their father.

Axis let out a heavy breath, shook his head, then turned to Elric. "You are brave, if foolish, to challenge me."

The Headmind looked at Wynn with his owl-like eyes. "But it seems I owe a debt, and therefore must forgive you. Thank you," he said. "For the life of my son. You, and those who matter to you, will always have the protection of the elves, even in the dark days to come. Now it is time to let the healers do their work. Guards, lock them back in the room."

Lexi jumped off the bed and grabbed her father's arm. "Father, no."

"I will not risk their escape. They are the most valuable thing in this entire wood. With them here, we have a chance to break the shield and take our crystal back."

"What?" Lexi shouted. "But that means war with the fairies!"

The Headmind patted his daughter on the shoulder. "We have been at war a long time. Don't worry for the humans. Humans and elves have always worked together. We will keep them safe. They can stay together. They can even keep the chicken. We will do what we can to save the gravely injured one, as is our way. Mortal lives must be protected. Now we must look forward."

"No!" Elric shouted as the guards grabbed him. One of them pulled his sword from his scabbard. "Give me that back. Let go of me."

The smiling guard grabbed Wynn's arms. Now his teeth looked sharp, and his grin terrifying.

Wynn didn't resist as they led her back to her room. They tossed her inside, followed by Elric, and Mildred.

Mildred squawked and flapped her wings in protest as she retreated to the corner. Elric went back after the guards, but they closed the door in his face. They heard the rough scrape of wood as the latch fell into place.

CHAPTER TWENTY-FOUR

Wynn

"HOW ARE WE GOING TO get out of here?" Elric pounded on the door with a heavy *thump, thump, thump*. It wouldn't do any good. Wynn already tried that the day before.

Wynn sat down on the bed. "We just have to wait."

Elric crossed over to her, holding up his hand to shade his eyes from the slants of light shining through the boards of the wall. Wynn could tell he really didn't want to sit. He was pacing. He wanted to break down the door, by the way he was pounding on it. He flopped beside her, then leaned in so that his shoulder touched hers. She liked that. "Why did you go into the woods, Wynn? You were safe in the gardens. I asked you to wait for me."

Wynn didn't say anything for a bit. Sometimes it took her a long time, but Elric waited for her words. She was glad he gave her a chance to speak.

"I saw Mildred," she said. "But it wasn't Mildred."

"What do you mean?" Elric asked. Mildred clucked sleepily as she settled down at the foot of the bed. She fluffed up the feathers at her belly and wriggled down over her white feet. Then her eyes drooped closed.

"It was a snake, but it looked like Mildred first," Wynn said. "It pretended to be sick. I tried to catch her, but she ran to the woods. It was the snake." Wynn didn't know how to make Elric see how desperate she was. She would have waited for him. But she was tricked.

"I was alone in the woods. Then my Mildred came. She pecked the bad snake in the eye. I hit it with a stick. Then I ran away. I got lost." Elric would never believe her. It sounded strange even to her.

Elric rubbed his chin. He looked like he was thinking hard. "So, the snake was magic," he said.

Wynn nodded. That was exactly it. "It had one of

Mildred's feathers in its mouth."

"Osmund and I found the dead serpent," Elric said. "It had spines down its back, didn't it?" Elric had a serious expression. He was a good thinker. "The only reason I left you was because a reaper was attacking the shield. It must have been a distraction so this serpent creature could lure you into the woods."

"Osmund?" Wynn brightened.

"He's here. He helped me find you, but he was bitten by a reaper and is very sick," Elric said. "I hope the elves will heal him."

"They healed Hob." Osmund would be fine. Lexi said the elves were very good at healing bodies.

"Hob is alive?" Now Elric looked happy. "I thought he might have been killed."

"I saw him. He was here. He ran away," Wynn said. She didn't get away like Hob did. She got caught, and now Elric was caught too. "I'm sorry," she said. "I was tricked. I should stay in the garden."

"It wasn't your fault," Elric said. "You thought Mildred was in danger. I would have done the same thing." He looped an arm over her shoulder. "I'm sorry too," he said. "I never should have left you alone."

"I can be alone." Wynn crossed her arms. She had

been alone a lot in the woods, and she didn't make any mistakes. She made new friends and did lots of things. Being locked in this room wasn't good, but now she was here with Elric and Mildred. And Osmund was here too.

"It's a good thing you have Mildred. She knew you were in trouble and ran after you." Elric reached out and stroked his hand over Mildred's back. "I'm glad she came to you. But this is troublesome. The fairies checked and fortified the barrier. Nothing could get through. How did this snake get inside?" Elric scratched Mildred on her neck and she cooed at him. "If it can change shape, it could have assumed the identity of anyone under the shield."

Wynn sat up straighter. "Hob said there was a secret crack. He tried to take me there, but the monster came."

"A crack?" Elric leaned forward. "And the fairies don't know? We have to get home, Wynn. The palace is vulnerable." A strange look came over his face. "What if this happened before," he said. "What if this snake creature you met transformed into the elf who kidnapped the Fairy Queen's daughter? What if it wasn't really Zephyr who lured Osmund away? Lord Raven believes there is a spy. What if this creature was the spy?" He stood up off the bed.

"Uh," Wynn said. She was very confused. "I don't know."

"If the Grendel has been using this snake as a spy," Elric said, pacing the floor, "then it means the elves never betrayed the queen. It was the Grendel all along. He wanted to drive a wedge between them to keep them both weak. It makes perfect sense."

Wynn nestled into the corner of the bed and yawned. "Wait until night. Lexi will come. She will help us."

"I'm not sure about that," Elric said. "She's the Head-mind's daughter."

"She is my friend." Wynn patted the bed next to her. Elric looked at her like he wasn't sure, but came and sat down next to her. She started to sing. They didn't need to find the way to the Silver Gate anymore, but she still liked to sing the song. It reminded her of home.

> *"The road begins at my feet,*
> *And leads me ever on.*
> *To the land that lies between,*
> *The first light and the dawn.*
> *I seek the favor of the queen*
> *Within that magic land.*
> *Please grant to me your silver branch,*
> *And through the gate I'll find you."*

Elric tipped his head and rested it against hers. "I'm glad to have you back, little sister."

"Me too."

Before long, the light shining through the walls faded, and it grew dark. Wynn stared at the loose boards, waiting for the moment when one of them would move.

Elric's head bobbed as he tried not to sleep. It took a very long time for Lexi to come. Wynn knew she would, but it didn't happen before Elric fell asleep, slumping on his side. It was hard for her to stay awake with him sleeping on the bed next to her.

Just when Wynn felt like she couldn't keep her eyes open, she heard the soft scrape of wood moving. She jumped forward and pulled the boards up. She reached for Lexi's hand, but instead she ended up with a lumpy mass of fabric. She pulled it through the hole and set it aside, but another one appeared, then a sack, then finally a small lantern that had been dimmed until Wynn could barely see the light. Last came the hilt of a sword. Wynn took that carefully, then finally, finally, Lexi rose up into the room on her moving plank.

She immediately hugged Wynn. "I'm sorry I took so long. I've had to be careful."

Wynn shook Elric awake. "Lexi's here!" she said. Lexi immediately shushed her. Elric woke with a start.

He reached for his sword at his side, but it wasn't there.

"I think you are looking for this," Lexi said as she picked up Elric's sword and handed it to him. "It wasn't right for Father to take it, or to lock you up. He's mustered all the fighters in the village. They are arming the siege weapons. They will attack the shield tonight. There are already deep cracks in the dome. It will not hold against the catapults."

Elric reached out and took the sword. He stared at it a moment, then looked to Lexi and pushed the sword into its sheath. "Shouldn't you be with them?" he asked as he glanced at the hole in the floor.

"I'm helping you escape," she said. "You helped me save my brother. It's the least I can do."

Wynn clapped her hands before she could help it. Elric lowered his hands onto hers to settle them down. "What is the plan?"

"I packed up as many things as I could, and snuck down here." Lexi smiled, her bright eyes glittering in the darkness.

Elric stared at her. "That's your plan?" He didn't sound very impressed.

Her eyes widened. "Oh, and I slipped a sleeping potion into the guards' water. We just have to wait for them to fall asleep now, and we can get out of here. I brought you disguises." She patted the bundles of cloth. Wynn picked one up and unwrapped it. Then she started to wriggle out of her dress to change. Elric turned his back to her and focused on Lexi.

"What do we do once we get out of here?" he said.

"I haven't thought that far," she admitted. "But if the dome shatters, the Grendel will come. No one will be safe. Not here, not anywhere. Father doesn't see that. He thinks the Grendel will ignore us and attack the fairies, and we will be protected because we're insignificant. I don't believe that." She got up and walked over to the door and pressed one of her large ears to it. "I can hear the guards stirring still. We have some time to wait yet." She sat down, then looked over at Wynn.

Wynn liked her new elf tunic and the loose leggings that went with them. They were dark red, and would be much better for hiding than her fairy dress. She pulled on a pair of boots, and kicked her old muddy dress. These clothes were warm and soft, and they came with a black hooded robe like Lexi's. Elric picked up a bundle and retreated to the corner to change.

Lexi turned to face Wynn. "People are talking all over town. They are saying you killed a reaper. Is it true?

How did you do it?" she asked as she pulled fruit and nuts out of her bag and offered them to Wynn.

Wynn screwed up her face to think. "I kicked it in the head. It dropped me," she said. "Shadow saved me."

"The Grendel found you?" Lexi looked very afraid. "Or do you mean the fire witch?"

"No, a girl." Wynn picked up another piece of fruit. "And her tigereon."

Lexi let out a high-pitched squeak. "That is impossible." She looked in the sack that she had brought with her, found an old book with a stained cover, and opened it. "Tigereons are extinct. We hunted the last of them decades ago before the dark times." She flipped through her book. "The skin of the last tigereon was given to the Fairy Queen as a gift on her wedding."

"Wynn, are you sure you saw a tigereon?" Elric asked.

Lexi interrupted. "They are large cats, but with heavy heads, and stripes. They can live at least a thousand years or more, and are immune to fairy magic. Their black stripes stay the same, but the white ones can—"

"Her stripes change colors," Wynn finished for her. "I stayed the night with her. Shadow is very nice. She didn't eat Mildred."

"Shadow?" Lexi leaned forward. "There's a legend

about a beast that lurks in the old ruins. It does the bidding of the fire witch, but no one has ever seen it. Could it be the last tigereon?" She inhaled and her eyes went wide, as if she were mystified by the idea.

Wynn huffed. "She doesn't like the name 'witch.' And she doesn't like elves, either. They stay far away so you won't see them and hurt Shadow."

Lexi tilted her head. "This doesn't add up. The witch is an old woman. She has haunted the woods for many years."

"No, she's a young girl. She's Elric's age. She is very nice. She likes Mildred." Wynn chewed on one of the nuts. It was very bitter, but she was hungry.

"An elf girl?" Elric asked.

Wynn shook her head.

"An Otherworld girl?" Lexi asked, searching through her book.

Wynn shook her head again. "No, she's a fairy. She can light rocks on fire. And her hair."

"But why would a fairy . . ." Lexi's voice trailed away as she looked very puzzled.

"Live alone out here instead of staying under the shield?" Elric finished for her. "That doesn't make any sense."

"No fairy would willingly live out here," Lexi said.

"It's miserable. Besides, I thought the queen forbid fairies from coming into the woods." Lexi turned another page, and squinted at it.

"She did." Elric shook his head as he picked up one of the pieces of fruit.

"Then how can she be a fairy?" Lexi asked. "Wynn, you might have mixed up a witch for a fairy. What does she look like?"

Wynn thought about it. It was hard to picture Flame in the dim light of the room. "She has brown skin, like the queen. She has dark hair that curls, like the queen. Sometimes there is fire in it. Her dress is smoke. Her eyes are dark, and she has bad scars across her face." Wynn made a slashing motion across her own face. "She has a very pretty smile, and a mark on her back."

"What sort of mark?" Elric asked. He was dressed now, just like Wynn, except she didn't have a sword. Wynn frowned as she thought about his question.

"It's a picture. It's round, like the queen's flower picture. But it looks like a star, and fire, so I called her Flame."

Elric paced around. He looked dumbstruck. Then he pulled his sword out of the scabbard and showed her the pommel. "Did it look like this?" he asked. A circle had been engraved on the bottom of the sword. It looked a lot like the great seal, only instead of flower petals, tongues of flame curled over the arms of a six-pointed star.

"Yes, that's right!" Wynn said. It was a pretty mark.

"When we first came to the Between, the queen gave me this sword. She told me it was meant for her daughter. The princess was destined to battle the Grendel with it," he said. Wynn didn't understand what he meant by that, but Lexi got very excited. Her mouth opened so far, a fish could jump in it.

Elric put the sword away and ran his hands over his hair. "I can't believe it. If what you say is true, there is one fairy left in these woods." The shadows flickered as he looked at them both. "The princess is alive."

CHAPTER TWENTY-FIVE

Wynn

"OH!" LEXI SQUEAKED AS SHE put her hands to her cheeks. "Do you think it could be true?"

Wynn nodded. Flame was definitely a fairy. It made sense.

"Wynn was lured into the woods by a snake-like creature that transformed into Mildred," Elric explained. "It's possible that years ago, a similar creature took the form of Headmind Reason and stole the queen's child while in disguise. And has been spying on the fairy court ever since."

Lexi held up her hand to stop him from speaking and rummaged through her sack to find another one of her books. She let the pages arch in a fan under her thumb, then suddenly stopped at one, slapping the book open. She showed them a sketch of the snake with the spines running down its back.

"That's it!" Wynn clapped her hands. "It was a bad thing." She scowled. "I don't like it."

"It's called an illusury. It lives in the Shadowfields beyond the woods. It can transform into anything, as long as it holds a piece of that thing in its mouth." She skimmed her finger over the pages. "It doesn't have to be much, even just a hair."

"It had Mildred's feather," Wynn said, and crossed her arms.

"That would do it," Lexi said. "They have very weak minds, and are easily controlled by fairy magic." Lexi traced over the words in her book with her finger. "But they are very rare and obviously difficult to capture."

"Master Elk said that the Grendel was a fairy once. Could he have controlled one of these creatures long enough to fool people?" Elric asked.

"Yes!" Lexi said. "Their illusions are perfect, but they can't talk. They can only hiss."

"Osmund said that Zephyr didn't speak to him when he lured him into the woods." Elric rubbed the edge of his jaw with his thumb. "It must have been an illusury. But how did a baby survive so long in the woods alone?"

"Shadow protected her," Wynn said. "They are good friends."

"And if she's a fairy, she can talk to animals." Elric looked stunned.

Lexi paced around in quick circles. "Oh my, oh my, oh my." She stopped very suddenly. "Do you know what this means?" she asked, grabbing Wynn by the arms, then letting her go just as quickly. "My people are innocent. The princess can stop this madness. She has the power to battle the Grendel."

"But we'd have to find her first," Elric said.

"I know where she lives." Wynn puffed up her chest. She glanced over at Lexi. "But she doesn't like elves."

"Well, that's going to be a problem." Elric turned toward Lexi. "You might have to stay—"

"She doesn't like fairies, either," Wynn continued. "Or strangers. She likes to stay alone."

"How can she not like fairies?" Elric snorted. "She is one."

"She doesn't know," Wynn said. Wynn was certain

Flame didn't know much about the fairies, only that she didn't like them.

"That doesn't make sense," Elric said. "She has a dress made of smoke and fire in her hair. How can she not know? How many other things in the wood can do that sort of magic?"

"Uh—" Wynn stammered. "I don't know."

Elric's face fell. "There's going to be a war. The shield will fall, and the only person who can possibly stop this mess doesn't know she's a fairy, and doesn't like anyone."

His shoulders slumped. He looked very frustrated for a moment, then he shot back up. He lifted one finger and tapped the air with it. He spun on his heel and pointed at Wynn. She blinked at him as a smile broke out over his face. "But she likes you. She likes you, Wynn! You have to find her. You have to speak to her. We have to convince her to go to the palace as the rightful heir and save the queen. If the shield falls and the Grendel comes, she may be our only hope."

They heard a loud thump outside. Lexi jumped, then moved to the door and pressed her ear to it again. Wynn didn't have to have her ear on the door to hear the snoring coming from the other side. Lexi scurried around the room to gather all her things back in her sack, then gently tucked Mildred inside it. "The guard is asleep. We have to go, now." She stood on the bar and lowered herself down the hole, pulling her sack after her.

Wynn followed, carefully balancing on the plank this time. Her stomach swooped, and she nearly fell, but Lexi caught her hands and steadied her. The machine lifted up one more time, and Elric rode it down before jumping onto the pile of sacks. Wynn walked toward the stairs, but Lexi caught her hand. "We can't go that way. There is a nurse staying with my brother tonight, and tending your friend. We can't let him catch us."

"Osmund?" Elric looked concerned. "Is he healing?"

"Yes, he will recover. We gave him medicine for the poison and tended his wounds, but he is still too weak to walk," Lexi said.

"Then I can carry him." Elric stood straighter. He looked tall in his elf boots. "We have to get him home."

"And your disguise won't work if you do. With the hoods on, you'll look like elves, and we can sneak away. We can't hide your friend under our robes. Besides, the nurse would notice him missing." Lexi crept over to a dark corner of the cellar. "No one should check on you two until morning."

Elric looked very torn. Wynn took his hand. "Don't worry," she said. "The elves will take good care of him. They are good healers. We will come back." Osmund needed to get better first. He should stay in bed.

A deep rumbling sounded outside. The blare of horns masked the sound. It was followed by the synchronized calls of the elves marching. It was the sound of war.

"They are moving the catapults through the gate," Lexi whispered. "We have to go now, while everyone is distracted."

Elric nodded at her. She climbed up on a crate and banged her hand against a pair of boards there. They came up, and she quickly shimmied up the hole. Elric gave Wynn a boost and Lexi helped pull her up.

They were in the hall, only a few feet from the sleeping guard. He had fallen off his stool and landed on the ground. His mouth was hanging open, but he had one hand curled under his cheek, like a sleepy baby.

Lexi pressed a finger to her lips, then tucked her hood over her head. Wynn did the same. Elric pulled himself up and replaced the boards. He put his hood over his head too.

"Whatever you do, don't look up. Your faces are pale and someone might notice. Stare at your feet so the hood keeps your face covered and keep your hands in your sleeves. I'll guide you," Lexi whispered.

Wynn did as she was told. She only looked up enough to see the hem of Lexi's long robe. She followed it through the building and out a side door.

The clattering noise outside seemed to shake the ground. The air filled with the creaking rumble of enormous machines rolling through the village on huge wheels. They had massive arms cocked back and held by heavy ropes. Great wagons filled with huge blocks of stone rumbled behind them. Wynn slapped her hands over her ears, but Elric pulled them down and tugged her behind the building.

They came out near the pigpens. The pigs were agitated by the noise, stomping around and squealing. Wynn didn't like that sound either, and the smell was even worse. She followed Lexi until they came to a shadowy alcove behind a small building.

"Now what?" Elric asked in a hoarse whisper.

"I don't know," Lexi said. "I didn't really think we would make it this far." She looked up.

"We can't go through the gate, that's where the catapults are." Elric looked up, but Lexi tugged on the front of his hood, forcing it back over his face. "We have to go over the wall," he said.

"We can't go over the wall," Lexi argued. "That's the point of a wall."

Wynn glanced up at the wall. Cut from tall young trees, the tops of each trunk had been shaped into a spike. Wynn wasn't good at climbing trees with branches. These trees had no branches. This would be even worse than climbing a tree. Elric looked determined as he stared at the wall. He walked forward and touched it, feeling the seam where two logs came together and looking for any place where they could get a hold.

Wynn glanced around. She thought she heard something. She wasn't supposed to look up, but she thought she heard the noise again coming from a tall tree on the other side of the wall. Something tapped her on the head. A small nut landed at her feet. She crept closer and peeked up from under the hem of her hood.

Two luminous eyes stared at her from beneath a mop of black hair and two large fox ears. Hob grinned.

"Hob!" Wynn clapped her hands over her mouth. They were being sneaky and she forgot to be quiet. Elric rushed to her side, followed by Lexi. She pointed up. Hob waved.

"Hob saw you, yes," he said. "I have been up here in this tree for days watching for my friends. I have been listening. I have been waiting. I have been tying vines into knots." The tiny creature held up a tangle of vines. "Just in case."

"Good work, Hob. Toss them down so we can climb up." Elric motioned to him, and he threw the vines over the wall. They cascaded like a heavy tumble of hair down to their feet.

Hob clapped. "Hob is always prepared, yes!"

"Shhhh." Elric pressed his finger to his lips. "Hurry, before someone sees." Elric grabbed the thick tangle of vines and pulled it to Wynn. "Climb as fast as you can."

"I can't," Wynn said. It was very high up.

Elric placed a hand on her shoulder. "Yes, you can."

She took a deep breath and looked up. She had to try. She gripped the mass of tangled vines and pressed her feet against the wall as she climbed up. Her arms hurt. If she let go of the vines, she would fall. She couldn't do that. She had to make it to the top. Wynn climbed and climbed. Her arms were shaking. Her teeth hurt from pressing them too tight together. Her foot slipped on the rounded wood poles. She tried to put her toes in the vines and climb up like a ladder, but the vines gave beneath her feet. She tried again to plant her feet on the wall, but her boot stuck in the crack. Slowly she inched her way up.

"Up here." Hob hung on to the sharpened spike of one of the cut logs and held a hand down toward her. He grabbed her wrist and guided her hand to the branch above her, then helped her foot into the gap between the two spikes. With one last push up, she pulled herself into the bendy branches of the tree.

Now how was she going to get down? She didn't like falling out of trees.

"This way," Hob said. He didn't have trouble in the tree. But he was very small. Wynn made the branch bend. She had to hold on to branches above as she shifted her feet toward the trunk, then walk her hands along the willowy branches above her head. Hob tried to help by placing her feet on stronger branches, and pointing where she should put her hands. Elric and Lexi climbed over the wall easily and into the tree. The whole tree shook, and Wynn held on tight. Once she got near the trunk, it wasn't as hard to climb down. There were many vines to hold on to, and Hob helped guide her. Finally her feet hit the ground.

Elric jumped down out of the tree, followed by Lexi. Elric bent on one knee as Hob bounded over to him. "I'm so glad to see you," he said, holding out his hand for Hob to shake. Instead Hob dipped his head down and wriggled under Elric's hand like a snuggly cat.

"Hob didn't think he would see the Otherworld prince again. I am very glad. Quick, follow me. I will take you back." He bounded forward and waved his hand. "The Grendel is at the edge of the wood. He is gathering an army under his storming clouds. He is waiting. And the elves are moving their weapons. This is bad. We must get you home."

"No," Elric said. "Not yet. We have to find the princess."

Hob looked over at Wynn and pointed at her.

Wynn tried not to giggle. "Not me. The princess in the ruins."

Lexi stepped forward and pulled Mildred from her sack and gently let her down on the ground. Mildred pecked at the old vines, then marched over to Hob. He patted her on the neck.

Lexi lifted her small lantern and pointed the way to go. "I know the way to the old city, but I don't know where the princess hides there. Be careful. Reapers aren't the only dangerous things in this wood, and we have to watch for traps."

Together they started walking through the dark woods. Strange sounds came from the trees. Wynn couldn't see the stars. They were covered by black clouds. The Grendel's storm was coming closer. The forest made everything seem darker. They walked on endlessly.

Wynn stayed quiet. She saw monsters in every shadow. Elric stayed close to Lexi, holding his glowing sword ready. Wynn followed behind him, and tried not to imagine that the branches of the trees were bony hands reaching for her.

It was still the dark part of night when they began to climb up a hill. Wynn saw ferns along the path, and things seemed less scary. As they climbed, she spotted one of the bright mushrooms that grew near where Flame lived; even though everything looked gray in the dark, she imagined their bright red and orange tops. They couldn't find a path, but Wynn did see the rocks that had been cut into squares poking up from the thick ferns.

"We're almost there," Lexi said. "We have to be quiet. Or we'll never find them."

A loud boom echoed through the woods followed by a sharp crack and a creaking, snapping sound, like ice breaking on a lake. Wynn covered her ears. She didn't like the sound. It was too loud.

"Those are the catapults," Lexi whispered.

Elric strode forward and climbed up the curling root of a tree. He craned his neck to see through the leaves, then looked at them with worry in his eyes. "Without any of us in the palace, the shield won't have the power to withstand such an attack. It's going to fall, and when it does, the Grendel will come. We have to hurry."

They climbed up the roots of the trees growing along a steep hill, but it was difficult to make their way up. The darkness didn't help. Wynn wondered if the dawn would ever come again—it had been so long since she'd seen the sun rise. She stumbled on another rock, then noticed one that looked like a step. Then another. Elric found the steps too and ran up them until he came to a stop beneath a crumbling archway.

Wynn knew where she was. She thought so, anyway. It did look familiar, and she smelled smoke on the breeze.

Elric stared into the darkness. "There's something out there. I thought I saw it move."

Hob lifted his pointed nose and sniffed at the air. "A big beastie is close. Don't know what it is."

Shadow was big. Wynn hoped it was her. She certainly didn't want to meet another reaper.

"We're never going to find the lost princess like this,"

Lexi said. Everyone turned to look at her. She clutched the strap of her sack as she lowered the lantern. "For years elves have been coming to this part of the wood for the sweet fruit that grows here, and we've never caught sight of more than a shadow. She knows we're here. She'll stay five steps ahead of us."

Wynn definitely remembered this part of the stair. She knew where she was, and where to go. "I can do it," she said, walking forward on her own.

"Not without me." Elric grabbed her shoulder and pulled her back.

"Flame likes me," Wynn said, standing her ground. "Not you. She is hiding."

"You'll get lost," Elric said.

"Mildred will come with me," Wynn said. She looked down at her hen. The hen gave a confident cluck, then strutted forward and began hopping up the broken steps. She looked back at Wynn to see if she was following.

"It's too dangerous," Elric said. "I don't want to lose you again."

"I can do it." Wynn gently pulled his hand from her shoulder. "Let me try."

Elric pulled her into a fierce hug, and she hugged

him back. Finally he let her go.

"I will be safe," Wynn said. Then she climbed after her hen. "I will find Flame."

The stairs were very scary in the dark. She didn't have Lexi's light. The light from the stars was blocked by the heavy clouds. She had to feel her way up the stones one at a time, and move very slowly. When she reached the top, she looked around at the ruins of the great city. She wondered if the elves could build it again. It must have been beautiful once.

Each doorway was dark and empty. Flame didn't mind the dark, but Wynn did. She didn't like it at all. Mildred clucked as she strutted ahead. Wynn followed, until they came to a familiar archway. Wynn knew this place. She'd found the chalky rock near here.

"Flame?" she called into the shadows. There was no fire, no light at all.

A low rumbling sound answered her.

Something pressed against her back, a heavy push and slide of an animal's head rubbing against her. Wynn jumped forward and spun around. She almost fell over. But there in front of her were Shadow's enormous eyes. They blinked at her as the tigereon changed her stripes from a very dark brown to white. It looked like she'd appeared from the air.

"You're wearing elvish clothes." Flame's voice came from the darkness. Mildred clucked in greeting. "Shadow was confused by your scent. Are you friends with the elves now?"

Wynn didn't know how to answer that. She was friends with Lexi, but she didn't like the elf leader very much. "They locked me in a room."

Flame stepped forward out of the dark shadows of her shelter. She didn't quite look at Wynn and kept her staff carefully poised in front of her. "How did you get out?"

"Elric found me," Wynn said.

Flame's forehead crinkled, making the scars across her face stand out. "He left the shield and braved the wood to find you?"

"He is a good brother." Mildred came over to her and Wynn picked her up as Shadow slipped beside Flame.

"If you have been saved, why are you here?" She placed both hands on her staff and leaned on it. Dark blue fire licked along the curls at her temples.

"You are my friend," Wynn said. "Come back with me."

Flame laughed.

Another loud boom echoed off the stones and old towers of the ruins. The sound of shattering ice was followed by a roll of thunder as the storm drew nearer. The Grendel was coming.

"Why would I want to live with the fairies?" Flame asked.

"Because you are a fairy," Wynn said.

"A fairy?" Flame didn't smile now. She looked very angry. "You think I'm one of those weak cowards? Can you believe this?" she asked as she turned her head toward Shadow.

"Fairies can talk with animals," Wynn said.

Flame snapped her head up and scowled. It made her scars look very frightening. "I have lived thousands of days in this wood. I should know what I am."

Wynn blinked at her. "Fairies don't get old."

Flame gripped her staff and pushed forward, but Wynn did not back down, not even when Flame's staff hit her legs. "I am not a fairy!" she shouted. The old pillars of the archway burst into a roaring inferno of white-hot flames.

"Fairies have magic." Wynn backed away from the wave of heat coming off the pillars.

They dimmed as Flame gathered control of herself.

Blue flames licked up either side of the archway.

"This can't be true," Flame said, her voice soft and sad. "I'm something different, like you are."

"I'm a fairy princess too." Wynn reached out and touched Flame's hand. She startled at the touch, then let out a heavy sigh and placed her own hand over Wynn's. Wynn closed her other hand over Flame's. "Even when I don't want to be."

"If I am a fairy, then why did they abandon me in the wood? Why did they throw me out here and then never come back for me?"

Flame sounded so sad. Wynn stepped forward and wrapped her in a hug. "The Grendel took you away."

Shadow suddenly crouched and hissed. Mildred let out a loud cluck and trotted down the path just as Elric came running up with his sword drawn. The tigereon leaped forward and took a swipe at Elric, who backed away from the enormous beast. Her striped tail lashed in anger.

Wynn ran forward and circled her arms around Shadow's neck. "No, Shadow, no. He is my brother."

Elric stepped forward as if he wanted to be with her, but Shadow growled at him and he backed away. "We saw the fire. Wynn, are you hurt?"

"I am fine." Wynn held tight to Shadow's neck.

"This is your brave and devoted brother, I take it?" Flame stepped into the cool blue light of the flaming pillars but didn't look at Elric. She stared somewhere past him. "The fairy prince?"

Elric crept forward waving his hand slowly. Flame still didn't look at him. As he stepped in front of her, she whacked him hard with her staff.

He shouted in pain and fell to the ground. "I'm sorry. For a moment there, I didn't think you could see me."

"I can't," Flame said as she leaned on her staff.

CHAPTER TWENTY-SIX

Elric

"YOU'RE BLIND." ELRIC COULDN'T BELIEVE it, but the scars across her face, slashing over her eyes, didn't lie. It explained so much. No wonder she didn't try to rejoin the fairies. She couldn't see the fairy realm, and her tigereon couldn't cross the barrier. She would have never set foot through the shield if she had to leave her only companion behind. For her, the fairy realm must have been like a legend that her tigereon told to her at bedtime, not the place where she belonged.

"I don't know what 'blind' means," Flame said as

Lexi came forward. Shadow slinked behind Flame, curling her body around Flame's legs. She put her head low to the ground and hissed. Her stripes shimmered between a harsh yellow shade and a vivid green. "Tell the elf to back away."

Lexi did so, pulling her lantern closer to her body.

"Your eyes are damaged," Elric said. "You can't see things." The reaper that captured her as a baby must have scratched her face, and cut her eyes. He wasn't sure how fairy wounds healed, especially in a baby, but her scars were deep. The streaks cut across the her forehead, slashed her cheek and the bridge of her nose, and crossed over her lip and jaw. Instead of changing color the way most fairy eyes did, the princess's eyes seemed fixed on dark brown.

"I can see things," she said as she brought her staff around and swung it dangerously close to his face. He didn't flinch, but he felt the muscles of his cheek twitch where her staff lingered. "Light, shadows, things moving nearby."

"But you can't see like us," he argued. Lexi and Hob shared a nervous glance as the flames on the pillars erupted in hot white fire. Wynn scooped up Mildred and scrambled toward Shadow.

"Can you see as well as her?" Flame tilted her head down toward her tigereon. Shadow bared her long fangs at him and hissed. "She tells me what she sees. That's all I need to know."

Another loud boom sounded as the catapults assaulted the shield. It could shatter at any minute. A flash of lightning illuminated the forest, and the rumble of thunder that followed made them all flinch. "We don't have time for this," Lexi warned from the edge of the forest. "The Grendel is coming. He will follow the storm and attack the fairy realm as soon as my father breaks through the shield."

"I'm not going anywhere," Flame said. "I am home." She crossed her arms, still holding her long staff ready as the sudden gusts of wind from the oncoming front stirred the billowing curls of smoke around her legs. "Come, Shadow." She turned with her staff, and the beast rose to take its place beside her.

"You can't run!" Elric shouted at her. The mark on her back stood out. It took up the entire width of her shoulders, a fiery star. The mark of a warrior. "You can't hide from this. War will tear everything good in the fairy realm and the Nightfell Wood apart. There is no safe place. The Grendel will take over everything. He will destroy everything. The only thing you can do is fight. It is your destiny." He held out his sword to her. It was hers by right. The silver sword glowed as if it too were on fire. Elric had to squint his eyes as he offered it to her. She was the one born to fight the Grendel, not him.

Flame scoffed and turned her head, not enough to actually face him, but that didn't seem to matter much to her at the moment. "You want me to fight for the elves?" she said. "Creatures that ruthlessly hunted down all of Shadow's kind?"

Lexi cringed.

"Or you want me to save the fairies. The ones who are so cowardly that they ordered others to hunt down and kill anything they couldn't control with their magic— anything with the strength to defy them. Both the elves and the fairies brought this storm upon themselves. The fairies hide under their precious shield. They gladly throw the rest of the world away to rot while they live in their perfect little bubble. And the elves? They are more than willing to destroy in the name of anger and let innocent life perish because it means nothing to them. They have their books, and make their terrible weapons. Yes, the storm is coming. Why should I right it? The world is already broken." She began to walk away. The fire on the pillars dimmed. The light in the sword slowly died in his hand.

"It doesn't have to be broken," Elric called after her.

She paused. He had to use his chance. She wouldn't listen to him long. He just wasn't sure the best way to reason with her.

"You can change things. You are the queen's daughter. She will listen to you."

She let out a choked laugh that almost sounded like a sob. "My mother? I never had a mother. I have always been alone. How do I know this queen even exists? Shadow has never seen her. If what you say is the truth, if it is real, then she never came for me." Flame took a step deeper into the darkness as the shadows of her dress swirled over her like a cloak. She turned back, and her hair lit with red fire. "She means nothing to me!" This time stones nearer to the ground burst into flame, and threatened to spread the fire to the trees. "Only Shadow has ever been there for me."

"The queen still loves you," Elric said. "Whether you love her or not." He paused, feeling a tug near his heart. He didn't have time to get distracted by his own feelings. He looked at Flame. "If the queen didn't still love you, Wynn and I would not be here. She brought us here to soothe her broken heart. It has never healed since the day she lost you. You are still precious to her—so precious, she named you Estaria, after the stars."

She turned to him, and Shadow circled around her body. "I don't know what those are," she said.

Elric took a step toward her. "They burn. In the deepest part of night, they shine. They give people hope that there is something powerful beyond this world. Even when we cannot see them. Even though we cannot touch them. We know they are always there."

Wynn came forward and walked past Elric. She held Mildred out and placed her in Flame's arms. Flame fumbled a bit with the hen, surprised.

"Come back with me?" Wynn asked. Flame gently stroked the bird in her hands. "I want you to be my sister." Wynn reached out to pet Shadow. "We can be princesses together. I will keep Shadow safe. No one will hurt her. I promise."

Shadow purred as she rubbed up against Wynn with enough force that Wynn almost toppled over. Elric helped steady her.

"If the Grendel comes," Wynn said, "he will kill the queen. My first mother died during a storm. I don't want that to happen again."

Wynn's words were jumbled, but Elric knew what she was trying to say. She had lost one mother already.

She didn't want to lose another. They finally had a place where they belonged.

But as he looked at Flame, Estaria, the lost princess, he saw a deep loneliness. An isolation as profound as the first star to appear in the night sky. She had never known what it meant to have a family. She only had her tigereon.

Thunder crashed, or it could have been a part of the shield collapsing. Elric couldn't tell. They were out of time. "I am going to return to the palace," he said. "I'm going to fight the evil that is coming. Go back to your dark little hole in the ruins. But if you do, know you are just as ruthless as the elves, and you are just as much of a coward as the fairies. Hide in shadows, or hide under a shield. In the end, it's all the same thing."

Elric turned away from her and walked back down the path as the first drops of rain fell on his face. "Come on, Wynn. It's up to us now." He held his hand out to his sister.

She hesitated a moment, looking back at the lost princess, then she tucked Mildred under her arm and ran to his side. He took her hand.

As they walked away, the roar of the tigereon shook the air as fiercely as the thunder.

* * *

Elric chased after Hob as fast as he could. He held tight to Wynn's hand and helped her over the rough forest path. "Lexi, you have to return to your village right away," Elric said as he dropped back next to the elf. "You have to evacuate everyone who is left—the sick, the elderly, children. The village will not be safe. The Grendel is right on top of us."

Lexi slowed for a second. "Evacuate?" She looked at him, stunned. "To where? Where can we possibly go?"

"To the palace," Elric said through gritted teeth. "Take as many as you can straight to the palace."

Lexi let out a gasping laugh. "Perfect, I'm sure we'll be welcome after our catapults attacked their shield!"

"The only way any of us is going to survive this is if we stand together," Elric said.

"I don't think that's going to work," Lexi said. "You can't shed years of resentment and suspicion like taking off a hood."

"You're innocent." Elric pulled himself over a fallen tree, and helped both Wynn and Lexi up.

"Sometimes that doesn't matter," Lexi said with a stern voice. Elric stopped in his tracks as she glared at him.

"I don't know if this is going to work," Elric admitted.

"But it's the only chance we've got. It will be easier to defend everyone if we are all in the same place, and having the vulnerable nearby may stop your father's attack long enough to make him listen. If people stay in the village, they will be caught behind an army of the Grendel's monsters. This is our only chance. I can't do this without you. The only way we're going to stop this mess is if we do it together."

"You are going to stand on the line for me?" Lexi challenged. "When the moment comes, you will side with the elves, not the fairies?"

"There is only one side now," Elric answered. "We have to make everyone see that. You can count on Osmund, he will help you. If he says anything to the contrary, tell him I said he's a fool. Go, and good luck." He placed his hand on Lexi's shoulder. She nodded.

"This way, quick, quick, hurry!" Hob said as he dashed forward. "We must reach the queen!" They ran hard through the woods, only pausing when Hob led them around a trap, or onto a path for the hog-carts.

Hob bounced only a pace or two ahead of them. Elric was afraid he was going to step on the creature's long and whipping tail as they ran. Mildred sprinted alongside them, her head bobbing furiously as she hopped over any obstacles in their path.

Drops of rain hit him relentlessly in the face, but it didn't matter. Time was their enemy now. They had to hurry before there was no hope left for this world.

They had to fight against the storm, and the mud, rocks, rivulets, roots, and branches. It was as if the forest itself was reaching out to grab them and trying to hold them back. Elric pulled Wynn up an embankment slick with dark mud. She didn't complain as she struggled, she just fought against the branches crossing the path, and the rain slicked leaves under their feet. Elric urged her along, not knowing how far left they had to go.

After what felt like hours of struggling down the narrow and twisted paths, they finally found the shield.

"Release the catapults!" The call rang out louder than the storm winds. It was followed by a creaking moan, then a loud crack like a whip. Elric watched in horror as a huge carved block of stone flew toward the shield.

It smashed against the gray wall with a sound that punched the air from his lungs. He clapped his hands over his ears as the stone tumbled down the shield and crashed into the trees to their right. Deep cracks appeared where it had hit. The fractures weren't healing themselves. The cracks only grew, and they were already as large as the trees.

He peered through the shield and spotted the curling oak where Zephyr said he would wait for them. "We're not far!" he called to Wynn, who had her whole body hunched over Mildred.

They scrambled along the edge of the shield until they reached the oak.

"Zephyr!" Elric called. "Zeph! Where are you?"

Elric waited, his heart in his throat. He called again, but there was no response. What if Zephyr had abandoned them? What if Osmund was right about him? It had been two days since he'd left.

Elric watched as a swirl of dried leaves spun upward in a twisting curl of wind. The wind formed together, then solidified into the familiar form of his friend. Zephyr flew toward them. His eyes were wide and yellow with panic. He swooped through the shield and knocked Elric over as he crashed into Elric and Wynn. He hugged both of them at once. "You are alive! I don't believe it."

He cradled Wynn's cheeks in his hands and stared at her with tearful eyes flashing in a rainbow of colors. "Even Mildred, you are alive! Hurry. The shield is failing. We have to get you to the queen. She is nearly gone. Where's Osmund?"

"He's coming soon," Elric said. Along with an entire

village of elves, but Elric didn't mention that part. He hoped Osmund was healed enough to make it. In his heart, he knew Lexi wouldn't leave him behind. She would hold up her end. Now he had to do his part. "Get Wynn to safety."

"Zeph," Wynn said, throwing her arms around him as if the shield weren't about to shatter at any moment. "It's so nice to see you again."

He returned her hug even as he pulled her toward the shield. Elric scooped up Mildred, placed a hand on Zephyr's shoulder, and pushed all of them through the shield. The fog passed over Elric like it was nothing, and suddenly he had to squint in the bright light of the heart of the fairy realm.

After being in the dim of the wood, the colors under the dome were so vibrant he could see lingering shadows of them if he closed his eyes. The weight that had been like a yoke around his neck lifted, and the oppressive dreariness finally left him.

The storm thundered outside the cracking shield, but it sounded distant, and the cold rain no longer fell on them. Elric looked back at the shield. Hob stood with his hands pressed against it, and his ears tucked back into his mop of black hair.

"Get him and bring him through," Elric demanded, pulling Zephyr up.

"But that's a darkling creature," Zephyr protested. Mildred pecked him on the foot. "Ow!"

"That darkling creature risked his life to save me and my sister. He belongs with us." Hob looked behind him, his small chest heaving in fright.

Zephyr twisted his expression into one of resigned uncertainty, but he flew through the shield and reached down for Hob. Hob jumped on his shoulder, then scrambled around and clung to the back of Zephyr's head. "Ugh, get off!" Zeph flew back through the shield while batting at Hob. He knocked him off into the flowers.

Hob bounced up, then scrambled to sit on top of Elric's shoulder. "Run!" Hob squeaked as he pointed toward the cracked dome above them.

Another large block of stone was flying toward the shield. It hit with a deafening crash and smashed through.

CHAPTER TWENTY-SEVEN

Elric

THE STONE HURTLED INTO THE old oak. Broken pieces of wood and dirt sprayed into the air. Zephyr pushed a gust of wind toward the blast, and blew most of the debris away from them. "The shield has been breached. It won't be long before it falls now."

Elric looked up at the gaping hole high in the shield. He could see the black clouds swirling above the trees and hear the wind howling on the other side. He turned to his sister. "Wynn, listen to me," he said. "You have to run. Run as fast as you can to the palace.

Find the queen. Heal her before the shield breaks. It's up to you."

Wynn blinked at him. "And what do you do?" she asked.

He drew his sword. "The Grendel is coming. So are the elves. Someone has to stand and fight."

Wynn threw her arms around him and clung tightly to his neck. He wrapped his arm around her and held on as long as he could. He could feel tears begin to sting his eyes. "No, no fighting," she said against his shoulder.

"Go, Wynn," Elric said, knowing this might be the last time he would ever see his sister. He was mortal, and this was war. "I will fight to protect you. I love you. You can do this. I'm counting on you to save us. Now go."

She gave him a teary nod and started off through the vivid green fields, Mildred only a step behind her.

Elric had to force himself to look away from Wynn. He wanted to watch her until he couldn't see her anymore, just to have one more moment with her.

A different sort of thunder rumbled through the hills to his left. An army of fearsome animals was charging over the rolling hill toward the broken shield. The fairies were coming. He had to stop them somehow. If they fought with the elves, they wouldn't have the strength to stand against the Grendel. "Zeph, come with me!" he shouted.

"We can't fight!" he shouted. "We're not warriors, Elric, we're just kids."

"We're not going to fight," Elric called back as he ran as fast as he could into the gap of land between the approaching army and the breaking shield. "But we have to stop them."

"Have you lost your head completely?" Zephyr flew in front of him and hit him with a gust. It made Elric stumble enough that he stopped.

He stared up at his friend. "You said you wanted to be a hero. Now's your moment. Are you with me? Or not?"

Zephyr looked up as the cracks in the shield turned into a dark web above them. "This is too big for us," he said. "The shield is breaking." The dome of the shield buckled, and pieces of it shattered, falling away and turning to glittering rain.

"I have to do something!" Elric shouted as he turned to run again.

Headmind Axis rode through the breach on an enormous boar. His army of elves rode behind him.

Elric had to stop this. He ran straight for the gap

between the elves and the fairies. Hob bounded along bravely at his heels. He didn't see Zephyr, but a strong wind at his back pushed him faster. To his right, a snow-white stag charged with the shining points of his antlers held low and deadly. To his left, Axis rode to battle, his arrow-slinger pointed directly at Elk.

Elric closed his eyes and ran with all his might until he slid to a stop between them. He drew his sword.

"Halt!" he shouted, and even though he could barely draw breath from his exertion, his voice rang out over the hillside. He held his sword aloft.

A powerful blast of wind pushed down from above him and out from where he stood. Elk skidded to a stop and shook his silver antlers. Axis pulled hard on the chain connected through the ring in his boar's nose. The beast squealed, but came to an unsteady stop.

Elk transformed in a flash of light and drew his broad sword as the fairy army fell into formation. The boar riders closed ranks and formed a protective line behind Axis.

"Elric, move aside," Master Elk commanded.

"I am your prince!" he shouted, and the authority in his voice shocked him for a moment. Elk took a step back and lowered his sword. "I command you to stand down," Elric continued in a slightly shakier voice.

Axis laughed. "How convenient. It will make it all the easier to take the crystal back to where it belongs." His orange eyes flashed in the dimming light. Thunder rolled overhead. "The fairies have used us too long."

Elric turned to him. "You will not fight."

Axis pointed the deadly weapon strapped to his arm at Elric. "Are you going to stop me?"

"You owe Wynn the life of your son," Elric said. He could barely speak the words through his clenching jaw. "A life debt. You swore yourself you would always protect us. Is this how you will repay her? By killing her brother?"

"Father, no!" Lexi ran as fast as she could toward Elric, clutching a book to her chest. She turned and put herself directly in the way of his weapon. "The fairies are not our enemy," she shouted. "And we are not theirs."

Elric watched as Osmund staggered toward them, supporting the thin frame of the Headmind's son. Behind them, a long line of pig-carts carried the vulnerable elves who had been left behind.

Lexi turned toward the fairies. "The Grendel lied to us all to drive a wedge between the fairies and the elves. He sent a creature called an illusury to make it look as if the elves had taken the queen's baby. It is a shapeshifter, and can be controlled by fairy magic. The Grendel's magic." She held up the book to the illustration that she had shown them earlier.

"It's true," Elric shouted to the fairies. "The same creature tricked Osmund and Wynn. It lured them both into the woods. But they survived, and so did the princess." Elric stepped closer to Elk. "I have seen her. She is real. There is hope. But the Grendel is on his way with an army of monsters at his heels. He wants us to fight each other. He wants us to be weak before he comes. The only way we can save this world is if we fight as one."

"How can you know this for certain?" Master Elk asked.

"Trust in me," Elric said. "I am not mistaken. I have spoken with the princess. All the queen's children are alive. There is a chance to save the queen. But we cannot make a stand against the Grendel without the help of the elves."

"They destroyed the shield," Elk shouted. "It was our only protection."

"They had a right to pull it down," Elric countered. "The crystal was a gift; the fairies have used it against them. Anger at their anger will not help us."

Elk considered this for a moment. His eyes changed color so quickly, Elric had a difficult time seeing one color before the next one flared. Elric wondered what thoughts were passing through the old warrior's mind. The old fairy looked up at Axis. "I remember the days of our friendship, and the feasts in the towers of the city in the woods. I remember fighting alongside your father in days gone by. We were allies once."

"Father," Lexi said, holding her book to her chest. "Did we come for revenge? Or justice?"

Axis looked at Elk. "That depends. To what truth do the fairies hold?"

"I choose to follow my prince," Elk answered. "If you fight with us"—he nodded slowly—"then we will fight for you."

Headmind Axis slowly lowered his weapon. He rode forward on his boar, and offered Elk an open hand. The leader of the guard took it. "Then I will follow the counsel of my daughter."

The dark clouds gathered overhead, casting a shadow over all of them. Elk lifted his sword. "We have to hurry. The power of the queen is diminishing. She is almost gone, turned to ice. We have to get those who can't fight to safety. To the grove over there." He pointed to a stand of trees.

"Wynn will save the queen," Elric insisted. "We have to give her time. Lexi, lead all those who cannot fight to that grove," Elric ordered, gesturing to the trees where Elk had pointed. She gave him a brisk nod and began shouting to the crowd of elves. "Osmund, go with her and protect them should the fight turn that way. Zephyr, cast your twilight over the grove to shield them. Then use your healing powers on the wounded."

"I've never done magic that big before," he said. He paled, and his eyes dimmed to a soft yellow.

"Now's your time," Elric stated.

Zephyr let out a slow breath, squared his shoulders, then flew off after the trail of the elf carts. He picked up an elven toddler and marched next to Lexicon as they headed for the grove.

"Prince Elric," Elk said as he placed a hand on his shoulder, "you must go too. You have to stay safe. You should aid your sister. Go to the queen. She is dying."

"The Grendel is coming. There will be nowhere in this world or the next that is safe," Elric said. "Wynn will reach the queen. I will do what you have ordered of me. I will use my life to distract the Grendel as long as I can and give Wynn the chance to save us."

"Elric, that was never—"

A loud clap of thunder sounded with such force Elric

felt as if the inner parts of his ears had broken. Several of the elves cried out as their boar mounts squealed in pain.

An ominous laugh circled around them like a carrion crow. Elric felt like the voice came from within his own head, but he noticed others looking around too.

"You fools," the terrifying voice said on the howling wind. It sounded like thunder and the distant howl of a fierce gale.

Elric gripped the hilt of his sword and took his place next to Elk.

"You think you have the power to stand against me?" It didn't sound threatening, though. It was worse than that: it sounded amused. Elric felt a wave of doubt and fear pass over him.

"Filthy elvish mortals, you will die. Those blessed with magic will diminish. And then the Between will belong to me. It is my right. I am its true king." He laughed again, and the sound made Elric feel sick to his stomach. "You have no hope left."

"Speak for yourself," Elric shouted. He still had hope, and he had faith in his sister. She knew what to do. He silently prayed for Wynn to reach the queen in time. "Your plan did not work."

"Brave words from a little boy." The Grendel laughed again. "Would you sound so brave if you had to face me?"

A final boom thundered through the air. Screams rose up around him as the clouds that had covered the Nightfell Wood rolled over the countryside. They cast the fairy realm in shadow, and seemed to steal the vibrant colors of the world as they went.

Forked lightning cracked overhead and struck the ground, sending the armies scattering. The shadows wrapped themselves together into a being as dark and as frightening as death. He wore a robe of black, billowing storm clouds that curled around his feet. His body was formed from the deepest darkness of night, and his eyes burned from the dark pit of a black hood with the frantic fire of lightning. He looked as if he were made from dark magic itself. He had lost everything that made a fairy seem human.

He floated forward and drew an obsidian sword that crackled with lightning around it. Elric felt as if he were staring at fear manifested into a single form. Elric shook with it, but he held the hilt of his sword tight. Now was the time for courage. Now was the time for strength.

"Go back to the Shadowfields, where you belong!"

Elric shouted at him, trying to keep his voice from shaking.

"I belong here," the Grendel said. "This is my kingdom. My sister stole it from me long ago. I have come to take it back, and then all of the world will be mine."

CHAPTER TWENTY-EIGHT

Elric

THE QUEEN'S BROTHER? ELRIC STEPPED back in shock. The Grendel was the queen's brother.

That meant he was just as old—and just as powerful—as the queen. They had no hope of defeating such an ancient fairy.

Elric's knees shook as he stared down the immortal. He couldn't see his face, only his burning lightning eyes. Bolstering his courage, he shouted, "There is only one of you, and we are a hundred strong."

Between the elven boar-riders and the fairies, they

had the Grendel outnumbered. But they were dealing with a force of darkness able to reach across the divide between worlds. Their numbers might not matter.

He smiled, a flash of white in a face hidden by shadows. His eyes sparked white-hot with lightning. "Oh," he said. "I have not come alone."

The Grendel lifted his arms, and the world seemed to fall into the dark of a winter night. In the depths of the woods, hundreds of burning eyes peered out at them. What little light remained caught on their sharp teeth as an army of fearsome beasts stepped forward out of the shelter of the trees.

Elric recoiled in terror. It was as if some horrible butcher had cut up several fearsome creatures and pieced them back together in terrible ways, then made them all enormous. There were bears covered in scaly armor like a lizard. Great insects with whiplike tails that ended in poisonous stingers, but were the size of oxen. Creatures with the head of a lion on the body of a goat. Giant spiders. Elric's mind could never have created such a nightmare on its own.

The monsters charged forward in a rush of snarls and grasping claws.

The boar-riders raised their weapons and shouted

as they kicked their pigs toward the Grendel's terrible army.

Their cry seemed to wake the fairies from their stupor as they too ran forward to meet the beasts. Magic swirled around them as they charged into the fray.

Elric stood his ground, sword in hand. An enormous spider scurried forward to meet him, but darkness enveloped the beast as the Grendel appeared before him. Elric brought his sword up out of instinct and it met the Grendel's obsidian blade as it came crashing down onto his. His fingers went numb as he squeezed his hilt with all his might. Lightning arched around the blades, but Elric held fast.

His arms shook as the Grendel crushed Elric under the strength of his blade. The churning clouds that made up the monster's robes surrounded Elric, and the darkness swirling around him seemed impossible to overcome.

Elric's sword glowed with cool, white-blue light but it was no match for the obsidian sword.

The shadows hiding the Grendel's face deepened, forming layers of shifting substance that weren't quite flesh and barely hid a grotesque white skull. The shadowy flesh pulled over the long teeth into a grimace.

Lightning flashed in the deep pockets of the Grendel's eyes.

"Fool," the Grendel said. "You have no hope. You have no power that can defeat me. Prepare to die. And then I will find that half-wit sister of yours. I will enjoy slowly ripping out her spirit, leaving her body as worthless as her mind. Then the queen will meet the same fate as the one she claimed to love."

The Grendel pressed down on his own hilt, and drove Elric into the ground. Elric cried out as he felt his strength giving way.

Just then a strange sound soared over the roar of the battle. Voices, a chorus of voices, were rising together from the grove. He didn't understand the words floating on the air. He didn't have to. The melody was strange— unearthly and haunting, but no less powerful for the emotion that it carried.

The elves were singing.

The Grendel staggered backward and flinched, as if he had just been struck by a physical blow. Light seemed to return to the battle. It was as if the cloud that had blocked the sun had rolled away. The magic of the fairies, locked in battle with the monsters of the Shadowfields, flared. They gained strength through the power of the song, and the darkness shrank back.

Elric used that moment to slip out from under the Grendel's sword. He rolled to the side, letting the Grendel's obsidian blade slice into the ground, and swung his sword at the back of the monster's leg. He sliced into the smokelike robes until his sword hit something of substance.

The Grendel screamed, and thunder rolled overhead. A bolt of lightning struck the ground nearby.

Elric tried to pull the sword back, but a powerful blow hit the side of his head. Pain erupted in his skull, giving way to a heavy thudding that seemed to block all thought. He had to force himself to open his eyes as he stumbled backward. His sword clattered from his hands, and he fell onto the grass. No. He had to keep fighting. But he couldn't seem to will his feet back under him. His head felt like it was being stabbed with a dagger from the inside.

"You will pay for that, boy." The Grendel lifted his obsidian sword high over his head. Elric panted through his pain and willed everything in his body to move at once. He watched the blade slice through the air, straight for his head.

Suddenly a white stag crashed into the side of the

Grendel, knocking him off balance. Pure darkness spread out from the wound in the Grendel's leg. It surrounded the Grendel in a cloak of night. Enraged, the Grendel swung his sword back around and sliced into Elk's side.

"No!" Elric cried out. Elk was disappearing. "No!" he cried again. He scrambled for his blade.

He reached the handle just as the Grendel swooped down on him. Elric couldn't see anything. He was surrounded in darkness. He lifted his sword and swung wildly, completely blind in the presence of the Grendel. The clouds of darkness poured out of the evil fairy like smoke billowing from a raging fire. It covered the battlefield. He could not see.

"There's no one who can save you now."

The Grendel loomed over him, his sword snapping with deadly energy that did nothing to light the dark. He was going to die.

A roar sounded nearby and Elric felt a sudden wave of heat.

"I can," a girl's voice said behind him.

Elric turned around. There stood Flame with Shadow at her side. Blue fire licked over the ground around her, burning back the darkness and illuminating her eyes that now glowed with the fire of burning stars.

"You came back." Elric couldn't hide the shock in his voice.

"Wynn asked me to," she said as she offered him a hand up.

The Grendel stumbled backward. "It can't be."

Flame let out a roar of her own as she charged forward into the darkness with her staff at the ready. The shadows didn't deter her at all. With a powerful blow of her staff, she hit the Grendel across his dark skull, then landed another blow to the bleeding wound on his leg.

The symbol on Flame's back began to glow with bright white light, and a great shout of triumph came from the fairies as the boar-riders charged against the monsters on the plain.

The Grendel gathered himself, building the shadows around him until he became a towering figure twice the size of a normal man. He swung the obsidian blade at Flame, the lightning sparking off it, crackling in the air.

"Flame! Get down!" Elric shouted, but he didn't have to. She ducked, but not before the blade hit her staff and cleaved it in two.

Elric ran forward with his sword in his hand. The mark on her back glowed like a star within her, shining through her skin. He touched her shoulder. "I'm here," he called, reaching down to place the hilt of the sword in her hand.

She grabbed it, her fingers wrapping around the hilt like it was a natural extension of her own arm. Elric could feel the dark energy crackling off the Grendel as he rose. Flame lifted the sword in front of her, and Elric fell back.

The sword had always glowed with a soft blue light, but now it burned with a bright white light as powerful as the sun. It flashed in Elric's eyes, and he had to look away. When he finally cleared his vision, he saw Flame clothed in a dress of pure starlight. She shone just as brightly as she battled the Grendel with her tigereon pacing behind her.

He didn't know how she was doing it. Perhaps she could see the darkness of the Grendel in contrast to the light pouring from her, or feel the foul presence of him. Maybe Shadow was telling her how to move, but in the midst of the vicious fight, Flame met the Grendel blow for blow. His darkness could do nothing to deter her.

Elric looked around, hardly aware of the pain in his own body. Swirling colors from the lingering effects of the light of Flame's new power danced in his vision.

As he pulled himself across the battlefield, a monster crawled through the grass toward him. It had the body of a snake, but with insect-like legs and large pincers that protruded from the front of its body. Its hairy mouth-parts clacked as it crept toward Elric.

A high-pitched cry drew the creature's attention as Hob leaped onto the creature's back and bounced up its scaly body. He grabbed the beast by the head, scratching at its mirror-like eyes. "I have you, yes!" Hob shouted as he grabbed its antennae and used them like reins to pull the monster away from Elric.

Elric turned as the faint body of Master Elk appeared next to him. He looked transparent, like he was slowly turning into a soft silver mist. He was diminishing.

No.

Fighting to his feet, Elric half stumbled, half crawled to Elk. He pushed under the ancient warrior's arm, and used whatever strength he had left to drag Elk toward the grove.

The elves still sang, but their voices were growing fainter. Monsters charged toward the trees even as elves and fairies battled together to protect those sheltered there.

Flame cried out. Elric looked back to see her locked

blade to blade with the Grendel.

They were running out of time. There was only one fairy with enough ancient magic to defeat the Grendel. Only one fairy who could draw the power from all the fairies in the kingdom. They needed the queen. Their only hope was Wynn.

"Come on, little sister," he whispered as he dragged Elk's fading body inch by inch toward the grove. "We need you now."

CHAPTER TWENTY-NINE

Wynn

WYNN RAN VERY FAST. HER mouth was dry and she could feel her heart pounding. The shield in the sky had fallen. The storm clouds gathered over the great tree at the heart of the palace. She had to reach the queen and help her get better. The Grendel was here and Elric needed her.

The sky thundered overhead and the palace looked darker than she had ever seen it. As she approached the great stone pillars circling the tree, the blue lights within them had faded away. They looked just like rocks.

Mildred strutted up to her ankle and clucked in alarm as they stepped into a soft drift of snow.

Wynn looked at the palace. It glistened with ice as heavy drifts of snow piled against the stone pillars and buried the gardens. Snow came from the queen's magic. When a fairy died, they turned into their magic. The queen was turning into the snow. This was very bad. She had to hurry. Wynn fought through the heavy drifts of snow in the courtyard. Mildred hopped and struggled in the ice. Wynn lifted her and tucked her in an alcove created by the curling roots of the massive tree. "Stay here, Mildred. You be safe," she said.

This time Wynn wouldn't be tricked.

The snow crunched under her boots as she climbed the steps and into the heart of the tree. The enormous room where she first met the Fairy Queen opened in front of her. The floor shimmered. Wynn took a tentative step on it and her boot slipped. It was covered in ice.

No one was around. The room was usually filled with fairies. Now it was empty. Snow settled along the wall, and ice dripped into sharp icicles in the windows.

In the center of the room, a single figure hunched over. His back was covered with a robe of black feathers. Wynn cautiously stepped closer to him, crossing over the edge of the great seal. It was dark in the room. She glanced up and realized the crystal that hung over the seal was gone.

No, it wasn't gone. It was lying shattered at the feet of the dark figure. "Lord Raven?" She stepped closer to him.

He didn't look at her. Wynn wasn't sure he really heard her. "The Grendel is here," he said without turning to her. He stood over the shards of the broken crystal. "It is over. The queen is dying. Save yourself while you can." In a flash he turned into a raven, and with a throaty caw, he flew out of the window without ever looking at her.

The sound of his cry chilled her. She had heard a raven's cry before, on the day she found her mother dead.

Tears filled Wynn's eyes. No. She didn't like this. She had to change things.

Her first mother had grown sick and died. There was nothing Wynn could do to save her. She had tried to bring wood for the fire, but she had failed. Elric said that the fire wouldn't have helped. That there was nothing Wynn could have done, but it still felt like she should have been able to do something. She hated that feeling.

The thunder rumbled overhead. She would not let

her second mother die. Wynn slipped and slid on the ice until she reached the great spiral staircase that led to the top branches of the tree.

The steps were coated in ice. Wynn put her foot up on the first one. She had to climb. Keeping a hand on the slippery wall, Wynn climbed the endless stairs. Her fingers burned at first, then turned numb in the cold. She could see her breath coming out in puffs around her. Through the windows, she caught glimpses of the storm clouds with their bright lightning and thunder. In the distance, she heard the sounds of a great battle.

Elric was there. So were Osmund, Lexi, and Hob. Biting her chattering teeth together, she climbed faster. Her foot slipped, and she fell hard, knocking her chin on a step before she slid down several more. She threw her hands out, and her legs crashed into the wall.

She touched her lip. It was bleeding. She couldn't worry about that. She had to get to Mother. She had to reach her before it was too late. She would build a fire if she had to and melt the ice. She would find a way. She tried to do that for her first mother, but she couldn't help in time. Now Wynn didn't have any sticks for a fire, and she didn't have any fairy magic.

Bruised and shaken, she got to her feet. A tear slipped

down Wynn's cheek as she moved up the staircase again. She wished Flame was with her now. Flame had magic.

Wynn stopped on the step. "Wait," she said out loud to let her thoughts gather. She did have magic too.

Wynn began to sing.

> *"My love, my love, my changeling child,*
> *You braved the wind and snow*
> *To find me here within the gate*
> *And make my magic grow.*
> *Please stay with me, my changeling child,*
> *And for all time I'll keep you."*

They were the last words the Fairy Queen had sung to her. Wynn watched in amazement as the ice on the steps at her feet thawed as she sang the words.

Hope flared in her heart. Singing was magic!

Wynn sang the song as she climbed the stairs. The ice melted before her. She found herself changing the words with every turn around the great trunk. By the time she reached her old room, she sang.

> *"My love, my love, my mother dear,*
> *I brave the wind and snow*

To find you here within the tree
To make your magic grow.
Please stay with me, my mother dear,
And for all time don't leave me."

She didn't know where the words came from. She wasn't very good at making up new words, but they were in her heart and she sang them. They were the best she could do for her fairy mother.

Wind howled down the high hallway leading to her room and Elric's. It seemed like a very long time since she'd been there. Wynn fell silent as she reached the bridge that she had crossed to warn Elric about the Grendel. The arching branch was covered in ice. It dripped over the branch, hanging in long icicles beneath the bridge that were as least as long as Wynn was tall. The ice reflected the stormy gray sky, and looked wet and dangerously slippery.

Wynn's heart leaped into her throat. A gust of wind blew past her and she clung to the doorway to keep from falling all the way down to the snow-covered courtyards below.

Reaching her toe out onto the branch, she tested her footing. There was nothing to hold on to. She held her arms out to balance and took another step. She wanted to sing, but her throat tightened. She couldn't say a word. She couldn't even breathe. One step. Another. Another.

The snowy ground was so far below, all she could see was mist beneath her. But she had to cross the bridge. On the other side was her room, and the treasure room she had found. That's where the Fairy Queen would be. The wind blew again, and she teetered, waving her arms through the air. One foot slid, and she balanced on the other. Slowly she reached the top of the arch of the branch. Now she had to walk downhill.

The wind blew a powerful gust that felt like a forceful shove at her back. It made her bend over to catch her balance as her stomach flipped. She sat down to save herself. She inched forward, but began to slip. She screamed as she slid on the branch, trying hard to stay on top of it. She skidded in through the other archway and landed with a crash against the wall.

She'd made it! Shaking all over, she picked herself off and dusted the snow from her backside. She ran past Elric's room, and then hers, and on to the room where she had seen the queen's treasures. She entered through the carved doors. On the far side of the room was another doorway. Wynn ran to it and climbed a short flight of stairs nearly buried in snow. She shivered as she reached a round chamber. In the center was a bed.

Curtains of frozen dew hung around it. Wynn crept forward and looked at the woman resting there. "Mother?" she called.

Instead of the warm, dark skin that glowed with health, the woman who lay on the bed looked like she was made of ice. Her skin was clear and blue, with white veins running through the cold crystal. Her hair looked as if it were made of snow as it rested in a soft drift around her head. Wynn ran to her side. "Mother?" she cried. Wynn crawled onto the bed and lifted the Fairy Queen's hand. It still felt like a real hand, not hard like ice, but it was very cold.

"Mother, I'm here," she called. "I'm safe. Don't die."

Wynn's heart would break forever if she lost her new mother now. She snuggled against the queen's chilled body, and lay her head on the frozen queen's heart. She could still hear it beat, but it was very weak and quiet.

With her arms wrapped around the queen, Wynn softly sang.

"My love, my love, my mother dear,
I brave the wind and snow

To find you here within the tree
To make your magic grow.
Please stay with me, my mother dear,
And for all time don't leave me."

She cried and her tears felt warm on her cheek. Wynn cried harder. "I'm sorry," she said. "I'm sorry I was lost. I came back. I came back to you. Don't leave me. I love you so much."

Wynn felt warm all over. A golden light glowed in her chest. It grew bright, and filled the room, taking the chill from the air.

She felt a hand touch the back of her head. Wynn looked up.

The fairy queen looked down at her. Her skin wasn't blue. It was still not quite the color it usually was, but it didn't look like ice anymore. "Wynn?" the queen said. "You're alive?"

"Mother!" Wynn cried, and wrapped her arms tightly around the queen's neck. Wynn laughed and cried at the same time and then began to hiccup. The queen held her and found the strength to sit up. "You are better!" Wynn cried. "I'm so glad. I love you."

"I love you too, my brave girl. How is this possible?

Where is Elric?" she asked. "What has become of him?"

"They saved me! Elric and Osmund saved me," Wynn said. "They brought me back to you. The elves helped, and Flame."

"Who is Flame?" The queen's eyes grew brighter as she was speaking.

"The lost princess," Wynn said. "I found her in the woods."

"What?" The queen sat up and swung her feet over the side of her bed. She placed her hands on the edge and took several deep breaths. "How can this be?"

"Elric sent me here to get you. The Grendel is here. The shield is broken. Elric is fighting," Wynn said.

The queen looked out the window and gasped. Then her eyes flashed bright red. "Sidian," she said between clenched teeth. "This ends now."

She took Wynn's hand and led her into the room with all her treasures. She grasped the staff and handed it to Wynn. "Hold on to this. Don't let it fall."

Wynn nodded. "Where are we going?" she asked.

"To save my children," the queen said, her voice a deep and resonant growl. She led Wynn to the icy bridge. The queen transformed in a swirl of silver snow.

Wynn gasped. Her mother stood before her as an

enormous white bear with flashing red eyes. She knelt down in front of Wynn, and Wynn climbed on her back. Clutching the staff in one hand, Wynn held on to the bear's snow-white fur with the other, then the queen charged over the icy bridge and down the stairs. She crossed the empty throne room, and ran out past the courtyard.

With a great roar she raced across the countryside to the black storm ahead.

CHAPTER THIRTY

Elric

THE GRENDEL'S STORM GREW INTO a tower of black clouds over Elric as he tried to pull Master Elk to safety. The enormous pillar thundered, and lightning flashed within it. The bodies of monsters and fallen elves littered the battlefield as weakened fairies dragged themselves toward the sheltered grove. A stand of elves fought off a flank of monsters as they approached the trees. Elric caught a glimpse of Osmund riding one of the boars as he fought with them.

The light surrounding Flame flickered. Shadow hissed, but still did not move forward. Flame threw a hand out toward her, warning the tigereon off. Elric heard a powerful roar. He turned to see a great white bear charging across the field, with Wynn riding on its back. She tumbled off into the grass.

Flame faltered, and the Grendel lunged toward her. Just then Shadow leaped up and attacked the Grendel, clawing and biting at his shoulder and arm. The Grendel threw the tigereon off him, twisted and stabbed Shadow with his black sword.

Shadow let out a fearsome and terrifying scream.

Flame turned around. "Shadow?" Suddenly she looked lost.

The Grendel laughed as he came forward. Elric left Elk in the grass and ran to meet him. He had to reach Flame in time.

"How sad," the Grendel taunted as he towered over Shadow's body. "The last of her kind, and now she's dead. As you will be too."

"Shadow!" Flame cried. She turned away from the Grendel, exposing her back to his blade. Elric ran faster and tackled her to the ground.

A chilling blast of ice-cold air hit them. It blew the clouds of the Grendel's cloak back.

The great white bear met him in a frenzy of black claws and sharp teeth.

Wynn stood up in the grass. She held a staff with a large blue diamond on the top as she watched the ice bear do battle with the Grendel.

The bear backed away and transformed in a burst of light and a flurry of snow.

Elric picked up Flame. He held her hand and tried to pull her toward Elk and the grove, but she called out Shadow's name again, and threw herself to the ground. She felt in the grass until she touched Shadow's tail, and she wrapped herself over the wounded tigereon's body.

They were too close to the queen and the Grendel. It wasn't safe here. Lightning crackled around the Grendel as the Fairy Queen's dress swirled around her with the force of a blizzard. Elric found Flame's sword in the grass and grabbed it. He stood on unsteady legs to protect her.

"Sidian, my brother," the queen said, holding her head high. "It has been a long time."

"That scepter belongs to me," the Grendel growled. "And I will have it. You are weak and broken. You never learned how to become truly strong."

"You think what you have is strength?" she said. "You are the one who has turned into a shadow of your former self. I pity you."

"You won't pity me when I control the palace, and

the portals to the Otherworld are mine," he said. "I know the crystal heart the elves gifted you has shattered. Your magic is broken."

Elric watched as a crowd of people slowly emerged from the wood, Lexicon and Zephyr among them. Osmund and the boar-riders halted their mounts. It seemed most of the monsters of the Grendel's army were dead.

Flame cried as she lay over Shadow. Elk wasn't far away. His body had almost disappeared completely into mist. He was only moments from diminishing to the point where his consciousness would be trapped for all eternity. Behind the queen, Wynn's head poked up out of the grass. She still held the diamond scepter. Hob perched on her shoulder.

Everyone he cared about was here. This is where it would end. For good or ill, at least they stood together.

The elves began to sing again. He could hear Wynn's voice as she joined them, though she sang a completely different song. Elric sang under his breath, the prayer he had sung to the queen when he was alone and desperate in the snow, and it seemed like all was lost.

The Grendel laughed, but his voice didn't resonate with the storm.

The queen glowed with a bright white light. She held

out her hand, and Wynn tossed the scepter to her. She caught it and held it high. "My heart is strong," she said. "My heart is here."

She raised the scepter to the sky.

A chord of light immediately connected Wynn to the Fairy Queen. It was the same powerful magic he had witnessed when Osmund returned and healed the fractured crystal. The queen seemed stronger, and glowed brighter.

Osmund swung off the back of the boar he rode and strode forward. A second stream of light burst from his chest and connected him to the Fairy Queen. The diamond in her scepter flashed with blinding light.

Elric felt a wrench in his chest, but he staggered away from it.

The queen turned to Flame, who lay over the still body of Shadow. Flame cried out as a stream of light burst from the symbol on her back, and connected directly to Wynn, then flowed through Wynn's link and back to the queen.

Elric felt the tug in his chest again, and he pulled away. The queen turned back to him. She glowed like the sun as she gazed upon him.

"My son," she whispered, "I need you."

Warmth, laughter, and a profound feeling of love and protectiveness poured through him. He watched as the light around the queen grew brighter. Her son. Not the extra. Not the one who was expendable. He looked at Wynn, his sister; Osmund, his mentor; and Flame, who had risked everything too because she also felt this connection.

Family.

Power flowed through him. He was a part of this new family. He exhaled as the cord of light burst from his chest and connected him to the queen.

Mother. Wynn. Osmund. Flame . . . Family.

The light connecting them flowed up the queen's arm and into the scepter. The diamond glowed with the brightness of the sun. It reached out into a hundred threads that touched each of the fairies. Their power flowed back like a flooding river. Zephyr, Elk, they were all connected.

The elves sang louder, and the power flared again, the glow of it raining down and touching the elves as well.

"You will never threaten this realm again," the queen said to the Grendel. She pointed the scepter at him, and the light shot forward, piercing the shadow that protected what remained of her brother. The Grendel seemed to shrivel before Elric's eyes as the voices raised in song grew louder. Elric felt swept away in the stream of power, and clutched the ground as it washed through him. The clouds and shadows that formed the Grendel's body pulled inward, sucked into the core of light that had pierced his heart. The storms above shot bolts of lightning into the ground, but they dissipated into the air without triggering the terrible thunder.

The Grendel screamed and howled. The clouds above him whipped with wind.

Elric thought about the love he felt for Wynn, the admiration he felt for Osmund, the strength he saw in Flame, and he gathered those feelings. The cord to his heart grew brighter and he let that love flow through the stream of magic coursing within him. This was his family. This was where he belonged. He gave the power of that love to the queen. She needed it, and for the first time he admitted to himself that he needed it too.

The clouds above dissipated as the voices of the elves rose, their song filling with joy and hope.

With a final cry, the Grendel became consumed by the glow of the scepter. He writhed until he became a dark mass. The queen waved the scepter and he pulled toward it. With an explosion of light and color, the darkness disappeared. The queen lowered her staff. The once clear blue diamond had turned opaque, dark, and murky; a storm of smoky malevolence trapped within a solid chunk of obsidian.

The cords of light slowly faded, and the queen took a deep breath. She hung her head for a moment, and touched the dark stone. Elric could feel her sadness through the magic still connecting them. But then he felt a pure, bubbly wave of Wynn's joy. The queen turned and looked back toward them. Wynn ran to her and wrapped her in a big hug. Elric dropped the sword, but he felt very weak and also relieved.

The Grendel was gone. He was finally gone.

CHAPTER THIRTY-ONE

Elric

OSMUND RAN OVER TO JOIN them, limping and swaying on his feet, but he laughed as he used his ax as a cane. The queen smiled at him and drew him in toward her side. Wynn hugged him, and he ruffled her hair.

Elric turned to Flame. The sound of her sobs reached him even through the cheers of the elves. Lexi and Zephyr came over the hill. Lexi knelt beside Flame. Blood stained the tigereon's white stripes as she lay in the grass.

Zephyr found Elk and his hands glowed as he tried

to heal their fading master.

Elric ran up next to Lexi. "Is Shadow dead?" he asked.

"Not yet, but it's bad." She rifled through a bag and pulled out a vial of liquid. She poured it into the tigereon's wound. The cat hissed.

"Don't touch her!" Flame shouted, her face streaked with tears. "Get away from her."

"I'm trying to help," Lexi answered.

The queen knelt beside her daughter and placed her hand on the girl's shoulder. "Estaria?"

The queen blinked as she looked at the scars slashing across her daughter's face and eyes. Her dark eyes were now speckled with the reflection of the light of a million stars. Her starlight dress made the edges of the queen's icy skirts glow. Flame remained hunched over her tigereon, stroking the dying beast's head.

Flame's tears fell as she tucked her head against Shadow's neck. "She can't die," she said, her voice choked with emotion. "She saved my life. She raised me. She is my only friend."

Wynn came forward and took the queen's hand. "She's a good tigereon," Wynn said, her own face streaked with tears. She reached out and pet Shadow's hip. Elric felt the sting of his own tears as he too stroked Shadow's beautifully striped fur.

"Then we must save her," the queen said. "There is only one way." She stepped back and transformed again into the giant white bear. Lexi motioned to the elves nearby.

"Help us get her up," Lexi said. Together they hoisted Shadow onto the queen's broad back. Flame looked like she didn't know what to do with herself, until Wynn reached out to her. Flame took her sister's hand.

The queen carried Shadow back to the palace on her back. Elric, Wynn, and Flame all followed. A long line of exhausted, wounded elves and fairies leaned on one another as they marched back to the safety of the palace. The queen entered the throne room, then carefully laid the tigereon on the great seal. The pieces of the shattered crystal lay around her.

The queen transformed back into her human self, and picked a small piece of the crystal and inspected it. She brought the crystal to her heart and it glowed.

"What is happening?" Flame whispered next to him.

"I don't know," Elric said. "The queen is using her magic."

The queen knelt beside the tigereon. She touched

the crystal shard to the beast's chest. It glowed with the golden light. "A piece of my life. A gift freely given. Your life is now bound to mine, and mine to yours." The queen pressed the shard of crystal to the center of Shadow's heart. It turned into a small golden light, and sank into Shadow's body. Shadow's large eyes slowly opened as Elric watched the wound on her side glow with light. Slowly it healed, and the tigereon pulled her head up and purred. "Thank you," the queen said, stroking the tigereon's head, "for saving my daughter."

"Shadow?" Flame cried. She pulled away from Elric and took a couple of tentative steps forward. Shadow huffed at her in greeting, and Flame fell to the floor, throwing her arms around Shadow's neck.

The queen touched her daughter's shoulder. Flame turned to her mother with a tear-stained face. "Thank you for saving her life."

"Thank you for saving all of ours," the queen answered. "My daughter."

The great seal glowed as the rest of the remaining shards of the crystal heart lit with a fire within. They rose into the air, spinning and twirling around until they came together and fused in a bright flash of blue-white light. The cracks and fissures in the heart were gone, save a small missing chip close to the center.

Blue light shot through the center of the tree. The hall full of elves cheered their greatest invention as the crystal heart glowed bright. They mingled together with the fairies and watched as the light spread out over the Nightfell Wood. There was no more shield surrounding the fairy lands. No more barrier between them. It would take time to heal all the rifts between them, time and patience. Some hurts would always leave scars, but for the first time, peace was possible, and that gave Elric hope. He caught Lexi's eye and smiled at her. Her cheeks turned a darker green and she looked away, then scooped up Mildred and went to join Wynn. He felt Zephyr blow past him with a hard knock to his shoulder, then felt the steady presence of Master Elk on his other side.

The queen walked over to Headmind Axis. "I understand there is a portal that needs repair," she said with a grateful smile. "Thank you, for your aid."

"It will take time to rebuild our city," Axis responded. "But we will. And we will welcome the fairies once more."

He bowed his head to her, and she returned his regal nod.

As dusk set in, the fairies poured into the courtyards of the palace. They watched the stars appear over the great tree for the first time in centuries. Bright pinpoints of light swirled in clouds of colorful dust shining in a clear and endless sky as the songs of the elves rose into the night. Streaks of light in gorgeous glowing greens and pinks flowed in waves of color through the night sky as the planets rose behind them.

Wynn came over holding Mildred. Elric reached out and stroked the hen.

"I like the stars," she said. "They're pretty."

She craned her neck to see the magical sky, before turning to Elric. "And I love my family," she said.

Elric watched the queen embrace Flame for the first time. Osmund gave him a proud nod.

Wynn stroked Mildred, then reached down to take Hob's hand. "Maybe now we can play in the garden," she said. "Or walk in the woods. Things are better now."

"Thanks to you, Wynn." He smiled at his little sister. She smiled back and nudged him with her elbow.

"And you too, big brother."

Elric watched the moon rise for the first time over the fairy realm. Its soft light smiled on them. They were free. And it was beautiful. "You're right, Wynn," he said as he threw his arm across his sister's steady shoulders. "Things are much better. We are together now."

ACKNOWLEDGMENTS

The first person I have to thank for every single book I write is my brilliant and tireless critique partner and friend, Angie Fox. We have been working together for over ten years of ups, downs, and a few books that went sideways. I always deeply appreciate her guidance and support. I wouldn't be a published author without her. She has the first eyes on every story and she makes me a better writer every day.

My editor is also deeply responsible for making me a better writer. Her insight with this book was especially helpful. There was a lot of work to be done to make this book shine, and Alex Arnold led me carefully and creatively to my best story. I appreciate all the work she does behind the scenes as an advocate and cheerleader. She is an amazing editor and it is an honor to work with her.

These books wouldn't exist without the support of my agent, Laura Bradford. She has never failed to fight in my corner. I rely on her cool head and dry wit in times of stress. No matter how much things have changed over the years we have worked together, she has my deepest trust, gratitude, and appreciation for all she does.

I was also very happy to have the assistance of Rebecca Aronson and the rest of the staff at Katherine Tegen Books. I'm deeply honored to work for such a wonderful publisher with such an amazing group of people caring for every detail of the publishing process. Once again, Lisa Perrin created a gorgeous work of art for the cover. I could not be more thrilled and delighted with the result. To Sharon Roth, you did an amazing job organizing events surrounding the launch of these books, and I appreciate all the hard work you do bringing authors together in our community.

I would like to thank all those who are working in advocacy for disability representation in children's literature. I have listened to your insights and voices, and appreciate all the things you choose to share about your experiences. For everyone who had a hand in shaping these two stories that are very dear to my heart, thank you so much. Thank you to my friends, my family, and to my beloved children for their joy and inspiration.

And finally, thank you very much to everyone who reads my books. I write for you. Thank you.